Join favorite author

Louise Allen

as she explores the tangled love lives of

THOSE SCANDALOUS RAVENHURSTS

First, travel across war-torn Europe with
The Dangerous Mr. Ryder

Coming

August 2008

The Outrageous Lady Felsham

September 2008

The Shocking Lord Standon

2009

The Disgraceful Mr. Ravenhurst

The Notorious Mr. Hurst

The Piratical Miss Ravenhurst

Author Note

Jack Ryder first appeared—of his own volition—in *No Place for a Lady,* and took on a life of his own. I found myself wondering about him, what his background was, where he had come from, and I realized I needed to tell his story.

Then I discovered that Jack is not alone—he has siblings, he has cousins, and some of them have a story to tell as well. So this is Jack Ryder's tale, but it is also the first of the stories of THOSE SCANDALOUS RAVENHURSTS, and of how they, like Jack, find the loves of their lives.

It is the start of a journey for me, and I hope you will come along and discover with me what befalls the Ravenhurst cousins.

Louise Allen

THE DANGEROUS MR. RYDER

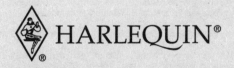

HARLEQUIN®

TORONTO • NEW YORK • LONDON
AMSTERDAM • PARIS • SYDNEY • HAMBURG
STOCKHOLM • ATHENS • TOKYO • MILAN • MADRID
PRAGUE • WARSAW • BUDAPEST • AUCKLAND

ISBN-13: 978-0-373-29503-6
ISBN-10:   0-373-29503-0

THE DANGEROUS MR. RYDER

First North American Publication 2008

www.eHarlequin.com

Printed in U.S.A.

DON'T MISS THESE OTHER
NOVELS AVAILABLE NOW:

#904 THE GUNSLINGER'S UNTAMED BRIDE—Stacey Kayne
Juniper Barns has sought a secluded life as a lumber-camp
sheriff to escape the ghosts of his past. He doesn't need
a woman sneaking into camp and causing turmoil....
Watch sparks fly as Juniper seeks to protect this vengeful beauty.

#905 A MOST UNCONVENTIONAL MATCH—Julia Justiss
Hal Waterman's calling on the newly widowed Elizabeth Lowery
is the caring act of a gentleman. He finds himself enchanted by the
beautiful Elizabeth and her little son—although he knows he can
never be part of this family....
*Follow Hal's emotional quest to win over Elizabeth's heart in this
long-awaited sequel to Julia Justiss's* The Wedding Gamble.

#906 THE KING'S CHAMPION—Catherine March
Troye de Valois, one of the king's own elite guard, has long lived
in Eleanor's heart and dreams. Dreams that are shattered
when he reveals his anger at their forced marriage,
and the emotions she is reawakening in him....
Drama and passion build in this stirring Medieval tale.

RAVENHURST FAMILY TREE

Francis Philip Ravenhurst, 2nd Duke of Allington = Lady Francesca Templeton

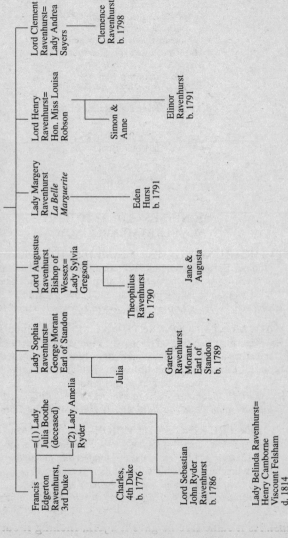

Francis Edgerton Ravenhurst, 3rd Duke
=(1) Lady Julia Boothe (deceased)
=(2) Lady Amelia Ryder

Charles, 4th Duke b. 1776

Lord Sebastian John Ryder Ravenhurst b. 1786

Lady Belinda Ravenhurst= Henry Camborne Viscount Felsham d. 1814

Lady Sophia Ravenhurst= George Morant Earl of Standon

Julia

Gareth Ravenhurst Morant, Earl of Standon b. 1789

Lord Augustus Ravenhurst Bishop of Wessex= Lady Sylvia Gregson

Theophilus Ravenhurst b. 1790

Jane & Augusta

Lady Margery Ravenhurst *La Belle Marguerite*

Eden Hurst b. 1791

Lord Henry Ravenhurst= Hon. Miss Louisa Robson

Simon & Anne

Elinor Ravenhurst b. 1791

Lord Clement Ravenhurst= Lady Andrea Sayers

Clemence Ravenhurst b. 1798

Chapter One

No one had told him that she was beautiful. Jack Ryder crouched precariously in a stone window embrasure two hundred feet above the ravine river bed and stared into the candlelit room. Inside, the woman he had been sent to find paced to and fro like an angry cat.

He kept his eyes fixed on the image beyond the glass as he wedged himself more securely into his slippery niche. Below, the void beneath the castle was shrouded in merciful darkness, the faint sound of the river floating upwards. Although his whole body was aware of it, he ignored the cold fingers of fear playing up and down his spine, knowing full well that if he let his imagination have full rein he would never be able to move at all. His studded boots ground on the stone, and he froze for a moment, but the sound did not seem to reach her.

Jack gave himself a mental shake and began to work on the knot that secured the end of the long coil of rope around his waist. As it came free he gave it a jerk, flicking it outwards, and the whole length detached itself from the battlement high above and fell out of sight into the void.

Now his only way down was through that window. Despite his perilous position, Jack had no intention of going through it until he had a chance to size up the woman inside. The woman he had been sent to bring back to England by whatever means he found necessary, including force.

It was for her own good, as well as in the interests of both countries, they had explained at Whitehall. The officials had spoken with the air of men who were glad it was not they who had to attempt to convince the lady of this. They had told him a number of things about her Serene Highness the Dowager Grand Duchess Eva de Maubourg. *Intelligent, stubborn, anti-Napoleonic, haughty, independent, difficult and demanding* was how she had been summed up by the various men who had gathered to deliver the hasty briefing, fifteen days before. *Half-French,* they had added gloomily, as though that summed up the problem.

She had not left the Duchy since her marriage and was likely to be near impossible to move now, the officials added. That was all right; he was used to being asked to do the near impossible.

But there had been no mention of darkly vivid looks, of a curvaceous figure or the lithe grace of a caged panther. And Jack was having trouble believing she could possibly be the mother of a nine-year-old son. It had to be the thick glass in the window panes.

She was alone in the room; he had waited long enough to be convinced of that. Jack shifted his position, focusing his mind on opening the window and not on what would happen if he lost his balance. The flat of a slim blade slid easily enough between the casement and the frame. Thankfully the window opened inwards, for its height above the floor would make it impossible to use otherwise. He eased it ajar by inches, waiting long minutes between each adjustment so there would be no sudden drop of temperature or gust of wind to alarm her. If she screamed this would likely end in bloodshed—he did not intend that it would be his.

Grand Duchess Eva ceased to pace and sank down in front of a writing desk, her back to the window, her head in her hands. Jack wondered if she was crying, then started, with potentially lethal result, when she banged her fist down on the leather desk top and swore colourfully in English. He could only admire her vocabulary—he was tempted to echo it.

It was definitely time to get off this window ledge. He grasped the frame, put his feet through and swung himself down into the room. There was no way he could land silently, not dropping eight foot on to a stone-flagged floor in nailed boots. She spun round on her chair, gripping the back of it, her face reflecting the gamut of emotions from shock, puzzlement, fear and finally, he was impressed to see, imperious anger masking all else. They had not told him about her courage.

'Who the devil are you?' she demanded in unaccented English, getting to her feet with perfect deportment, as though rising from a throne. Her right hand, Jack noted, was behind her; he searched his memory for his survey of the room. Ah, yes, the paperknife. A resourceful lady.

'You speak English excellently,' he commented. He knew from his briefing that she was half-English, so it was only to be expected, but it was a more tactful beginning to their conversation than *Put down that knife before I make you!* might be. 'But how did you know I would understand you?'

She looked down her nose at him. Jack registered dark eyes, thinly elegant eyebrows arched in disdain, a red mouth with a fullness that betrayed more passion than she was perhaps comfortable with and one deep brown curl, disturbed from her coiffure and lying tantalisingly against her white shoulder. He focused on those eyes and banished the fleeting speculation about just how the skin under that curl would feel.

'You will address me as your Serene Highness,' she said coolly. 'I was thinking in English,' she added, almost as an afterthought.

'Your Serene Highness.' He swept her a bow, conscious of his clothing as he did so. He was dressed for the purpose of shinning down castle walls, not making court bows, but he managed it with a grace that had one of those dark brows lifting in surprise. 'My name is Jack Ryder.' He had wrestled with whether or not to tell her his real name and decided against it. His *nom de guerre* would be safer in the event they were captured.

'Then you are English, Mr Ryder?'

'Yes, ma'am.'

'So you have not come to kill me?'

That has taken the wind out of his sails, Eva thought, watching the narrowing of the deep grey eyes that had been studying her with what she could only describe as respectful insolence. There was absolutely nothing in this Jack Ryder's expression to which she could take exception, yet somehow he managed to leave her with a distinct awareness of her own femininity and his appreciation of it. It seemed a very long time since anyone had looked at her quite like that and longer still since she had felt her pulse quickening in response.

She managed to keep her breathing under control with an effort, and flexed the fingers cramped around the paperknife. If he was English it was highly unlikely that he was a danger, but she could not afford to take the risk, not after what had happened yesterday. And his unconventional entry through the window had to mean trouble.

'No, ma'am, I have not come to kill you.' A smooth recovery. Why had he not asked her what she meant? Eva studied him while she pondered the disturbing implications of that thought. Some years older than her own twenty-six, but far from middle aged. Slim, dark haired and grey eyed and in obvious control both of his body—given the way he had gained entry to her room—and his face. She had a vivid mental image of him with a sword in his hand; he had a duellist's balance. He was showing no emotion now, after that first fleeting reaction to her statement.

'Convince me,' she said, hoping he had not noticed the tremor that vibrated the hem of her evening gown. 'If you do not, I will scream and there will be two guards in here within seconds.'

He produced a pistol from one pocket. 'And one of them will be dead in as short a time. There is no need for this, ma'am.' The sinister black shape slid back into his coat. 'I am here at the behest of the British government. Your son's god-father is of the opinion that it would be better for the young Grand Duke if you were with him.'

'The Prince Regent? He has hardly shown any interest in Fréderic since he wrote to send the christening gift.' She wished she could move, but the necessity to keep the knife out of his sight kept her pinned against the desk.

'Nevertheless, ma'am, the British government keeps an eye on the Duchy of Maubourg and its affairs, and has done ever since the outbreak of war. To have a neutral country embedded within France can only be a diplomatic asset, however small it is.'

'Of course.' Eva shrugged negligently. He was telling her

nothing she did not know all too well. 'Presumably you are aware that my late husband did what he could to mitigate the situation by acting as a go-between. He opposed the French, naturally, but he was too much of a realist to think we could resist in any way.'

'I believe you first met the late Grand Duke in England.' Ryder shifted position, his eyes skimming over the furnishings, searching the corners of the room. She felt it was more an habitual wariness than a search for anything in particular. His knowledge of her history did not prove he had received a government briefing; anyone with an interest in her affairs could have discovered that easily enough, it had made a big enough stir in the news sheets.

She inclined her head. 'We were in exile at the time. My father had died in the Terror, Mama returned home to her father, the Earl of Allgrave. I had my come-out in London and I met the Grand Duke at my very first ball.'

It had seemed like a fairy tale, looking back now. Louis Fréderic, tall, darkly handsome, sophisticated far beyond her experience, an exotic presence on the English social scene, was a catch outside her wildest dreams. The fact that he had been thirty years her senior and that she was barely seventeen had weighed neither with her mother, nor with her.

The Grand Duke carried out his mission by negotiating for an exchange of prisoners, enjoyed a whirlwind courtship and returned to Maubourg with his future Grand Duchess at his side. Eva stared back down the years of memory at herself. Had she ever been that young and innocent?

'And since your husband's death almost two years ago, his brother Prince Philippe has acted as Regent and you and he are joint guardians of your son.' Ryder was not so much asking, as establishing to her that he knew the facts. It seemed he was not completely up to date, but she did not hasten to inform him that Philippe had been confined to his room with some mysterious illness ever since the news about Napoleon's escape from Elba had reached them. That was almost three months ago and she was beginning to despair of his recovery.

'Yes.' Her legs had stopped trembling. Eva shifted her position slightly, resting her left hand casually on the chair back. She could swing it across his path if he lunged for her. 'I have not seen my son for four years. My husband judged it best that he should be educated in England.'

The pain of that, the sense of betrayal, still stabbed like a knife. Louis had not even given her the opportunity to say goodbye, justifying it by saying her tears would weaken the boy. First a private tutor, shared with the sons of a ducal family, then Eton. *Little Freddie, will he even recognise me now?*

'There is no easy way to say this…' Ryder began, and Eva felt the blood begin to drain from her face. *No…no…they have sent him to tell me he is dead…* 'Your son has been the victim of a series of accidents in the last month— No! Ma'am, he is quite well, I assure you!' She felt herself sway and he was at her side supporting her even faster than her own disciplined recovery.

'I am quite all right,' she began, then, as his solicitous fingers closed around the paperknife and whipped it from her hand, 'Give me that back!'

He lobbed it through the open window with scarcely a sideways glance to take aim, but stayed at her side. 'I prefer to remain unpunctured, should I happen to displease you, ma'am. Your son is alive, despite his run of bad luck, and even now, I am certain, is ploughing through his Classical studies.'

'What accidents?' Eva demanded, moving away. Mr Ryder's proximity was strangely disturbing. If she had not been a sensible widow she would have put it down to the close presence of a handsome, dangerous man. But it could not be that. It must be the relief at hearing that Freddie was all right.

He made no move to follow her, simply shifting his position to keep her in view. 'First, in the middle of May, there was a fall down a stone staircase, which was fortunately interrupted by a number of youngsters on their way up. They shared a number of interesting bruises I gather, but that is all. Then on the eighteenth, there was a runaway carriage in the High Street, which only missed the Grand Duke because he was pushed to safety by a passer-by. The carriage and its driver could not be traced afterwards. Then—'

'Hoffmeister should have been taking better care of him,' Eva interrupted angrily.

'His personal secretary and tutor can hardly be expected to keep a lively nine-year-old in leading strings, ma'am. And to his credit Hoffmeister became suspicious enough after the third incident to make contact with Whitehall.'

'Third incident?'

'The inexplicable appearance of one poisonous toadstool in a fricassee of mushrooms that was set before Fréderic for dinner on the twentieth.'

'How…' Eva swallowed, fighting to keep her composure '…how did he escape that?'

'By being immediately and very thoroughly sick. His personal physician tells me that his Serene Highness has a very sensitive stomach.' She nodded, dumbly. 'On this occasion it probably saved his life. He has additional security now, believe me.'

This time she made no pretext of hiding her shaking limbs. Eva sank down on to the chair and tried to tell herself that Fréderic was safe, that all his servants, and especially Hoffmeister, would be guarding him closely now.

'I realise this may be hard to accept, ma'am—' Jack Ryder began, then broke off as she lifted her head to look at him.

'No, Mr Ryder, it is not at all strange. I am fortunate, it seems, that Fréderic gets his sensitive digestion from me, for I spent a miserable few hours with a badly upset stomach two nights ago. At the time I put it down to shock after the accident when the wheel came off my carriage as we were crossing a narrow bridge. Only the parapet stopped it tipping into the gorge. And then yesterday I slipped on the top step of the stairs outside my room; it seems someone had carelessly stood there with a dripping candle for some time. The stone was quite encrusted with wax.'

'Were you hurt?' His instant concern sent a flash of warmth through her and she found her cold lips were curving into a small smile for the first time in days.

'No, I thank you. But the tapestry hanging beside the staircase is the worse for being torn from its hooks as I clung to it.'

'And how did Prince Philippe react to this chapter of accidents?' Jack Ryder took a chair, swung it round and straddled it, his arms along the back. He had stopped calling her *ma'am*, his behaviour was shockingly casual, but somehow none of that mattered just at the moment.

'My brother-in-law has been indisposed—in fact, in a state of mental and physical collapse—since the news of Napoleon's escape from Elba reached us. We assumed at first it was a stroke. He has been in that condition now for three months. My personal physician and a bodyguard are with him around the clock.' She stared at him, seeing her own scepticism reflected in the steady grey eyes. He looked like an austere priest hearing a confession, with his straight nose and his tightly closed lips.

'You suspect poison. And who rules Maubourg now?'

'My younger brother-in-law, Prince Antoine.'

It was obvious that had been a rhetorical question—this Englishman knew exactly who would be holding the keys of the Duchy. 'Ah, yes, the gentleman who was so anxious to persuade Price Philippe to end your neutrality and join forces with Napoleon after the death of your husband?' Eva nodded. 'And the man who would become Grand Duke should your son and Prince Philippe die?'

'Yes. That is why Philippe is protected as he is. I had not thought Antoine's arm would reach as far as England,' she added bleakly. It had never occurred to her that Freddie would be in danger; she had believed up until now that it was a struggle for power between two brothers.

'It is very likely that an enemy from here could strike at the young Grand Duke, and they could certainly reach far enough to remove the one person who has the authority to protect the Regent,' Ryder pointed out, resting his chin on his clasped hands. It was a well-sculptured feature, she noted absently.

'Myself. Yes, I had thought of that. And I have had time to realise that Philippe's illness happening as Napoleon lands in France is too much of a coincidence. Antoine worships the Emperor—he will throw Maubourg on to the French side in the hope of patronage from Napoleon.'

'Forgive me, I do not wish to insult your country, but while a neutral Maubourg has proved very useful to the Allies in the past, why should Napoleon be bothered with it now, one way or the other?'

'In the past, he was not, or we would never have stayed untouched as we have. But now, I think we may have something he would want.' Jack raised a sceptical eyebrow, but she shook her head. 'I am not certain, it is only a suspicion. What do you know about explosives?'

Instead of answering, Ryder got to his feet and walked quietly to the massive panelled door. He eased the key round, cracked the door open and looked out, then, apparently satisfied, locked it again and came back to her side. 'There are guards at the end of the passage—are they loyal to you?'

'I…I think so.'

'Hmm. I know less about explosives than I suspect I am about to need to. What is going on?'

Eva so far forgot herself as to begin to run her hands through her hair, then caught herself. A Grand Duchess did not give way to displays of weakness, nor was she ever anything but coolly immaculate under all circumstances. She folded them elegantly in her lap.

'The main industry of the Duchy is perfume.' Ryder nodded. It seemed he knew that, too. 'The State perfumery employs a number of chemists, for it is very much a process of distillation and blending. I take an interest in the enterprise and I was looking through its books last week. Antoine has taken on a number of new men without asking myself or Philippe—professional men by the size of their salaries, not workers or craftsmen.

'And then there have been explosions up in the mountains. That is where I was driving on the day of the accident. We found deep craters, signs of burning, but that is all, although I had the feeling we were being watched. The wheel came off on the way back.'

'So, Prince Antoine is possibly experimenting with some new form of armament, just when the greatest general of his generation lands on the doorstep. And everyone who stands between him and the title suddenly becomes ill or has accidents.'

'Yes.' They stared at each other, Eva wondering suddenly why she had found it so easy to blurt all that out to a complete stranger. He might be a spy of Antoine's, he might be a free-lance, after some end of his own. She had been completely naïve to have trusted him. 'Have you any credentials, Mr Ryder?'

'A little late to think of that, ma'am,' he said, echoing her thoughts. The way his lips twitched with amusement had her eyes flashing.

'Better late than never, sir.'

He raised a hand, its long fingers unadorned by rings, and flipped back his lapel to reveal a small silver greyhound pinned there. 'I am a King's Messenger, ma'am.'

'A glorified postman?' She was feeling chills running up and down her spine as the extent of her indiscretion grew on her. If she could only be certain he was just what he said.

'We do rather more than deliver the diplomatic post,' he said mildly.

'How do I know you haven't murdered the real King's Messenger?'

'You do not. What did you intend to do about all this before I came through your window?'

Eva found her thoughts were suddenly running very fast, very cold. He wanted to know too much. She got up and began to walk up and down the chamber, her crimson skirts brushing against the bed hangings. It did not take much skill to pretend agitation. 'I was thinking how I could get out of the castle and raise the population against Antoine.'

'Madness,' Ryder said flatly, just as she reached her bedside nightstand.

'Oh!' Eva raised one hand to her face and feigned a sob, then opened the drawer and began to fumble in it as though looking for a handkerchief. It was in her hand as she straightened up. 'I think it would be *madness* to trust you any further with the scant identification you have, sir. I am going to ring this bell and when my maid comes I shall send her to fetch my private secretary and my personal bodyguard. Then we shall see.'

'No.' Ryder took two long strides across the room and had his hand outstretched to intercept hers on the bell pull as she flicked aside the handkerchief and revealed the little pistol beneath it.

'Thank you for coming so close, sir. This is not much use over a long distance, but, near to, I believe it would seriously inconvenience you.'

How he did it she had no idea. One moment the muzzle of the pistol was virtually pressed to his waistcoat and he was staring at her in apparent shock, the next the pistol was flying across the room and she was picked up and thrown on to the bed, Jack Ryder's long body pinning her into the yielding mattress.

He stared down into her furious face, his own showing nothing more extreme than irritation. He was, damn him, hardly breathing any harder than he had before. '*Madame,* you may walk out of here and come with me to England willingly, or you may leave this room unconscious and make the journey under restraint. It is your choice.'

Chapter Two

As a way of restraining her it was remarkably effective, Eva admitted to herself as she lay glaring up at the man pinning her to the bed. She could struggle—fruitlessly no doubt, given the size of him and the strength he had already demonstrated—but that would simply press her body into even closer contact with his. She had far too much dignity to do so and he obviously knew it. He would probably enjoy it, too.

She regarded the wicked glint in the grey eyes stolidly for a moment, then said, 'Would you kindly remove your person from my bed?' She could only admire the steadiness of her voice, especially as some part of her, a tiny, suppressed sensual part, was aching to arch against the hard masculinity that was dominating her. She fought down the urge; she had, after all, been fighting that particular instinct for two years.

Jack Ryder responded by raising himself on his elbows, the better to look down into her face. The movement caused even more disturbing pressure on her pelvis; Mr Ryder did not appear to be fighting his own inner sensuality very energetically. His eyes were hooded, watching her with speculation. 'In a moment, ma'am, when we have sorted this out. I am not sure what written proof of my identity and mission you would accept, given that, as you say, I could have stolen it. Will you accept your son's word?'

'Freddie? What do you mean?'

'When I was talking to him, telling him I was coming to fetch you, I asked him if there was a password I could give you in case you did not believe me. He thought for a moment, then said, "Ask Mama how Bruin and the Rat are. It's all right for me to say it, because we aren't at home."'

'Bruin? Oh, the little wretch! Mr Ryder—' She gave him a shove. It was like trying to shift one of the castle's wolf-hounds when they got on to the bed. 'Please get off—I believe you.' Too relieved to be indignant with him any longer, Eva sat up as Jack rolled off the bed to stand leaning against the bedpost, his eyebrows raised interrogatively. 'They are his nicknames for his uncles and I made him promise never to use them to anyone but me because they might be offended. At least, Antoine would be.'

'The Rat I presume?'

'Exactly. He has a long nose that twitches when he is agitated. I believe you, Mr Ryder—now, will you get me out of the castle?'

'That is my intention.'

'And help me raise resistance to Antoine?'

'No.'

'Why not?' Eva swung her feet off the bed and confronted him, all her indignation surging back. This official, this *postman* for the English government, had no right to dictate to her. He was obviously a man of action, just what she needed in these circumstances—he should do as he was told. 'It is your patriotic duty, sir.'

'Humbug.' Eva gasped. No one spoke to her like that. It was

so unexpected that she gaped at him. 'Leaving aside the fact that I have no allegiance to this Duchy, it is not my duty to get most of its male population massacred by French troops, which is what will happen if Bonaparte wants this place and you resist. If he doesn't, then you are risking a civil war for nothing. My duty, as I have already explained to you, is to remove you safely to England where you have the legal authority to look after your son until all this is over. It will also remove one hostage from Antoine's grasp.'

'What, slink off and abandon the Duchy to Antoine and the French just because I am a woman?' He obviously thought she was some milk-and-water English miss. Despite him remembering—occasionally—to address her with due respect, he had no idea of the role she had had to play these past two years since Louis's death, nor the iron that had entered her soul as she had done so.

'No, execute a strategic retreat because that is the sensible thing to do,' he retorted. 'You do understand the concept of sensible action as opposed to romantic gesture, I presume?'

'How dare you speak to me like that? You insolent oaf—I can perfectly well look after myself.'

'Indeed, ma'am? You have escaped two accidents and one poisoning by the merest chance. If I was an assassin, you would be dead by now. Your son needs you, and you need me. Now, are you going to sit there on your—' his eyes flickered to her body '—dignity, clutching an invisible coronet to your bosom, or are you going to come with me?'

I should slap him, but he is too quick for me. How can I leave? This is my duty, my country now...but Freddie. This Jack Ryder thinks I am an hysterical woman...

'What about Philippe? He cannot be moved.'

'Then we leave him. He is the Regent, he accepted the risks

along with the office.' He spoke as though it was a matter of leaving someone behind while they went on a picnic, not that they might be abandoning a man to his death. Dear Philippe, Freddie's favourite Old Bear… 'Can you help him if you stay?' She shook her head dumbly. 'Then we go.'

'Now?' Her head was spinning. For so long it seemed she had had to think for herself—now this man was calmly taking over her decisions and her actions and the frightening thing was, it felt like a relief to let him do so. Eva straightened her spine and tried to think this through, ignoring the hard grey eyes fixed on her.

'Yes, now. Unless you can think of any reason why leaving in broad daylight might be safer. Can you change into something completely neutral—a walking or carriage dress with a cloak or a pelisse? Something an ordinary lady would wear, if you own such a thing.' His gaze swept down over the rich figured silk of her crimson evening gown to the tips of her exquisite slippers, assessing it, and probably, she thought irritably, pricing it, too.

'I will need to pack,' she began. How was he going to get them out of there?

'A valise only. Essentials—one change of outer garments at the most. A discreet gown, nothing showy.'

'But it will take us days to get back to England, I need more clothes than that.' Court routine, even on a quiet day, demanded a minimum of four changes from rising to retiring.

'We can buy more as we go. Have you any luggage here?'

'Of course not. I will have to ring for my maid to help me change, and how am I going to explain why I need a valise at this time of night?'

'Tell her you want to pack up some clothes for the poor— No, better, you know of a deserving young woman in the town who has the opportunity for a post as a governess and you want make her a gift of a valise and have decided to give her one of your old ones. Then tell her you want to change into your nightgown because you have a headache and do not want to be disturbed again tonight.'

'And how, pray, am I going to get into a walking dress by myself?' She knew the answer as soon as the words left her lips and spoke before he could. 'I presume you are going to tell me that King's Messengers have training as ladies' maids?'

'No, but I am capable of tying laces with my eyes closed,' he confided.

'I am quite sure you are, Mr Ryder,' Eva said grimly. And untying them, too, no doubt. He would have a certain appeal for some women who liked the quietly dominant type, she could see that. It was fortunate that she was inured to male appeal. She tugged the bell pull and watched with a certain malicious interest to see where Mr Ryder was going to hide himself. It was a positive disappointment to see him drop to the floor and slide under the bed without any apparent discomfort.

She was beginning to wish she could catch him out in some way—he appeared to have an answer to everything. In fact, the only sign of humanity she had witnessed so far was the occasional glint in his eyes which, in anyone else, she would put down to mischief.

'Your Serene Highness?' It was Hortense, her dresser, slipping into the room with her usual soft-footed discretion.

'Fetch me my valises, Hortense, if you please.'

'Now, ma'am? All of them? You want to pack?'

'Yes, all. And now, and of course I do not want to pack, Hortense. I am thinking of ordering a new suite of hand baggage from Paris and I want to see what I have.' There was no reason why she should not have used Mr Ryder's ingenious excuse—it was sheer stubbornness on her part and she knew it.

She was not given to issuing capricious orders and made a point of being considerate to the castle staff, so such a quixotic demand at that hour of the evening was unusual. But Hortense was too well trained to register surprise. 'Yes, ma'am, right away.'

It took almost twenty minutes, but eventually the dresser was back with four menservants carrying fifteen bags between them. 'Thank you, Hortense. I had no idea I had so many. Put them over there, please.' She waited until the men had gone, then added, 'Help me undress, please. I am a little fatigued and I will not need you after that.'

'Yes, ma'am.'

It felt decidedly risqué to be undressing with a man under the bed, even if he could see nothing. Eva slipped her arms into a wrapper and tied the sash firmly. 'Good night, Hortense.'

As soon as the door shut behind the woman, she ordered, 'Stay there,' and began rummaging through her clothes presses for a suitable walking dress. She was answered by a faint sneeze as she threw her wrapper and nightgown aside and began to pull on her underthings again. A simple pair of stays which she could lace from the front solved one problem, but what to wear on top?

Finally she struggled into the plainest gown she had, which by almost dislocating her shoulder she could button up behind by herself, and found a stout pair of walking shoes to match. There was a large, but rather worn, valise in the pile and she added a good selection of undergarments before announcing, 'You may come out now.'

Jack Ryder slid out from beneath the bed and got to his feet as she was gathering up toothbrush and toiletries. 'That bag?

No, far too large.' As Eva gasped, he delved into the valise, extracted the pile of frills, fine lawn and filmy silk and deposited it on the bed.

'*Mr Ryder!* That is my underwear!'

'How very dashing of you to mention it, I was endeavouring not to. French, I observe,' he added outrageously. 'That bag there will do, but you will need to halve that pile of frippery. Here.' He flipped through the pile, sorting it into two, and handed half to her.

Eva contented herself with one glare, dumped it into the small bag, then began to find the other items, trying to think which were the essentials to take. 'What about money?'

'I have enough. The journey to the frontier should only take us just over a week.'

'But Napoleon controls France!'

'He is in Paris, massing his troops. It would not do to show we are foreigners, but we should have no trouble passing as French travellers—it worked well enough on my journey down. Your French is perfect, mine good enough to pass as regional.'

Eva shrugged; he had got to Maubourg, true enough, now she just had to trust he could get them both back to England. 'How do we get out of the castle?' Travelling virtually the length of France seemed simple in comparison to walking out of her own castle with a strange man and a valise.

'Have you a cloak with a hood?' Eva nodded and went to take it from the press. Ryder folded it, placed it in another of the valises, then stripped off his own coat and added that to it. 'I need a sash.' He stood there, waiting for her to catch up with him; of course, in shirtsleeves with his dark waistcoat and breeches, he could be taken at a distance for one of the menservants, except that they all wore a red sash around their waists. But what did that achieve? She could hardly disguise herself the same way.

And if he could see from his hiding place under the bed the way that the footmen were dressed, what else had he been able to see?

Eva forced that worry away and rummaged in the press until she found a long scarf of almost the right colour. 'Let me.' She was so focused on being brisk and matter of fact that her arms were round his waist before she thought what she was doing. Jack stood very still for her, his arms lifted. Eva felt the colour rising in her cheeks; it was impossible to do this without touching him.

'The way it is knotted is distinctive,' she said briskly. 'There, that should do.' She stepped back, hoping her blushes would be taken for general agitation. The heat of his body had been disturbing for some reason. She forced herself to think clearly—it had to be the shock of the whole situation, otherwise what could account for the way she was reacting to this man? 'Now what?'

'Do you know which way to go to reach the lower courtyard without passing many guards?' Ryder was securing the pistol out of sight in the swathing sash, his movements crisp.

'Yes, of course, but we cannot avoid them all, there are two at the end of the corridor, for a start—my bodyguard.' She watched him, puzzled. 'I doubt I can disguise myself to deceive them, nor any of the others, for that matter.'

'You don't even try. Just walk with me, scolding me for something or another, then take the route for the lower courtyard using the least frequented areas.' He swung the small valise up on to his shoulder, casting his face into shadow, and lifted the other one in his other hand. With only the cloak and coat in it, it hung in his grasp, obviously light and apparently empty.

'I understand.' Eva found her face relaxing into a smile. It felt strangely stiff and she realised how long it was since she had found anything genuinely to smile about. 'Come on.' She pressed open the door and led the way out into the corridor. A short distance ahead, where the passage to her private suite joined the main gallery, guards stood on either side, pikes at the slant. At the sound of her voice, they snapped to attention, their weapons crashing upright.

'I cannot imagine how it can take one man so long to mend a simple strap,' she complained, remembering at the last minute to speak the Maubourg *patois*. 'And how you can say you do not understand which valise I want to replace it with, defeats me! I suppose it will be faster to come and look at them myself. How long have you been employed here? I must speak to the major-domo about his selection of staff.'

They passed between the guards, Eva, nagging away, keeping herself between Jack's unprotected side and the right-hand man. There was no response from the guards as she marched along, her heels clacking on the stone floor, her voice raised peevishly. 'This way, man, I do not have all evening!'

Jack strode along in Eva's wake, suppressing a grin at her tone. Although, if she was this bossy in real life, it was going to be a tense trip back. It was hard to understand how such a feminine-seeming creature could be so hard. He had seen genuine tears when she had feared for her son's life, but beside that she seemed cold, arrogant and wilful. As he had been led to believe.

He kept his head down as they passed a knot of female servants, all too busy bobbing curtsies to look at him, and followed the willowy figure of the Grand Duchess.

She wound her way down spiral stairs, along narrow passages and through what were obviously the working areas of the castle with surprising confidence. Perhaps, despite her autocratic manner, she took a practical hand in the supervision of the household. Jack found himself admiring the way she moved, the swing of her hips in the plain gown, then made himself concentrate on trying to maintain his sense of direction and to keep count of floors.

Eva opened a heavily studded door, then stopped. Puzzled, Jack glanced at her and saw she had gone pale. There seemed nothing to account for it, no voices, nothing but the start of a dark spiral staircase. It seemed she braced herself, her fingers white on the ring handle, then she stepped forwards.

After that hesitation she led the way unerringly down the precipitous flight to the solid oak door at the bottom. She pushed it and they stepped out into a brightly lit hubbub of steam, cooking smells and bustling women. In the centre of the room a massive, florid-complexioned individual brandished a ladle and harangued his subordinates. 'Which criminal idiot put cream in this?' he was demanding. 'Do you not know what her Serene Highness likes? Do you wish to poison her?' He glanced across the room, caught a glimpse of the newcomers through the steam and gasped. *'Madame!'*

'Just carry on.' The Grand Duchess waved a hand imperiously and the workers turned back to their tasks, leaving the maestro goggling amidst his cooking pots. 'Through here,' she murmured and Jack found himself outside in the wood yard. A lad staggered past carrying a basket of logs, then the door into the kitchens swung shut and they were alone in the dark.

He put down the lighter valise and took out her cloak and his coat. 'Here, pull up the hood and hide your face as much as possible.' He kicked the empty bag into the shadows, took her arm and began to walk steadily towards where he guessed, if his internal compass had not failed him, the lower courtyard would be. The townsfolk had unrestricted access there; in a few moments they would be simply two passers-by.

It proved easier than he had hoped, although the Grand Duchess was stiff at his side. She was obviously unused to being manhandled by subordinates. There were guards, but only on the main entrance to the inner courtyard, and no one took any notice of one couple amongst so many townsfolk.

'I've a carriage waiting down by the East Bridge,' he said as he steered her out of the gates and past a group laughing as they headed for a tavern, then dodged a stallholder who had finally given up for the night and was packing his wares into a handcart. 'This is busier than I expected.' At least the woman was less trouble than he had feared she might be from the way she had been described. She had a cool head, even if she had a sharp tongue.

It was hard not to give in to the temptation to run—the slope of the street towards the river encouraged haste—but that would only draw attention to them. Below, Jack could just make out the glint of water and ahead was the creaking inn sign he had used earlier as a landmark. 'Down here.'

It was a steep lane, almost an alley, with steps down the centre and cobbles at the sides, and it led directly to the riverside. Beside him Eva was walking briskly along, clutching her cloak at the throat and showing no sign of fear. Now they were well embarked on their escape she was still calm. Jack offered up thanks for being spared an hysterical female and allowed himself to think they were going to make it.

Then, only yards down the alleyway, Eva slid away from him with a little gasp of alarm, her feet skidding on the greasy stones. He dropped the valise and used both hands to reach for her, but she tripped on the steps and was down with a loud noise of rending cloth.

'Ouch! Oh, that is *hard.*' She sat up, batting irritably at the tangling folds of the cloak. In the gloom he could make out the white oval of her face, and the moth-shapes of her moving hands, but that was all.

'Are you hurt?' Jack dropped to one knee and reached out to support her.

'Bruised, I expect, nothing serious.' Eva began to get up, then clutched for her cloak. 'Oh, the wretched thing! The fastening at the throat has broken.' Jack helped her to her feet and steadied her. She moved well, he noted automatically. She was fit, slender, active. That was a relief—he had feared finding a pampered, plump princess on his hands. The cloak slipped away, invisible in the shadows at their feet.

'Just stand there a moment, I'll find the cloak and bag,' Jack began, then froze at the sound of loud voices. The flare of torchlight lit up the mouth of the alley with dramatic suddenness as booted feet hit the cobbles. He spun back against the nearest shuttered shop front, pulling Eva to him. The narrow lane filled with torchlight. 'Make this look good,' was all he had time to say before he bent his head and fastened his lips over hers.

'Mmmf!' she protested against his mouth, trying to jerk her head back. Jack applied one palm firmly to the back of her head, held her ruthlessly around the waist with the other hand and focused on giving a demonstration of blind rutting lust in action. It was not easy when the lady in question was trying to bite your tongue with vicious intent.

'Hey! What have we here?' The voice was loud, cultivated and arrogant. 'Can we all join in, friend?'

Jack raised his head, catching a glimpse of furious, rebellious brown eyes in the second before he pressed Eva's face into his shoulder, muffling her snarl of fury in the cloth. 'Sorry, but this lady's all mine.' There were half a dozen of them, officers in the pale blue-and-silver Maubourg uniform that he had learned to recognise as he had scouted the castle and its defences. They had been drinking, but only enough, it seemed, to make them boisterous and over-friendly.

He kept his accent pure Northern French, gambling on them finding that more intimidating than provocative—which was more than could be said for the Grand Duchess's efforts to free herself from his grip. He had his hands full of scented hair and sweet curves and she was pressed intimately against him. He tightened his hold, which had the unfortunate result of pressing her harder against the part of his anatomy that was entering into the deception with enthusiasm, and growled, 'Patience, sweetheart, wait until these gentlemen have gone at least.' Her reaction was to attempt to plant a knee in his groin. 'Friends, give us some privacy, the lady's husband will be looking for her—have some fellow feeling.'

That provoked the predictable lewd reaction, guffaws of laughter and cries of encouragement. They turned away, beginning to descend again to the river, when one, the most senior by the glimpses Jack had of his epaulettes, stopped.

'Why, the lady has dropped her cloak. Allow me.' He stooped, gathered it up and stepped close to lay it over Eva's shoulders, holding up the torch, all the better to see exactly what he was doing, and, Jack guessed grimly, to catch a glimpse of the lady in the case.

Chapter Three

*C*olonel *de Presteigne!* At the sound of his voice Eva stopped her efforts to free herself from Jack's outrageous embrace and clung to him instead, pressing her face into the angle of his neck. This was not a group of young subalterns who could be relied upon not to recognise their Grand Duchess in a plainly clad figure glimpsed in a dark alleyway. This was a senior officer who knew her all too well.

Against her lips she could feel the pulse in Jack's neck, strong and steady, and tried to stay as calm. 'Here, allow me, *ma chère.*' The weight of her cloak settled heavy on her shoulders and the colonel's fingers trailed, lingering, across the nape of her neck. He had done exactly the same thing two nights before as he had restored her gauze shawl at a reception, counting on her not knowing whether it was deliberate or accidental. Now she could recognise that it was quite deliberate, no doubt a favourite ploy of his he could not resist trying on any female, whether noble or bourgeoise.

'*Merci.*' Jack's hand came up, ostensibly to smooth the cloak around her shoulders, in effect bringing the edge of his palm sharply against the colonel's groping fingers. '*Bon nuit,*' he added pleasantly. Under the words the threat of violence hung like a lifted rapier.

Eva could feel the atmosphere crackle between the two men and knew instinctively that Jack had let his gallantry override his common sense. It was foolhardy, yet she felt a *frisson* of pleasure run through her that he had reacted that way. To be protected as a woman and not as a grand duchess was so novel she felt quite flustered. Or was that simply the effect of his outrageous kisses?

She felt Jack's arm tighten and could tell from the way the muscles flexed that he was preparing to push her out of harm's way if the other man reacted. There was a second where everyone seemed to have stopped breathing, then de Presteigne laughed. *'Bon nuit. Bon chance, mon ami.'* The officers clattered off down the hill, leaving them in darkness and silence. Eva felt herself slump against Jack in relief as she felt both her poise and her balance desert her. She dragged down a deep breath and tried to stiffen her shaking knees, even as her arms clung to him.

Before she could free herself, Jack lifted both hands, cupped her face and kissed her again with a fierceness that spoke of relief, tension released and, quite simply, sexual demand. His mouth was hot, hard and experienced and Eva surrendered to it, swaying into his embrace again with a sensation of letting go. Physical pleasure, direct and straightforward, was such a liberation that she felt her mind go blank and let herself slide into the moment, ignoring the squalid little alley, the greasy cobbles underfoot, the danger of pursuit.

Her mouth opened to the thrust of his tongue, its message echoed by the hardness of the male body she was clinging to. Behind her closed lids stars spun against blackness. Need flooded her body like the kick of a glass of spirits at the male taste of him, the scent of his skin.

'Hell.' He lifted his head, still holding her tight against him, and reality and reaction hit her simultaneously.

Hell? They were very nearly making love on the cobbles and all he could say was *Hell?* She must have been mad—what would have followed if that moment of insanity had happened in her bedchamber? How dare he presume to touch her? How could she have allowed it?

'You…' she began furiously.

'I forgot myself, indeed.' The rueful admission was tinged with a satirical note, reminding her of her own part in what had just occurred. In the darkness she could not read his face; it was perhaps as well he could not see hers. 'Relief and tension do strange things to us. Shall we go on?'

It was, certainly, the most dignified course to say nothing at all about the incident. Discussing it would lead nowhere but into more embarrassment—as it was, thinking about it made her skin hot all over. 'Certainly, Mr Ryder,' she said haughtily. 'Have you the valise?' Eva clutched the broken cloak clasp at her throat, feeling her pulse race against her knuckles.

'Here.' He stooped, a dark shape in the shadows, then took her arm. Knowing another fall risked injury, she made herself accept his touch, and tried to focus on something other than the newly re-awakened demands of her body.

'Who is looking after the coach?' She had not thought to ask, but this was the real world outside the castle, the world where coaches did not appear with drivers, grooms and out-riders ten minutes after one had the whim to drive out. In this world people stole horses if you left them unattended. It was a world she had been insulated from for almost ten years, one she was going to have to learn to understand and survive in very rapidly.

'My groom, Henry.' Jack's pace increased as the hill

levelled out and they reached the quayside. Light spilled out from taverns and bawdy houses all along its length; the destination, no doubt, of the colonel and his companions.

'What if someone speaks to him?' Eva pulled up her hood and watched her feet as they stepped over mooring ropes stretched taut across the quay.

'He spent two years in a French prison, so his grasp of the language is adequate, if colourful.' Jack sounded amused and alert, not at all like a man who had been indulging in a torrid kiss with a virtual stranger not minutes before. She only wished she had his *sangfroid*. Perhaps he had not found her very exciting. Now, that was a dampening thought. 'Here we are.'

The carriage was drawn up opposite the entrance to what Eva was quite certain was a brothel, as though waiting for its owner to return from his pleasures. A group of men were standing outside, talking over-loudly, and a bruiser with fists like hams stood watching them in the doorway. From the brightly lit windows came the sound of music and laughter.

The driver must have been on the lookout, for Eva saw a figure in a greatcoat sit up straight from its huddled position on the high box seat. 'There you are. *Quel surprise.*' He bent down as they came alongside and addressed Jack in accented French and with a familiarity that amazed her. 'Thought I'd be picking your broken bones off the rocks come morning. Quite resigned to it I was. This the lady, then?'

'No, just one I picked at random,' Jack said sarcastically, opening the carriage door and helping Eva inside. 'Of course it's the lady. Did you have a scout round this afternoon like I told you to?'

'Yes, guv'nor.' The man had dropped into English. 'And a very nice little burgh it is, too, not up to Paris, of course, or even Marseilles, but a man could have a bit of fun here, given the time.'

'Well, we haven't got any time, and speak French, damn you,' Jack retorted. 'Did you see the perfume factory?'

'I did. Ruddy great place and smelling like a Covent Garden flower stall. Why? Were you wanting to buy any presents?'

'No, I want to break in to it. Take us there now, and go steady, I don't want to attract attention.' Jack swung into the carriage, closed the door and lay back against the squabs opposite her. He breathed out a heartfelt sigh and Eva glimpsed the flash of white teeth. 'Phew. That all went better than I had expected.'

There did not seem to be much to say to that, at least, not anything that didn't risk an allusion to that episode in the alleyway. 'Do you really intend that we break in to the factory?'

'I am going to, you are not.'

'Mr Ryder, do I need to remind you who I am? I say where I go and do not go. Besides, I have the key.' The lights from the various establishments flickered into the carriage, illuminating Jack's face in flickering bursts. She caught a look of surprise before he had his expression under control again.

'Here? You have the key here? Why on earth would you bring it?'

It was tempting to pretend that she knew he would need it, but honesty got the better of her. 'It is in the pocket of this cloak; I forgot I had put it there last time I visited. It was when I discovered about the chemists Antoine is employing—I had gone down one evening to look in the old recipe books, because I had found a perfume receipt up at the castle that sounded promising and I wanted to see whether we had it at the factory already.

'I used to visit all the time, but since Philippe became ill I had stopped going. I don't think Antoine knows I have a key to the offices. What are we looking for?'

'*I* am looking for formulae, drawings, equipment—anything that might give me an inkling of what they are up to.'

'*We* will need to start in the offices, then,' Eva said, loftily ignoring his carefully selected pronouns. 'Then we can move to the laboratories if we find nothing there. The actual workshops are unlikely, I think—after all, the production of perfume is continuing as normal, or I would have heard about it.'

'It will be easier if you draw me a sketch.' Jack rummaged in one of the door pockets and came out with some paper and a pencil.

'I told you, Mr Ryder, I am coming with you.' Eva pressed them back into his hands. Even in the gloom of the carriage with the occasional flashes of light, she could see from his expression that he had no intention of agreeing. 'I have a perfect right to be there,' she said, with sudden inspiration. 'I can walk in with whomever I like—who is to refuse me? And the caretaker will not think to wonder what I am doing, he is so used to seeing me. It will reduce the risk, and hasten things, if you do not have to break in.'

'That is true,' Jack conceded. He must have sensed her surprise at his capitulation. 'I am not in the habit of turning down perfectly good arguments just because someone else makes them.'

'I thought you objected because I am a woman. Or because of my position.'

'Neither. What you do in your position is your choice. I have a history of disagreements with dukes, but not grand duchesses, and in my experience women have an equal tendency to good and bad sense as men.'

'Oh.' He had taken her aback and it took a moment to recover. Whatever their station, the men in her life made it quite clear—deferentially of course—that she must be treated with respect for her position and with patronising indulgence for her opinions. Even dear Philippe was prone to treat her as though she had hardly a thought in her head beyond gowns, good works and her son. A grand duchess was expected to be a dutiful doll.

She was beginning to relax a little too much with this man, beginning to like him. In her position it was dangerous to do any such thing just because someone did not treat you like a brainless puppet—and kissed like a fallen angel. 'Do you treat the dukes with as great a familiarity as you treat me? I have a title which you should use—'

'Your Serene Highness, if I address you as such, then not only will every sentence become intolerably prolonged, but we risk exciting interest at every point along our journey.'

'*Ma'am* would do excellently,' she retorted, finding all her irritation with him flooding back.

'What is your full name? Ma'am,' he added belatedly just as she drew in a hissing breath of displeasure.

'Evaline Claire Elizabetta Mélanie Nicole la Jabotte de Maubourg.'

Jack whistled. 'I can see why you are referred to as the Grand Duchess Eva. I think we are here.'

Eva looked out at the high wall and the double gates with a little wicket set in them. 'Yes, this is it.' She found the key and handed it to him. 'I shall tell the watchman that you are a French visitor from Grasse, interested in seeing how we make perfume here. And do try to remember to address me properly,' she added as Jack handed her down from the carriage.

'Yes, your Serene Highness.' The click of his heels was a provocation she decided to ignore.

Old Georges, the watchman, came out with his lantern before they were halfway across the courtyard. He was pulling on his coat one handed, his wrinkled face a mask of concern at being caught out. 'Your Serene Highness, ma'am! I wasn't expecting you, ma'am—is anything wrong?'

'No, nothing at all, Georges. This gentleman is from Grasse where they also make fine perfumes, as you know. He has no time to visit tomorrow, so I am showing him the factory tonight.'

'Shall I light you round, ma'am?'

'No, that is quite all right, just give *monsieur* your lantern. We will let you know when we leave.'

She opened the door into the offices, nodding a dismissal to the old man. Jack followed her in and closed the door. 'That was almost too easy,' he observed.

'What do you mean?' Eva opened the heavy day book and began to scan it. 'There is always just Georges on duty at night. Now, this is the outer office; I doubt if we'll find anything in here and the day book seems innocuous.'

'If you were operating a secret laboratory, would you leave just one old man on duty? He did not seem at all alarmed by our presence, so he cannot be in on the plot.' Jack scanned the room, opened one or two drawers, then moved into the next room. 'Therefore it must be well hidden.'

'I see what you mean.' Eva picked up her skirts and followed. 'The laboratories are through here; I have the master key.'

One after another the doors swung open until she reached the last one. 'We do not use this one any more. Oh, look— the lock has been changed.' Suddenly the familiar surroundings of the factory, which she had often walked through at night without a qualm, seemed alien and full of menace. She found she had moved closer to Jack and bit her lip in vexation at the betraying sign of fear. 'This key will not work on it.' She held it out as though to explain her instinctive movement towards him.

'I'll have to pick it, then.' Jack fished in his boot top and produced a bent piece of thin metal, then hunkered down and began to work on the lock. Eva picked up the lantern and came to hold it close. 'No, I do not need the light, thank you. I do this by feel and by sound.'

She watched, fascinated by his utter concentration. Again, the image of a swordsman, balanced and focused, came to her as she studied, not his hands, but his profile. His eyes were closed, his face relaxed as though listening to music, hearing and analysing what he heard at the same time.

Dark lashes fanned over tanned cheekbones. She saw a small crescent scar at the corner of his eye and observed the darkening growth of evening stubble begin to shadow his jawline. He was a very masculine figure, she thought, aware of the ease with which he balanced, the way his breeches moulded tightly over well-muscled thighs, the warmth of his body as she stood close.

I am too used to courtiers, too used to velvets and satins and posturing politicians and officials. Even the officers wear uniforms that speak more of the ballroom than the battlefield. This man looks dangerous, feels dangerous. And the biggest danger was, Eva realised, dragging her gaze away from his body to concentrate on the movement of the picklock, that she found him exciting to be with. Infuriating, insolent, casual and peremptory—and exciting.

It was something she had been wary of, these two years of widowhood, letting herself get close to another man, allowing the chill of her lonely bed to drive her into some rash liaison. You overheard too many people sniggering behind their hands as they recounted the tale of yet another widow of high rank taking a lover. It was risky, demeaning and ruinous to the reputation, for the secret always seemed to get out and, of course, it was inevitably the woman who was the butt of the jokes and the object of censure.

This feeling of arousal, this sense of hazard, was simply due to the shock of Jack Ryder's eruption into her life and the stress of her worries for the past weeks. Everything was heightened, from her fear, her anxiety, to her sensual instincts. That was all it was, all it could ever be.

'Got it.' The lock clicked and the door swung open. Inside was a room laid out as a drawing office, with two desks on one side, a wide, high table in the middle and two drawing slopes with stools on the other side. Along the back of the room was a range of chests fitted with wide drawers.

'Not a scrap of paper.' Jack pulled open the desk drawers. 'Empty except for pens and ink and rulers.'

Together they went to stand in front of the chests. Eva reached out a hand and touched the dark wood, noticing how heavily the piece was made. 'Look at the locks. I have never seen anything like that before.'

'Neither have I, and I will tell you now, I cannot pick these.' Jack straightened up from a minute inspection of the locks, each made of steel, with double keyholes and strange rods and bars on its surface.

'We will just have to smash the chests, then,' Eva said robustly. 'There are fire axes in all the rooms. Look, here.' She lifted the axe from the corner where it stood next to a pail of water and swung it experimentally. It was heavy.

'If I do that, then there is no hiding the fact that we have been here.' Jack leaned back against the chest, folded his arms and regarded her steadily.

'Of course.' That much was obvious.

'When Prince Antoine discovers your disappearance from the castle he may give chase, he may not. It is unlikely to be a matter of such desperate urgency to him that he will throw great resources into the pursuit. But if he links your disappearance with a raid on his secret laboratory, he is going to tear the countryside apart to find you.'

'But we must find the proof of what is going on.' Eva knew she was frowning in puzzlement. Was he really asking her if she would put her personal safety before her duty?

'We have enough to confirm that Prince Antoine is experimenting with explosives. My orders are to get you back safely, not to engage in espionage.'

'Are you telling me that you will walk away from this?' Eva demanded.

'No, I am asking you whether you want to. It is your life. It is your son waiting in England.'

Eva found the axe was still dangling from her hand. She propped it against the nearest chest while she tried to sort through her thoughts. Jack was offering her the choice, as he would to another man. He was not trying to hide the dangers from her. He wasn't happy about it, but she was here inside the factory with him because he was prepared to listen to her ideas.

'If there is a risk that some weapon that might aid him falls into Napoleon's hands, then I would never forgive myself,' she said, meeting the cool grey eyes. 'I married a ruler of a country, albeit a small one. This goes with the territory.' And she knew that if her life was at risk, then so was Jack's—at greater risk, in truth, because she was coming to realise that if Antoine wanted her, he would have to go through Jack to get to her.

His lips curved in a smile that held admiration and a certain wry acceptance that she had just raised the odds stacked against them and that the counters she was pushing on to the gaming table represented both their lives. He held out his hand for the axe. 'Right, let's get started.'

Eva picked up the rough wooden handle, set her teeth and tightened her fingers. 'No, let me.' She raised it, her arms aching at the weight, and smashed it into the first lock. Wood splintered and the jolt as the blade hit metal ran up her arm. 'That is for Fréderic. How dare Antoine try to take what is my son's? I wish he was here at this moment!'

Chapter Four

Jack reached across and prised Eva's fingers from around the axe handle. 'Allow me. I fully appreciate your wish to decapitate your brother-in-law, but I think I may be faster at turning these into firewood.'

She nodded abruptly, letting him take the axe and stepping back, her eyes fixed on the chests with angry intensity. *God, that's a woman with backbone!* he told himself as he set to work to hack the locks out of their setting. She should be the Regent, she deserved to be. The way he was addressing her, the approach he had taken to their relationship, was simply because he could not afford for her rank to stand in the way of the mission. It was not through any lack of respect, whatever she might believe.

What the Whitehall officials who had sent him on this mission would say to him embroiling her in breaking and entering and spying, he shuddered to think.

The final lock in the first chest yielded in a mass of splinters and Jack began on the next. Beside him he was aware of Eva pulling open drawers, taking out piles of papers and laying them in order on the big table.

The physical effort of swinging the axe, hacking into the solid wood, made the sore muscles around his ribs where the rope had cut earlier ache savagely. He had not realised the strain his body had been under while he was doing it—the mentally numbing effect of the drop beneath him as he had lowered himself over the battlements was probably enough to account for that.

Jack made himself concentrate on breaking into the chests as fast as possible. There was too much distraction already in this mission to be thinking about bruised ribs. The revelation about the Regent's health, the positive identification of Prince Antoine as the source of the treachery, the discovery of this factory and its secrets, were all outside his briefing and must be factored into his plans. And the impact that Eva was having on him was entirely unexpected and was going to need more than a change in tactics to neutralise.

He was not surprised to find himself admiring her for her coolness and courage, but he had not expected to find himself lusting after her. And that was what it was, there was no excuse for blinking at it. And it wasn't just beauty that was having this effect. Jack delivered a final blow to the last chest and began to wrench out the drawers. There was something else—a passion behind those steady brown eyes, an energy and anger concealed under cool grace and dignity. And her body in his arms, the sweet fury of her mouth under his when he had kissed her…

He stepped back as Eva came to lift out the sheets of drawings from the drawers he had just opened. She moved as though in a state reception, but her hair was coming down and her face was flushed from hurrying backwards and forwards in the stuffy room. Her cloak was in a crumpled heap on the floor and she had pushed back the sleeves of her gown to expose strong, slender forearms and fine-boned wrists.

The drawings were already arranged on the table, he saw, as she darted about, brow furrowed in concentration, sorting the latest collection. Jack put down the axe and leaned back against the splintered chest to watch her. He should never have kissed her, of course, although as a ruse in the crisis they had found themselves it, it had worked very well.

The frankness of her kiss when she had stopped fighting him, when the officers had gone, should not have surprised him, either. She had been a married woman, she knew what she was about. From the briefing he had received, if she had taken a lover she had been very discreet about it—he may have been receiving the benefit of several years of chaste frustration.

They had both been under pressure, in danger, and that embrace had been a response as natural as two soldiers going out and getting drunk after a battle—a life-affirming release. It seemed she had dismissed it now, and so should he. Which was easier said than done.

'Mr Ryder. Have you gone to sleep?' The tart enquiry was sufficient to dampen any wandering fantasies of unpinning the rest of her coiled conker-brown hair and letting it flow over her shoulders.

'No, ma'am, merely keeping out of your way until you had finished.' The meek response had her narrowing her eyes at him, but he kept his face straight and she turned back to the table with nothing more than thinned lips to show her displeasure. Grand Duchess Eva had a knack of ignoring unpleasantness and skimming straight over it—presumably a useful skill in court life. 'How have you sorted the papers?'

'These are drawings of different mechanisms, but I think they all go together.' She frowned and Jack found his hand lifting to smooth away the little crease between her brows. He jammed his fists in his pockets and came to stand next to her. 'I have stacked each one with the most recent drawing uppermost; they are all dated.' Eva pointed to a pile of black-bound notebooks. 'Those are all figures and calculations. Formulae. They make no sense to me.'

'To me, neither.' Jack flicked through the topmost one and turned his attention to the drawings. 'These are rockets.'

'Fireworks?' Eva leaned over close to his side to see and Jack drew in a sharp breath between his teeth. Her body was warm and fragrant and conjured immediate memories of how she had felt in his arms.

'No, artillery weapons.' Jack shifted round away from her as though to show what he was talking about. 'They were invented by Congreve and the British have been using them at sea and on land since about 1805. Napoleon offered a reward for anyone who could invent one for the French army—but they haven't got them yet. They aren't very accurate, though.' He leant over to study the other drawings. 'See, these are frames and carriages for firing the things—I wonder if they have worked out a way to aim them better?'

'And the notebooks might be formulae for the explosive powder?'

'Yes, that could be it. We need to get these back.' A look which could only be described as smug passed fleetingly over Eva's face. 'Ma'am, if you are about to say "I told you so"—'

Her eyes opened wide in hauteur. 'I would say nothing so vulgar, Mr Ryder. Just how do you suggest we get them all out past Georges?'

'We don't. Not all of them.' Jack picked up a pair of shears and began to cut down the top drawing from each pile, removing every scrap of waste margin. 'We take the most recent of each of these, the most recent notebook, and we destroy the rest.'

'The fireplace.' Eva nodded and began to scoop up the remaining drawings, jamming them into the cold fireplace in the
corner of the room. She picked up the notebooks and started
to tear the pages out. 'They'll burn better loose.'

The half-dozen reduced drawings folded into a neat packet
with the notebook. Jack jammed them into the breast of his
coat and lit a spill from their lantern. The paper flashed into
flame, blackening and falling apart in moments. Jack beat out
the ashes with the poker and straightened up, observing, 'How
to make a prince angry in one easy lesson.'

'Antoine will be beside himself,' Eva agreed, picking up
her cloak and shaking the dust out of it with a *moue* of distaste.
Jack took it and put it around her shoulders. 'Thank you, Mr
Ryder. We had better be off, had we not?'

'Indeed.' Jack scanned the floor until he found what he was
looking for: a shard of broken metal smaller than his little fingernail. 'I'll lock the door behind us.' It was a matter of
moments to flick the lock shut with the pick, then he eased
the fragment of metal into the keyhole and tried it again. The
fine pick jammed and grated against the foreign body. 'There,
they won't be able to get the door open, but at first they will
simply think the lock is faulty. It might buy us a little time.'

Eva led the way back out into the yard, keeping up a steady
flow of polite chitchat that could only have come from years
of practice at mind-numbingly tedious parties and diplomatic
events. The caretaker came out and stood waiting for them.
'Ah, there you are, Georges. We are off now; I am sorry to
have disturbed you. Is your daughter well? Excellent.'

Jack paused to hand the lantern to the old caretaker and
followed his gaze as the Grand Duchess made her way across
the cobbled yard with all the dignity and grace of a woman
stepping on to the ballroom floor. Her hair was coming down

at the back, her face was flushed and there was dust around the hem of her skirt. Her dirty, crumpled cloak looked as though it had been used as a bed by a pair of hounds. It gave him an idea.

'Thank you.' Jack pressed a coin into the gnarled hand and lowered his voice. 'Her Serene Highness can count upon you to be discreet, I am certain.' The man stared at him, comprehension dawning on his face, then he nodded vigorously.

'God bless her, *monsieur,* she deserves someone to care about her.'

Jack let one eyelid droop into a slow wink and sauntered out of the yard in Eva's wake, the bulge of the documents flattened under his arm.

Eva allowed herself to be assisted back into the carriage and sank back against the squabs. 'That wretched little rat! If Philippe recovers, he is going to make himself ill all over again when he finds out about Antoine. To ally us with Bonaparte is treachery enough, but to create weapons to put into his hands, that is beyond forgiveness or understanding.'

Now they were out of the factory, the full magnitude of what they had found was beginning to dawn on her. Inside it had all seemed an adventure. She had found it exciting, even though she had been frightened. She had enjoyed the give and take with Jack, both of words and, as she had swung that axe, of physical effort. He brought something alive in her, something that had been repressed for a very long time. It was enjoyable, and it must be resisted.

'How long will that lock hold them, Mr Ryder?'

'Quite a while. They will have to get a locksmith and although they will be impatient, I do not think they will realise it has been sabotaged. A locksmith will realise at once that it has been jammed, of course, then they will break the door down, I should imagine.' He sounded as though he was frowning in thought. 'From the weight, it may have been re-inforced—they'll be cursing their own precautions by the time they get inside.'

'And then they will ask Georges who was there and he will tell them, he has no reason not to. I should have spoken to him.' Eva shook her head, angered at her own lack of fore-sight. 'Although what I could have said to explain such a request without exciting curiosity, I do not know.'

'I think he will be circumspect.' There was something in Jack Ryder's voice that made her suspicious. Perhaps if it had not been almost dark, she would have missed it, but relying only on her hearing seemed to make her more sen-sitive to his mood.

'Why?' she demanded, suddenly suspicious. 'What did you say to him?'

'Nothing at all of any significance. I tipped him, said I was certain he would be discreet…'

'And why should he think that was needed?' A stray lock of hair tickled the dip of her collarbone. Eva put up a hand and discovered that half of it was down. As she touched her face, she felt how warm and damp her skin was. Her cloak, she recalled now, was crumpled and dusty from being on the floor.

'I walk in to a deserted building after dark with a man and I emerge an hour later, dishevelled and flushed and crumpled and he asks the caretaker for discretion,' she said flatly, working it out as she went. 'Georges thinks…you *encouraged* him to think…that we were making love in there!' The mag-nitude of it swept over her, leaving her hot faced and sick inside with humiliation. 'How could you?'

'It will be effective. And he appeared most sympathetic. I

imagine your people would not grudge you a little harmless diversion.'

'Harmless? Diversion? Is that how you categorise adultery and dissipation? Is it?' She kept her voice down with an effort. A grand duchess does not shout. Ever. 'Think of my position!'

'It could not be adultery,' the infuriating man pointed out. 'Neither of us is married.'

'Oh! You render me speechless.'

'Patently not, ma'am.'

Now he was being literal with her! He deserved to be thrown into the castle dungeons. If only she had access to them now—they would be full of rats and spiders and he could hang there in chains next to Antoine, she thought vengefully. They deserved each other. Then the memory of what else lay under the castle sent a shudder running through her. No, best not to think of that, not here, not now, in the darkness.

'Mr Ryder. Let me be plain. If I were to so far forget myself—and what is due to my position—as to take a lover, I would not chose an insolent, ill-bred adventurer and spy.'

'You made me a spy,' he countered.

That was true. Eva caught herself on the verge of an apology. This was outrageous—how was Ryder managing to put her in the wrong when he was quite obviously the one at fault? 'Just because I did not remonstrate as I should when you took those outrageous liberties with me in the alleyway, there is no reason to assume you can blacken my name—'

'Liberties, ma'am?' His voice, with its faintly mocking edge, cut into her diatribe like a knife into butter. 'Forgive me, but when those officers had gone I do believe that you returned my kisses with as much enthusiasm as I gave them. Either that, or you are an exceptionally talented actress.'

'I was in shock,' Eva protested, guiltily aware he was perfectly correct.

'Of course you were,' he agreed smoothly. 'I perfectly understand. And, please forgive me, but that incident had nothing whatsoever to do with my exchange with Georges just now. I am afraid he leapt to a conclusion and it seemed to fit our purposes all too well.' There was a pause, which Eva filled by gritting her teeth together and concentrating on breathing slowly and calmly through her nose. 'Would you like me to go back and explain he has jumped to an incorrect conclusion, your Serene Highness?'

'No!' Deep breathing was not as calming as it was supposed to be. 'It is too late now. The damage is done. Where are we?' She looked out of the window and saw the glint of the river below. 'Driving back into Maubourg? But why?'

'Because it is the last place they would expect you to be by now if you have been missed. This coach is going to drive slowly, and very visibly, through the middle of the town. Henry is going to ask the way for the Toulon road at least three times, at each point making certain that the rather gaudy red door panels are well illuminated. We will then drive into a dark alleyway, remove the door panels to reveal a tasteful—and fictitious—crest, and equally sedately, make our way out of the Northern gate with me driving. By the time daylight comes Henry will be driving again, the door panels will be plain and to all intents this will be a third carriage, one which has not been seen in Maubourg.'

'And if they have not missed me yet?' The precautions and layers of planning took her aback. If she had thought at all about what would happen after they had left the factory Eva had simply envisioned driving as fast as possible towards the coast. 'No,' she answered her own question. 'I see. They will question the guards and time my escape by us leaving my bed-chamber, so they will be checking up on the coaches leaving tonight. Mr Ryder—do you do this sort of thing a great deal?'

'Abduct royalty? No, this is the first time.' He must have felt the intensity of her glare in the gloom, for he continued before she could explode. 'Missions into Europe during the war, yes, some. Mainly I carry out intelligence work for the government, and occasionally for private individuals.'

'What sort of thing? Following errant wives?'

'Checking that suitors are what they seem, occasional bodyguard work. Recently I assisted a gentleman who had misplaced his wife ten years ago.'

'Goodness. How very careless of him. And you earn your living from this?' He spoke like a gentleman, with the hard edge and decisiveness of a military man. Her jibe about lack of breeding had been far from the mark. He wore no jewellery and she could make no judgement from his clothes, other than they seemed suitable for climbing down walls.

'I have an adequate private income. I do this because I enjoy it.'

'You do?' How very odd, to enjoy fear and danger. Then Eva realised that she was enjoying it, too, in a perverse sort of way. She was scared, worried sick about Fréderic, embarrassed by much of what had happened today, but she was also alive. The blood was pumping in her veins, her mind was racing, she had been pitchforked from a life of predictability and privileged powerlessness into one of complete uncertainty—and she felt wonderful.

Only the day before she had gazed at her own reflection in the mirror and struggled to accept the fact that all that lay ahead of her was a decline into graceful middle age.

In a few months she would be twenty-seven. For nine

years she had been a dutiful wife, then a dutiful Dowager Duchess. She had done nothing rash, nothing impulsive, nothing exciting. As Freddie grew up, then married, she would step further and further back into respectable semi-retirement. It was her duty. She might as well be dead.

'Ma'am?'

'Yes, Mr Ryder?'

'You sighed. Are you all right?'

'I am contemplating the thought that it is dangerous to wish for things. I had been finding my life a trifle dull and wanting in diversion recently. Then Napoleon returns, Philippe is struck down, someone tries to murder Freddie and me and you leap through my bedchamber window and take me burgling. I appear to be about to enter an adventurous phase in my life.'

'I can promise you that.' The coach stopped again, for what must be the third time. Eva listened to Henry's rough French accent and the response from the watchman standing under the streetlight. She drew back further into the shadows.

'Why are we not taking the Toulon road?' she asked as they started forward once more.

'Because, although it is faster, it is also riskier. Support for Bonaparte is strong to the south, and it is the obvious route for us to take. Then how do we find a boat to take us to England from a French port? I am going north, up into Burgundy, and then north-east towards Brussels, which is where the king has fled. Wellington has had his headquarters there since early April. We will go from there to Ostend.'

The coach turned sharply, lurching over a rougher surface, and pulled up. 'Excuse me, we will be on our way in a moment. Henry will sit with you for a few miles.'

After some scraping and banging at the sides of the

vehicle, the coachman climbed in, doffing his hat. 'Begging your pardon, ma'am.'

'That is quite all right.' This at least was easy. One's entire life appeared to be made up on some days of holding conversations with tongue-tied citizens. 'Have you been a coachman long, Henry?'

'I'm a groom, ma'am. Least, that's what I am official-like. Most of the time I'm whatever the guv'nor wants me to be, depending on what we're about.'

Hmm, not so tongue-tied, which could be useful. 'So sometimes you have to be a gentleman's groom, when Mr Ryder is at home in London?'

'Aye, ma'am. When the guv'nor's being himself like, which isn't often.'

'That must be difficult for his family,' Eva persisted, fishing as carefully as she could. 'For his wife, for example.' Though he had said he was not married… 'Or his parents.'

'Would be, indeed, ma'am, if he'd a wife. As for his respected father, top-lofty old devil he was, if you'll pardon me saying so; nothing the guv'nor did was ever right for him, so I don't reckon he'd give a toss, even if he was alive. Which he ain't.'

That had not got her very far. He was not married and a *top-lofty* father confirmed his origins were respectable. It was an odd choice of words, *being himself*—it implied two very different lives. And London was *home.* Just who was Jack Ryder?

'We're out the Eastern gate,' Henry observed. 'Another hour and we'll be snug at the inn, ma'am. I'll wager you'll be glad to be settled for the night.'

'You know where we are staying tonight, then?'

'Why, yes, ma'am. The guv'nor doesn't leave things to chance. All booked, right and tight on the way down, and the landlord expecting us late, so no suspicions there. It's a nice little place used by gentlemen on hunting expeditions in the foothills, but it's quiet now.'

Eva sank back against the squabs and fell silent. Henry was certainly not in need of setting at his ease in her presence, so, strange as it felt, she did not have to make conversation. It was curiously peaceful to realise that she had no duties, none at all, other than to survive this adventure and reach England.

'Ma'am!' She jerked upright, startled to find they had stopped moving and there were lights outside. 'You'd dropped off, ma'am,' Henry added helpfully.

'Yes, thank you,' Eva said repressively. Goodness knows what sort of appearance she must present with her gown crumpled, her cloak filthy and her hair all over the place. She pushed it back and pulled her hood up to shadow her face as best she could. People saw what they expected to see, and this innkeeper would not be expecting a weary traveller to be his grand duchess. She must just be careful to do nothing to attract his attention.

The door opened, Jack helped her down and the landlord came bustling out to greet them, cheerfully prepared for their arrival at this late hour.

'Welcome, sir, welcome, madam! Come along inside, if you please.' Eva let the familiar local patois wash over her as the horses were sent off to the stables, their luggage carried in and Henry vanished in the direction of the taproom. 'The room is just as you ordered, sir. The bed has been aired and I am sure your wife will be comfortable.'

The man led the way up the stairs. Eva stopped dead at the bottom, the last traces of sleep banished. 'Room? Wife? Which room are *you* in?'

'Ours.' Jack took her arm and began to climb. Without

actual violence she had no option but to follow him. 'Thank
you.' He took the branch of candles from the landlord's hand
and pushed her gently through the open door at the head of
the stairs. 'This looks excellent. Some hot water, if you will.'

Eva stood in the middle of the room and looked around.
One dresser, two chairs, a rug before a cold grate, a clothes
press, a screen and a bed. One bed. 'And just *where* are you
sleeping?' she enquired icily. Beneath her bodice her heart
was thudding like a military tattoo.

'With you. In that bed. Why? Where else do you expect
me to sleep?'

Chapter Five

'I expect you to sleep in your own bed, in your own room.' Her mouth had gone dry, her stomach was full of butterflies.

'I am your bodyguard. I need to be close to you.' He was touching the flame to the other candles in the room, his hand steady as he did so. Eva felt her irrational panic building. What was she afraid of? That he would ravish her? Ridiculous. Somehow common sense did not stop the unsettling physical reactions.

'Then sleep on the floor.' She pointed to the far corner, hidden behind a screen.

'Why should I be so uncomfortable?' Jack enquired. 'The role of the modern bodyguard does not include sleeping at your threshold like a faithful troubadour. I have had a long hard day. That looks like a very large, very comfortable bed. I'll put the bolster down the middle of it if that would make you feel any better.'

The click as he turned the key in the lock brought the panic bubbling closer to the surface. 'It is scandalous,' she stated. 'I am—'

'My wife,' Jack said, turning from the door to face her

across the expanse of snowy-white quilt. There was not a trace of amusement on his face. 'For the rest of this journey you act, think, live as my wife.'

'No!'

'Eva, what are you afraid of? Do you think I am going to insist on my conjugal rights? That would be carrying the deception a little too far. This is for your safety.' It was not a small room, but his masculine presence seemed to fill it. Part of her mind registered that he had called her by her first name; part of it dismissed that as an irrelevance. The forefront of her consciousness was full of the reality that she was going to have to spend this night, and goodness knows how many nights after it, in bed with this man.

'Of course I do not think that.' She was fighting *not* to think of it! 'And I am not afraid of you.' She tilted her chin haughtily and tried to stare him down.

No, she was not afraid of him, she was afraid of what he was reminding her she missed, afraid that every hour spent with him would tear away a little more of the screen she had erected round her needs and desires. Afraid that she might turn to him in the night for strength and comfort and… It was easy to resist temptation when it was not a fingertip away, easy to ignore yearnings when there was no way of satisfying them.

'You are tired. We both are. They will bring hot water up soon and you can wash and go to bed.' As he spoke there was a tap at the door. Eva watched, startled, as Jack slid a knife from his boot and went to open the door. By the time the little maid had come in with the pitcher of water, the knife was out of sight. He turned the key in the lock again once she was gone and gestured towards the washstand and screen. 'Go on.' He lifted her valise and placed it behind the painted wooden panels.

'Thank you.' Eva forced the words out of stiff lips and

stepped past him into the fragile privacy. She was going to have to use her cloak as a dressing gown. Her hands shook as she delved into the valise, but she lifted out the scanty contents, shook out the one spare gown he had allowed her and sorted through the rest. *Oh, no!*

'Mr Ryder.' It was the tone she used to point out some grave dereliction of court protocol and it normally produced a reaction of instant, anxious, attention on the part of the person so addressed.

'Yes?' His voice sounded muffled, but unconcerned. Eva had a momentary vision of his shirt being pulled off over his head and turned her back on the join in the screen panels resolutely. For a moment she had wanted to peep, like some giggling maidservant spying on the grooms.

'When you took those things out of my valise at the castle, you apparently removed my nightgown. What, exactly, do you expect me to sleep in?' If she hadn't been so angry, she would have considered her words more carefully. As it was, there was a long silence from the other side of the screen. *He is laughing at me, the beast,* she decided grimly, just as a white linen garment was tossed on top of the screen.

'Have one of my shirts.'

'You have plenty, I assume?'

'Of course, I knew how long I was packing for.' *He is laughing.* Eva fumed as she stripped off and washed hastily, then dragged the shirt over her head. It came midway down her thighs, the cuffs dangling well below her fingertips. She pulled it down as much as possible, rolled up the cuffs and unpinned her hair. At least he had left her hairbrush in the case.

The long, regular strokes had the soothing power of routine. She did the requisite one hundred and hesitated, half-tempted to do another set. Then another. She braided it hastily. 'Where are you, Mr Ryder?'

'In bed.'

'Then close your eyes.'

'Very well. They are closed. Will you snuff out the candles?'

A cautious look around the edge of the screen revealed that Jack was indeed in bed, his eyes closed as promised. There was no doubting that he was awake somehow; he seemed to radiate alertness. The covers were pulled up to his chin, not giving her any hint as to what he might—or might not—be wearing and the odd lump down the centre of the bed showed that he had inserted the bolster as a gesture to modesty.

Eva emerged, resisted the undignified urge to scuttle from candle to candle and then dive into bed, and instead went round carefully snuffing each until the bed itself was just a white glimmer in the room. She slid under the sheet, pulling it up tight to her throat.

'Good night, Eva.'

No more *ma'am*, not until they reached safety. It was a curiously liberating thought. 'Good night,' she responded coldly. *Jack.* Liberating, or dangerous? Protocol was a straitjacket, but it was also an armour. Behind it one could maintain a perfect reserve, perfect privacy for the emotions. This adventure was going to throw her into an intimacy of thoughts and fears with this man that was at least as perilous as any physical closeness.

She should have been exhausted, ready to drop into sleep the moment her lids closed. The bed was comfortable, clean, and there was the reassuring touch of the bolster down her spine to remind her that she did not need to fear turning and touching Jack in the night. Of course she trusted him, and really, it was no different to him sleeping on the floor on the far side of the room, she told herself stoutly.

So why could she not sleep? Eva closed her eyes and tried to relax, starting with her toes and working up. She tried counting sheep, reciting recipes, recalling Italian irregular verbs. Hopeless.

Was he asleep? She held her breath to listen to his, steady and even. There was an interruption as he shifted slightly, a soft sigh, then the even rhythm resumed. Jack Ryder was obviously one of those infuriating people who could sleep anywhere, under any circumstances. She just hoped he would wake up as quickly if danger threatened.

Eva turned her thoughts resolutely to her son, her lips curving into a smile as she did so. How soon before she could see him? He would have grown so much. What new clothes would he need? Would he look more like his father now as he grew up, or less? Would he still throw himself into her arms to be kissed, or was he too grown up for that now? Without realising it, she relaxed and drifted off to sleep.

Jack opened his eyes on to darkness and lay still, trying to work out what had woken him. Eva's breathing was soft and regular, she was lying curled up with her back turned and had managed to push the bolster a good three-quarters of the way across the bed towards him. A woman used to sleeping alone.

Distantly a dog was barking, the bored yap of a lonely animal, not the aggression of a threatened one. The yard below was silent. He dredged into his mind and came up with the sound of a closing door outside. It must be about three o'clock—who was abroad at this time? He had chosen this inn, a hunters' favourite off the main road, for its isolation.

He eased out of the bed, pulling on his breeches before taking four silent strides to the window. He unlatched the shutter, pushed it back and stood looking down until his eyes adjusted to what dim light there was. Minutes passed, then he saw a familiar figure come out of the shadow of the stable opposite and walk across the yard. In the centre the man stopped and looked up, directly into his eyes, although he could not have seen Jack.

He eased the window wide and leaned out. 'What's the matter?' He pitched the whisper to reach Henry and no further.

'Nothing,' the groom hissed. 'I was restless.'

Jack raised a hand in acknowledgement and silently closed the window again. Henry was lying, of course, he had probably been prowling about every half-hour or so throughout the night. He never seemed to need much sleep—the result, he claimed, of becoming accustomed to very little when he was a prisoner of war.

The man drifted out of sight as soundlessly as he had appeared. Jack turned to go back to bed and found himself face to face with a white spectre. 'What the hell!'

It was Eva, of course. How she had got out of bed and across the room without him hearing her was a worry—was he losing his sharpness of hearing, the instinct that warned him of danger? But, of course, Eva was not a danger. Not, at least, in the sense that she was likely to knife him in the back.

'It is me,' she whispered. 'What's wrong? Is it Antoine's men?'

'No, nothing's wrong. I was simply checking. Henry is on guard below,' he said reassuringly. 'Go back to bed.'

'Very well.' Eva started to turn, stumbled, put out her hand for balance and hit it sharply against his naked ribs. The gasp of pain as her nails grazed across his bruises was out before he could choke it back. 'What's the matter?'

'Nothing. You scratched me slightly and made me jump, that's all.' She stood, looking up at him as though she could read his face in the near darkness. Her own was a pure oval of white, only the shadow of her eyes discernible.

'I do not believe you,' she said after a moment, and spun round towards the bedside table, the movement sending a faint rumour of warm skin and gardenia wafting, achingly, to his nostrils. 'Stay there.' There was a scrape and a flame flared up. She touched it to the candle and carried it over to where he stood. '*Mon Dieu!* Your ribs, your chest! Turn around.'

'It is nothing, just bruises from the rope.' Jack tried to urge her back to the bed, but she stood her ground. Eva should have looked ludicrous in his oversized shirt, her slim legs and slender feet emerging from beneath the hem, but she looked tousled and delectable and the fact she was wearing something of his was oddly arousing. No, *extremely* arousing.

'What rope? And turn around, I am not going to hurt you, you foolish man.' She seemed to have no conception that he might not obey her.

The implication that he was frightened had him turning before he could catch himself. Then he froze as a cool palm touched lightly on the diagonal welt across his back. 'You didn't think I climbed down the castle wall to your window like a lizard, did you?' It was suddenly difficult to control his breathing.

'Rational speculation about how you appeared in my room was the last thing on my mind,' Eva said drily. 'You could have flown there on a broomstick for all I knew.' She made a soft sound of distress as she moved the candle to see the full extent of the damage. Jack stood watching their shadows slide across the bedchamber wall and fought the urge to turn and take her in his arms. Her feminine concern, the gentleness of her touch, almost banished the constant awareness of who she was. But the Grand Duchess was all too aware of it; Jack reminded himself grimly of the fact, and turned round.

It did not help that the suddenness of his movement gave her no time to move her hand and they ended up almost chest to chest, her right arm wrapped around his naked ribcage, her left hand holding the candlestick out to the side in an effort not to scorch either of them. Oddly, the intimacy did not appear to be concerning her.

Eva tutted again, moving away to put the candle down safely. 'I don't suppose you have anything useful like medical supplies along with all those clean shirts, have you?' He was breathing like a virgin on her wedding night now and Eva was perfectly composed. *For God's sake, man, get a grip.*

'Of course.' Offering up a quick prayer of thanks that he had stopped to put on his breeches, Jack lifted one of his valises on to the bed and opened it. 'There. Not that I need anything.'

'I will be the judge of that.' Eva began to lift things out of the case. 'What on earth are these?'

'Probes for removing bullets.'

'Urgh.' She opened her fingers fastidiously and dropped the instrument on to the bed. 'I hope Henry knows what to do with them, or that you stay well out of the line of fire, because I am certainly not using them. Here, witch hazel, that is just the thing. And some lint.' She shook the bottle and pulled out the stopper, releasing the strange astringently aromatic smell into the room. 'Sit on the corner of the bed, please.'

The liquid was cold on his sleep-warm skin and Jack could feel the goose bumps forming as she dabbed her way up his back and across his shoulder along the lines left by the rope. He found himself wondering with a sense of detachment if she was going to deal with his chest with such aplomb. It seemed she would. For some reason a woman who baulked at sharing his bedchamber could cope quite easily with his half-naked body provided there was an injury to deal with.

Eva moved round, tipping the bottle on to the lint again to re-dampen it. She paused to survey the darkening bruise, then caught his eye. 'What is it?' *Damn the woman, can she read minds?* His ability to keep a straight, unreadable, face was one of his most valuable professional assets. So he had believed.

'I was wondering why you do not appear to find this embarrassing,' he answered frankly. 'We are both half-dressed and in a bedchamber, and earlier that appeared to be a major obstacle to a good night's sleep.'

She looked down her nose, suddenly every inch the Grand Duchess, despite her makeshift nightshirt and bare feet. 'You are injured; that is something that must be dealt with, whatever the situation. On the other hand, finding myself constrained to share a bed with a strange man was something I would hope to avoid if at all possible.'

'So modest behaviour depends on circumstance? Ouch!'

'Sorry.' She peered close to see why he had jumped, then carried on dabbing. Her breath fanned warmly over his collarbone, playing havoc with his pulse rate. 'Of course it depends. If I was in my bath and the place was burning down, I would not expect you to wait politely outside the door until I got dressed before breaking in to rescue me.'

Jack fought with himself, biting the inside of his cheek in an effort not to laugh, then he caught Eva's eye and watched while she imagined the scene she had just described. Her lips twitched, the corners of her eyes crinkled and she burst out laughing. He had never seen her laugh before; he hadn't known whether she had a sense of humour. The only smiles he had seen were polite social expressions, but this was another woman. One hand pressed to her lips, she hurried to put the bottle down safely, then collapsed on the bed in a paroxysm of giggles.

'Oh, Lord! I can just imagine our chamberlain doing just that! "I regret to inform your Serene Highness that the castle is on fire. Might I suggest you complete your coiffure at your earliest convenience, ma'am, as the flames are licking around my feet, ma'am…"'

She looks eighteen, a girl, so fresh, so natural, so sweet. The laughter drained out of Jack as he stared at her. Eva sat up at last, hiccupping faintly and mopping her eyes with the cuff of the shirt.

'I am sorry, it must be the strain.' She smiled at him hazily. 'I can't remember the last time I laughed out loud, or even found something silly enough to laugh about.'

Jack put out a hand towards her, not knowing what he wanted, only knowing he needed to touch her. Eva put her hand in his, her eyes questioning. He did not speak—there was nothing to say, nothing that he could articulate. For a moment she held his gaze, then awareness of who she was and where they were became clear from her expression and she looked away, chin up. Jack freed her hand and stood up.

'Back to bed, we will need to be up in a couple of hours. You require your sleep.'

She nodded haughtily, very much on her dignity and got up, skirting carefully around him to slide under the covers on her side. 'Good night.'

'Good night.' He stoppered the bottle of witch hazel, grateful for the way its heavy odour blanked out the feminine scent of her, and pulled the covers up firmly over his shoulders.

It was no part of his plans to be attracted to a woman, least of all a grand duchess. He had not thought himself so susceptible, nor so unprofessional. It was not as though he was short of feminine comfort for his physical needs—a succession of highly skilled barques of frailty made quite certain of that—for he had long since recognised that his chosen path was not one a wife could be expected to tolerate.

Not that the examples of marital life about him had made him eager to commit himself to such a relationship, so it was not such a deprivation. His recently widowed sister, Bel, had once confided that her husband was so dull she could hardly stay awake in his presence, his father had been a serial adulterer, and his friends, one after another, appeared to be sacrificing themselves on the altar of respectability by marrying simpering misses straight from the portals of Almack's.

Flirting with young ladies of good breeding was boring and risked raised expectations and broken hearts. Flighty matrons and dashing widows required more emotional commitment than he was prepared to invest—which left the professionals, with whom one could at least be assured there was no hypocrisy involved.

So why was this woman making him hard with desire? Why did he want to shelter her to an extent that went way beyond his brief to bring her back safely to England? She was hurt, anxious and vulnerable despite her efforts not to betray that and she had got under his skin in a totally unexpected way.

It was the novelty, obviously, Jack decided, stopping himself turning over restlessly for the third time. He was unlikely to find himself on such intimate terms with a member of a royal family again, that was all it was. Satisfied he had put that anxiety to rights, he closed his eyes, willed himself to sleep, and forbade himself to dream.

On the other side of the bolster Eva was wrestling with her emotions, her body's reactions and her sense of decorum and duty. She had woken, roused by instinct—for she was certain Jack had made no sound—and had lain for a moment looking

at the silhouette of his head and torso against the pale frame
of the window. His body was a beautiful shape, the classic
male outline of inverted triangle over a narrow waist,
enhanced by a musculature in the peak of fitness—hard,
sculpted and wickedly exciting to a woman who had lived a
life of celibate respectability for over twenty months.

Then the sleep had cleared from her mind and she forgot
erotic considerations in anxiety about what he was looking at.
That anxiety had carried her across the room to his side
without self-consciousness, or any modest concern for how
she was dressed, and no sooner had she recollected these
things than she had been distracted again by the realisation
that he was hurt.

Small boys with scraped knees were a matter of routine for
a mother; grown men needing bandaging and nursing were
part of a wife's duties, and somehow that had carried over into
caring for her brother-in-law, and now Jack. She simply had
not thought of him as anything but a body to be mended until
he had looked into her eyes and held out his hand to her.

What was he asking? What did he want? After the skill of
that kiss in the alleyway she had no doubt he could make a
fine attempt at seducing her, if that was what he desired. She
would find him hard to resist, she acknowledged that. Eva had
long since abandoned self-deception as a method of dealing
with her situation in life, and she was not going to risk everything by pretending she did not know temptation when she
saw it. For years she had been able to turn away flirtation,
thinly veiled offers and outright attempts at seduction without
the slightest quickening of her pulse rate, not a moment's
sleep lost. Now she felt as unsteady as a young girl in the
throes of her first infatuation.

Was it simply friendship she had seen in Jack's gaze, in his outstretched hand? Or was it the first move of a skilled seducer? She could afford neither, for if friendship brought her closer to him she feared her own need would betray her, and if he was intent on seduction, then only a rigorously maintained distance and discipline would save her from herself.

Eva closed her eyes and made herself lie patiently waiting for sleep.

There was no virtue in remaining chaste while there was no temptation, she told herself severely. The morning would bring new resolution and greater strength, she had to believe that.

Chapter Six

The sound of booted feet on the floorboards brought Eva awake with a start of alarm. Sunlight was flooding through the window, morning had broken and she was still abed while pursuit could be at the door. She sat bolt upright. 'What time is it?' How could she have slept so soundly? 'How are your bruises?'

'Six, that is all. But time you got up, all the same. And my bruises are much better, thank you.' Jack straightened from fastening a valise and smiled at her, a casual smile that held none of last night's unspoken complications. He was fully dressed, clean shaven and alert. It felt very odd to have a man in her bedchamber while she was still in bed. 'There is warm water on the washstand. I'll wait downstairs unless you need any help with…er…' he waved one hand in an effort to find an acceptable word '…buttons or anything.'

'Thank you, no,' Eva replied, suppressing the information that she had carefully selected garments that did not require assistance with laces, buttons or any other fastening. Yesterday she would have probably blurted that out; today she was resolved to retain the utmost dignity compatible with sharing a room with a man to whom she was not married.

'Very well, I will order breakfast for twenty minutes' time.' He paused, one hand on the key. 'Lock the door behind me.'

She made it downstairs with five minutes to spare and was rewarded by a raised eyebrow as Jack stood and held a chair for her in the deserted parlour. 'I have a busy schedule that requires frequent changes of clothing,' she explained, answering the unspoken comment on her punctuality and accepting a proffered napkin with a nod of thanks. 'Where is Henry eating?'

'In the kitchen, I imagine.' Jack helped himself to a hearty slice of ham, two eggs and a length of sausage.

'I would prefer that he join us.' She poured coffee into the large cups and added a generous amount of milk, still frothy from the milking pail.

Jack accepted a cup, frowning. 'Why? He can hardly chaperon us in the bedchamber, so his presence at breakfast seems a touch superfluous.'

'Even so. I wish to retain the appearance of respectability so far as I am able.' How direct he was! She had hoped to raise the matter without mentioning chaperons or bedchambers, but, no, Jack made no concession to conventions, or to the mild hypocrisies that oiled the wheels of real life. Eva tried not to either blush, or look like a prude, and suspected she had ended up merely looking starched-up. Not such a bad thing.

'As you wish.' Jack got up, put his head round the door to catch a passing potboy with the message and resumed his seat. 'I am not sure Henry would add to any lady's credit, but I cannot provide you with a lady's maid.'

'No, I agree. It would not be fair to her, and she could slow us down in an emergency.' Eva buttered bread sedately, resisting the fragrant dish of ham and eggs until she had taken the sharpest edge off her appetite. Dinner last night had been unusually early and she had had nothing since, but she was not going to bolt her food. Years of eating in her room so she could be seen dining in public with the appetite of an elegant bird had left her awkward about tucking into a meal in company.

'Quite. A very practical assessment.' Jack was regarding her with a quizzical air. Eva stared haughtily back and carried on nibbling her bread and butter. 'Is anything wrong?'

He was always catching her off-balance, she thought resentfully. Half the time he was coolly expressionless, practical and seemed to expect her to just get on with things as he did himself. Then there would be a flash of sympathy, of understanding or concern, and his grey eyes came alive with a warmth that made her want to reach out and take his hand again.

'Whatever could there be wrong?' she said lightly, feeling her smile tighten. She added, with an edge of sarcasm, 'This is all quite in the normal run of my experience, after all.'

'Treating me like a awkward ambassador is not going to— Henry, good morning. *Madame* would like you to join us.'

'Strewth.' The groom stood turning his hat round in his hands. 'You sure about that, ma'am? I mean, I've been seeing to the horses this morning and all.'

'Entirely sure. Please sit in that chair there, Henry. Now, would you care for some coffee?'

Eva poured, served herself ham and eggs, made careful conversation with both men in a manner that effectively forbade the introduction of any personal matter whatsoever and finally rose from the table, satisfied that she had set the tone for the rest of the journey. 'Where are we travelling to today?' she asked over her shoulder as Jack pulled out her chair for her at the end of the meal.

He shook his head slightly and she caught her breath. She had been beginning to feel safe, lulled by the routine domesticity of breakfast. Of course, walls had ears, people could be bribed to pass on tittle-tattle about earlier guests. The cold knot in her stomach twisted itself together again, not helped by the squeeze he gave her elbow as she preceded him out of the room. She was not used to being touched. It was meant to be reassuring, she was sure, but it succeeded all too well in reminding her just how much she needed him.

Jack waited until the carriage had rattled out of the inn yard and Henry had turned west before speaking. 'Grenoble, Lyon, Dijon, then north to the border with the Kingdom of the Netherlands by whatever seems the safest route at the time,' he said without preamble as she folded her cloak on the seat.

'Through so many big towns? Is that wise?' The watchful grey eyes opposite narrowed and Eva caught a glimpse of displeasure. *He does not like my questioning his judgement,* she thought. *Too bad, I want to understand. I need to.*

'In my judgement it is,' Jack responded evenly. 'We need the speed of the good roads and travellers are less obvious in cities. However, if we run into trouble, then I have an alternative plan.' She nodded, both in comprehension and agreement. 'I am glad you approve.'

'It is not a question of approval,' Eva snapped, then caught at the fraying edge of her temper. Grace under pressure, that was what Louis had always insisted was the mark of rulers. Grace under pressure at all times. 'I wish to understand,' she added more temperately. 'I am not a parcel you have been charged with delivering to the post office. Nor does my position make me some sort of mindless figurehead as you seem to think. If I understand what we are doing, why we are going where we do, then I am less likely to make any mistakes to earn your further displeasure.'

'It is not my place to express displeasure at any action of yours.' Jack's retort was even enough to tip her emotions over into anger again. He was humouring her, that was what he was doing. He wanted it both ways—he wanted to call her by her first name, carry on this pretence of marriage and sharing a room, yet the moment she tried to take an active part in their flight he fell back on becoming the respectful courtier.

'No, it is *not* your place, Mr Ryder, but I thought we had agreed that for the duration of this *adventure* I was not a grand duchess, that you would call me by my given name. I had assumed that meant you would also stop treating me as if I was not a real person. I hate it when I visit a village and they have painted the shutters especially. How do I know what lies behind them? Are they prosperous or are they poor? How much money was wasted on that paint? I want the truth, Mr Ryder, not platitudes, not your equivalent of painted shutters.'

Her angry words hung in the air between them. She saw the bunching of the muscles under the tight cloth of his breeches and wondered if he was about to jump up, pull the check cord and transfer to the box, leaving her in solitude to fume.

Then Jack leaned back into the corner of the seat and smiled. It was not a sign of humour, it was the kind of smile she produced when she was deeply displeased, but it would not be politic to say so, a curving of thinned lips. Had that hard mouth really been the one that had slid over her warm lips with such sensual expertise?

'Very well.' Eva jumped, dragging her eyes away from his lips. 'If you must have it without the bark on it. The amount of danger we are in all depends on whether Antoine wants you back, and, if he does, whether he has a preference for alive or dead.' Eva tried not to flinch at the brutal analysis. 'He might simply be satisfied with you disgraced, in which case we are doing his work for him—last night was enough to ruin you. Or, of course, an accident on the road has the advantage of simplicity.

'If he wants you ruined, he just has to leave us alone, spread the rumour that you have fled with your lover and make sure every newspaper in Europe picks up the tittle-tattle.'

'When I get back to England and I am seen to be received by the Prince Regent and the Queen—'

'The damage will be done by then, the dirt will be on your name. No smoke without fire, they will say.'

'I wonder, then, that you chose to share my room last night.' Cold shame was washing over her body—what would Freddie think? Small boys were cruel; someone would make certain he heard of his mother and the smutty tales about her. 'It was poor judgement on your part.' All this time worrying about her reputation and knowing that taking a lover was out of the question, and now this.

'I put safety above respectability. Better slandered than dead.' There was a flash of white teeth in a sudden grin, then the grim humour was gone. 'And besides, Prince Antoine has all the ammunition he needs without confirmation from an innkeeper about which beds were slept in. You were seen leaving with a man and some baggage.' He paused, watching her face. 'If I had pointed this out, back in the castle, would you still have come?'

'Yes, of course I would have come!' Of course she would have. 'What does my reputation matter against Freddie's safety or my duty? And what difference does it make to our choices whether Antoine wants me alive or dead?'

'If he wants you back in Maubourg so that people can see you, while he controls you as a puppet by threats to your son, then he will have to capture you and transport you home. That requires some logistical planning, more people. It may be easier to spot. If he wants an accident…well, then that is harder to see coming.'

'Yes, that is putting it without the bark on,' she agreed, trying not to let her voice shake. This was the man she had begun to think she understood and now realised she had been underestimating. Jack seemed so cold, so unmoved by the fear and danger behind his analysis. 'Are you ever afraid?' she demanded, the words leaving her lips as she thought them.

'Of many things,' he said evenly, surprising her. 'The knack is not to admit to it, not even to yourself.'

'I am scared of spiders,' she confessed. 'But I am not prepared to say what else.' Even referring to her recurring nightmare obliquely made it hideously real. Those dark passageways under the castle, the shifting lift of the torches making half-seen shapes move in corners. The rectangular shapes and the knowledge of what was in them… She pushed it away with an inner shudder. 'I understand what you mean; it does not do to conjure such things up. Instead, tell me what I should to do to help protect us all.'

'Do what I tell you, always, at once and without question.'

Eva blinked. She had been hoping he would give her a pistol, and show her how to use it, or demonstrate how to hit an assailant over the head, or some other active form of defence. 'That was very peremptory, Mr Ryder.'

'Are you going to argue about it? And call me Jack.'

'Yes, I am going to argue, *Jack,*' she said. 'What if I do not agree with what you are telling me to do?'

'We stand there and debate it while the opposition takes the advantage, or I hit you on the point of your very pretty chin and do whatever it is anyway.'

'My… What has my chin got to do with it?'

'It is the easiest part of your anatomy to hit in a crisis.' He appeared to have regained his good humour. 'Then Henry and I bundle up your unconscious body and make our escape with you slung unflatteringly over Henry's shoulder.' The smile reached his eyes, crinkling the corners in a way that was infuriatingly attractive.

'There is the death penalty in Maubourg for striking a member of the Grand Ducal family,' Eva stated. *And see how you like the thought of a coarse hemp noose around your neck, Mr Ryder!*

'What a good thing we will not be in Maubourg if such an eventuality transpires.' They sat in silence. Eva glared out of one window, Jack looked out of the other, his lips pursed in a soundless whistle.

Eventually the coach turned, lurched and began to ride more smoothly. Eva dragged her attention back to the landscape and away from a satisfying daydream of seeing Mr Ryder dragged off in chains to the scaffold. They had reached the post road to Grenoble.

'Are you going to sulk all the way to Brussels?' Jack enquired.

'I am not sulking. I have simply not got anything to say to you, you insolent man.'

'I see. I apologise for the remark about your chin.'

'What part of that remark, exactly? Threatening to hit it?'

'No, making an uncalled-for personal remark.'

'Has anyone told you how inf—' She broke off at the sound of a fist being banged on the carriage roof.

'Hell.' Jack sat upright. 'That means trouble. We are almost at the border—do you normally have it guarded? There was no check when we entered the Duchy.'

'No, never. Our army is minute and there are far too many passes and back roads to make it worthwhile putting on border guards. What do we do?' Jack would have a plan for this, he couldn't intend that they stop, surely? Eva braced herself, expecting the horses to be whipped up to ride through whatever obstruction lay in their path.

But Jack was on his feet, balancing against the swaying of
the coach as Henry began to rein in. Eva stared as he groped
under the edge of the seat he had been sitting on. There was
a click and the whole top folded up leaving a rectangular
space. Jack threw her valise into one end and gestured. 'In you
get. There are air holes.'

'No!' It gaped, dark and stark as a sepulchre. Eva could feel
the panic constricting her throat. *Don't talk about night-
mares...it makes them come real...* The edges of her vision
clouded as though grey cobwebs were growing there. The
shadows in the corners shifted... the sound of stone grinding
on stone...the scratch of bone...

'In!' Jack gestured impatiently, his attention on the scene
outside as the carriage came to a halt. There were voices
raised to give curt orders. 'Now!'

Duty. It is my duty to survive. It is my duty to be strong.
Eva scrambled in, and sat down. The air seemed to have
darkened, she was light-headed. *Don't shut it, no! Don't!* The
scream was soundless as Jack pushed her down until she was
lying prone. He said something, but the roaring in her ears
made it hard to hear. Then the lid closed on to darkness.
Forcing herself to breathe, she raised both hands until the
palms pressed against the wooden underside and pushed up.
It was locked tight. *Trust him, he will let you out. Trust him.
Trust...he will come.*

Jack sat down in the corner of the carriage, ran his hands
through his hair, crossed one leg negligently over the other
and drew a book out of his pocket. He raised his eyes to look
over the top of it as the door was flung open. 'Yes?' It was a
soldier in the silver-and-blue Maubourg uniform. Sent by
Prince Antoine, no doubt.

'Your papers, *monsieur.*'

'But of course.' Jack put down the book, taking his time, and removed the documents from his breast pocket. His false identity as a Paris lawyer was substantiated by paperwork from a 'client' near Toulon who wished for advice on a family trust. He fanned out the documents without concealment, extracted the passport and handed it across.

The man took it and marched away towards the front of the vehicle without even glancing at it. Damnation. That probably meant an officer. Jack climbed down and walked forward to where a young lieutenant was scanning the papers, three soldiers at his back.

'You are on your way back to Paris, *monsieur?*'

'Yes. I have been on business near Toulon.' The young man's thumb was rubbing nervously over the wax seal. The lieutenant was inexperienced, unsure of himself and probably wondering what on earth he'd been sent out here to deal with.

'What other vehicles have you passed since yesterday?'

'I have no idea.' Jack stared at him blankly. It was a useful trick. People questioning you expected you to lie, to make up an answer, to be able to catch you out. An honest admission of ignorance took the wind out of their sails and made you seem more credible. 'I have been reading, sleeping. I take no notice of such things. *Henri,* what have you seen?'

Henry shrugged. 'All sorts, *monsieur,* all sorts. What is the lieutenant looking for?'

'A woman,' the young man began, then reddened at the grin on Henry's face and the sound of his own men choking back their laughter. He glared at his men. 'A fugitive. A woman in her mid-twenties, brown hair, tall. With a man. Probably in a travelling carriage.'

'No idea.' The groom was dismissive. 'Can't see inside

anything closed from up here. Could have passed the Emperor himself and a carriage full of Eagles for all I know.'

'Very well. You may proceed.' The officer handed Jack the passport and stepped back.

Jack climbed into the carriage and sat down without a glance up at Henry. Inept and badly organised was the only way to describe that road block. It must have been the first response last night, to send troops out on the main roads. He did not fool himself that this would be the extent of Antoine's reaction to the disappearance of his sister-in-law.

The rapid tattoo on the roof told him that no one was following them. All clear, he could let Eva out. What a fuss she had made about getting in—no doubt she thought the box contained the dreaded spiders she had confessed to fearing.

Jack unlatched the seat, lifted the lid and caught his breath. For one appalled moment he thought she was dead. Her face was grey, her eyes closed, her hands, clasped at her breast, had blood on them. Then her eyes opened, unfocused on some unseen terror. 'No,' she whispered. 'No! Louis—don't let them in!'

Chapter Seven

'Eva.' A dark shape loomed over her. *He* had come, just as she knew, just as she feared. The figure reached down, took her shoulder and she gasped, a little sound of horror, and swooned.

'Eva, wake up.' Her nostrils were full of the smell of dust, of the tomb he had just lifted her from. She was held on a lap, yet the male body she rested on was warm, alive, pulsing with strength, not cold, dead…

He shifted her on his knees so he could hold her more easily. 'It's all right, we are quite safe, there is no one else here.' *Jack?* She could not trust herself to respond. A hand stroked her cheek, found the sticky traces of half-dried tear tracks. Flesh-and-blood fingertips against her skin, not the touch of dry bone. She came to herself with a sharply drawn breath. 'Eva, you are safe,' he said urgently.

'Oh. Oh, *Jack.*' She burrowed her face into his shirtfront.

'Are you all right now?' He managed to get a finger under her chin and nudged it up so he could look into her face. 'You frightened me. What was all that about?'

'I am sorry.' She tried to sit up, but he pulled her back. 'It is just that that was…is…my worst nightmare. A real nightmare. I keep having it.' *I am awake, I am safe. Jack kept me safe.* He *did not come.*

'Tell me,' he prompted.

She had never spoken of it to anyone. Could she do so now? Admit such fear and weakness? 'When I first came to the castle Louis, my husband, took me down to the family vault under the chapel. At first it was exciting, fascinating, like a Gothic romance—the twisting stairs, the flickering torches. I didn't realise where we were going.'

The smell of the air—that was what had hit her first. Cold, dry, infinitely stale. Old. Louis had held, not a lantern, but a torch, the flames painting shapes over the pillars and arches, making shadows solid. 'Then he opened the door into the vault—it seems to go on for ever, right under the castle, with arches and a succession of rooms.'

She had been a little excited, she remembered now. These must be the dungeons. It was all rather unreal, like a Gothic novel. Until she had realised where they were.

'We were in the burial vaults. All there is down there are these niches in the walls, like great shelves, each one with a coffin on it.' Jack must have felt her shudder at the memory and tightened his hold.

'The newer ones were covered in dusty velvet, there were even withered wreaths.' How did the flowers and leaves hold their shape? she had wondered, still not quite taking in what she was seeing. They had moved on, further and deeper into the maze of passageways. 'The older ones were shrouded in cobwebs. Some of them were cracked.' There had been a hideous compulsion to move closer, to put her eye to those cracks and look into the sarcophagus as though into a room.

'Then Louis started to show them to me, as though he

were introducing living relatives; it was horrible, but he seemed to think it quite normal, and I tried not to show what I was thinking.' Already, by then, she was learning that she must not show emotion, that she must show respect for Maubourg history and tradition, that weakness was unforgivable. Somehow she applied those lessons and did not run, screaming, for the stairs. Or perhaps she had known she would never find them again.

Then they had moved on. She had felt something brush against her arm and had looked down. 'There was one—an old wooden casket where the planks had cracked and a hand had come out.' She had tried never to think about it while she was awake, but whenever the nightmare came, this was the image that began it. 'A skeleton hand, reaching out for me as we walked past. It touched me.'

Her voice broke. Jack made a sound as if to tell her to stop, that it was too distressing, but she was hurrying now. It must all be said. 'And then he came to two empty shelves and said "And these are ours". I didn't understand at first, and then I realised he meant they were for our coffins.'

One day she would lie there, enclosed in a great stone box, sealed up away from the light and air for ever. There would not even be the natural, life-renewing embrace of the soil to take her back.

'I don't know how I got out without making a scene. That night I dreamt I had died and woken up in my coffin. I knew I was down there, and *they* were all out there, waiting, and that any moment Louis would lift the lid and he would be dead, too, and— I am sorry, such foolishness.'

Eva sat up, smoothing her hair back from her face with a determined calm. *Discipline, remember who you are.* There was pity and respect in Jack's grey eyes as he looked at her.

She could not let it affect her. 'Ever since then, I have been afraid of very tight, dark, spaces.'

'I'm not surprised, that is the most ghoulish thing I have ever heard. Did your husband not realise what an effect it was having on you?'

'Louis was a firm believer in self-control and putting on a good face,' Eva said with a rueful smile. 'I soon learned what was expected of me.'

'Did you love your husband?'

'No, of course not, love was not part of the expectation,' she said readily. She had just confessed her deepest fear—to tell the tale of her marriage was easy in comparison. 'I was dazzled, seduced and over-awed. I was seventeen years old, remember! Just imagine—a grand duke.'

'A catch, indeed,' Jack agreed. There was something in his voice that made her suddenly very aware of where she was and that Jack's body was responding to holding her so closely

'I… Mr Ryder, Jack, please let me go.' She struggled off his lap, suddenly gauche and awkward, knowing the colour flaming in her cheeks. 'Thank you. I appreciate your… concern.'

She settled in the far corner, fussing with her skirts and pushing at her hair in a feminine flurry of activity. 'You say you have the dream quite often?' Jack said slowly.

'Yes.' She nodded, keeping her head bent, apparently intent on a mark on her sleeve.

'Very well. You must remember, the next time, that when the lid begins to move, it is me opening it. I will have come to rescue you. There will be nothing unpleasant for you to see, and I will take you safely up those winding stairs, up into the daylight. Do you understand, Eva? Remind yourself of that before you go to sleep.'

'You? But why should you rescue me in my dream?' No one has ever rescued me before.' He had her full attention now. She fixed her eyes on his face as she worried over his meaning.

'You did not have me as a bodyguard before,' Jack said simply. 'All you need to do is believe in me, and I will be there. Even in your dreams. Do you?'

'Believe in you? Yes, Jack. I believe you. Even in my dreams.'

It was a fairy tale. Eva looked down at her clasped hands so that Jack would not see that her eyes were suddenly swimming with tears. Such foolish weakness! She was a rational, educated woman; of course he could not stride into her nightmare like a knight, errant to slay the ghosts and monsters. And yet, she believed him. Believed *in* him.

Only the year before she had found an enchanting book of fairy stories by some German brothers and had been engrossed. What was the name of the one about the sleeping princes? Ah, yes, 'Briar Rose.'

And it was a dangerous fairy tale, for she wanted more than protection from her knight errant—she wanted his lovemaking, she wanted him to wake her from her long sleep.

Jack wanted her, too, she knew, if only at the most basic level of male response to the female. He could not hide his body's response from a woman nestling in his lap. And that frightened her, for she realised that she had responded to it, been aroused by it, before her mind had recognised what was happening to them. She should have been alert to that danger, she had thought she was. Had she not resolved to maintain everything on a strictly impersonal level, as recently as this morning? That attack of panic had upset all her carefully constructed aloofness like a pile of child's building blocks.

'What are you thinking about?' He was matter of fact again. It almost felt as though he was checking on her mental state in the same way as he would check on the condition of a horse, or test the temper of a blade he might rely upon.

'Fairy stories,' she said promptly, looking up, her eyes clear. Telling the truth was always easiest, and this seemed a safe and innocuous subject. Her early training came back—find a neutral topic of conversation that will set the other person at their ease. 'I found a wonderful book of them last year.'

'The Brothers Grimm? Yes, I enjoyed those.' He grinned at her expression. 'You are surprised I read such things?'

'Perhaps you have nephews and nieces?' she suggested.

'No, none. And I do not think it is a book for children, do you? Far too much sex, far too much fear and violence.'

Flustered by how closely this was impinging on her fantasies, Eva said hastily, 'Yes, of course, you are quite correct. It is not a book I would give to Freddie.'

'I doubt he sits still long enough to read anything except his schoolbooks,' Jack said.

'Oh, of course. I forgot, you actually spoke to him.' How could she have forgotten that? She had been fighting her fears about Freddie, fretting over how he was, and here was someone with news of him that was only weeks old. 'Tell me how he looked.'

'As well as any lively nine-year-old who has just had a severe stomach upset,' Jack said. 'A touch green round the gills, but so far recovered that he was able to enjoy describing exactly, and in minute and revolting detail, how his mushrooms had reappeared and what they had looked like.'

'I am sorry.' Eva chuckled. 'Little wretch.'

'He's a boy. I was one once— I am not so old that I cannot remember the fascination of gory details.'

'How tall is he?' Eva asked wistfully. 'Hoffmeister writes me pedantic reports on a regular basis. "HSH has attained

some competence with his Latin translation, HSH has been out-
fitted with new footwear, HSH smuggled a kitten into his room.
It has been removed." But it doesn't help me *see* Freddie.'

Jack stood up, braced himself against the lurching of the
carriage with one hand on the luggage rack and held the other
hand palm down against his body. 'This high. Sturdy as a little
pony now—but any moment he is going to start to grow and
I think he will be tall. His hair is thick, like yours, and needs
cutting. His eyes are hazel, his face he is still growing into.
But I saw he was your son when I first set eyes on you.'

He sat down again and Eva felt the tension and fear of the
past hour ebb away into relief and thoughts of Freddie. 'Oh,
thank you so much, I can just picture him now! He was such
a baby when Louis insisted he went to England. The first
thing I am going to do when I am settled there is to have his
portrait painted.'

'With his mother, of course?'

'No,' she said slowly, thinking it out. 'Alone. His first
official portrait. I will have engravings done from it and flood
Maubourg with them. It is time people remembered who their
Grand Duke is.'

'Ah.' Jack was watching her, sizing her up again in a way
that made her raise her chin. 'The Grand Duchess is back.'

'She never goes away,' Eva said coolly. 'It would be as well
to remember that, Mr Ryder.'

His half-bow from the waist was, if one wanted to take
offence, mocking. Eva chose to keep the peace and acknowledged it with a gracious inclination of her head. Then she let
her shoulder rest against the corner squabs and closed her
eyes. One could never take refuge in sleep in public as a
grand duchess, but she was coming to see it was a useful
haven in everyday life.

* * *

'Grenoble.' Jack spoke close to her ear and Eva came fully awake as the sound of the carriage wheels changed and they hit the cobbles.

'What time is it?' She sat up and tried to stretch her neck from its cramped position.

'Nearly eight. We made faster time than I feared we would.'

'And where are we staying?' Water glinted below as they passed over a bridge. The Drac or the Isère, she could not orientate herself.

'Another eminently respectable bourgeois inn. And this time we have a private parlour adjoining our bedchamber, Madame Ridère.'

'So that's who I am, is it? I suppose it is easy to remember—Ryder or Ridère. And this was all booked in advance for tonight?' He nodded. Eva could make out his expression with some clarity, for the streets were well lit. 'You were very confident that we would get here, were you not?' Jack smiled, looked as though he would reply, then closed his lips. She added sharply, 'I suppose you were about to say that you are very confident because you are very good.'

'It is my job.' Infuriatingly he did not rise to her jibe. Eva was stiff, hungry and tense, for all kinds of reasons. A brisk exchange of views with Jack Ryder was just the tonic she needed. It seemed she was not going to get one. 'We are here.'

'Bonsoir, bonsoir, Monsieur Ridère. Madame! Entrez, s'il vous plaît.' The innkeeper emerged, Eva forced herself to think in French again, and the ritual of disembarking, being shown their room, ordering supper, unwound.

'That bed is smaller,' she observed as they sat down in the parlour to await their food. 'In fact, it is very small.'

'Indeed.' Jack was folding a rather crumpled news sheet into order in front of the fireplace. 'No room for the bolster, then, which is a good thing—you nearly pushed both it and me out last night.'

'I am *not* sleeping with you in a bed that size. There is a settle in here.' She pointed to the elaborately carved example of Alpine woodwork on the far side of the room.

'That is a good foot shorter than I am, as narrow as a window ledge and as hard as a board. And it appears to be covered in very knobbly artistic representations of chamois. I am not forgoing a comfortable bed.' She bristled. Jack snapped the newspaper open and regarded her over the top of it. 'Do I appear to you to be crazed with lust?'

'I… You… *What* did you say?'

At this critical juncture the waiter appeared with a casserole dish, followed by various other persons bearing plates, bread, jugs and cutlery. Eva folded her lips tightly and went to take her seat at the table.

Jack put down his newspaper and joined her. *'Du pain, ma chère?'*

'Don't you *my dear* me,' she hissed, only to subside as the waiter returned with a capon and a dish of greens. *'Merci, c'est tout,'* she said firmly.

'Non, non, un moment, la fromage.' Jack wielded the bread knife and passed her a slice.

'Coward! You cannot hide behind the servants for ever.' She forced a smile as the waiter brought the cheese. The door closed. 'How dare you?'

'I thought the *my dear* added verisimilitude. Some wine?'

'Yes, please.' A stiff drink was what she really needed. Brandy at the very least. 'That was not what I was referring to and you know it. How dare you refer to lust in my hearing?'

'I apologise for my choice of words.' Jack passed her a glass of white wine and took a thoughtful sip from his. 'Amorous propensities? Uncontrollable desire? Satyr-like tendencies? Ardent longings? Any of those any better?'

All or any of them involving Jack would be sinfully wonderful, as would throwing the cheese board at him. Eva gritted her teeth and persisted. 'It would be highly improper for us to share that bed. It is far too small.'

'And you expect what, exactly, to occur as a result?' Jack began to carve the legs off the capon. Something about his very precise knife work suggested repressed emotion at odds with his dispassionate tone.

'We might touch. Inadvertently.' Eva took a deep swallow of wine, nearly choked and took another. A capon leg was laid on her plate. 'Thank you.' Even when discussing lust one could maintain the courtesies, she thought hazily, reaching for the decanter and refilling her glass. 'Some greens?' She lifted the serving spoons competently.

'Please.' Jack passed her the butter and took the lid off the casserole with a flourish. *'Pommes Dauphinoise?'*

'Allow me…' *To upend it over your head.* Eva wielded a serving spoon with practised elegance.

'Thank you. Has it occurred to you that we have been touching—inadvertently or otherwise—all day?'

'Of course. It was unavoidable. Butter?'

'Thank you, no. And?'

'And nothing. Touching in bed is quite another matter.'

'That, my dear, is indubitably true.'

Eva almost choked on a further incautious mouthful of wine and stared at Jack across the steaming dishes. 'I do not need you to tell me that. I am a mur…married ludy. *Lady.*'

'Widowed lady,' he corrected gently. 'More wine.'

'Yes.' She was obviously tired, despite that nap in the carriage. Otherwise why was her tongue tangling itself? 'Please.'

'So.' Jack chewed thoughtfully. 'How to avoid this undesirable inadvertent touching? Whilst allowing me a decent night's sleep.' He reached across the table and lifted the second bottle of wine and the corkscrew. 'What forethought on my part to order two bottles.'

'It is a tolerable vintage,' Eva allowed, fanning herself with her napkin. It really was warm in here. 'As to the bed, thatsh— I mean, that's your problem, Mr Ryder. You arranged it.'

'What if I sleep on top of the bedclothes and you under them? More capon?'

'Thank you.' She was obviously hungry or why was her head spinning so? 'Wearing what?'

'Me or you?'

'You, of course.' Her glass was empty again. It really was a most excellent vintage.

'A nightshirt.' He lifted his wineglass, then glared at her over it as she snorted. It wasn't a very elegant reaction, Eva acknowledged vaguely. Grand duchesses never snort, but really!

'What, exactly, is there in that to provoke a snort?' Jack demanded.

'Men look ridiculous in nightshirts. Hairy legs sticking out of the bottom.' *Did I just say that?* She blinked at the wineglass. It appeared to be half-full now. How many had she drunk?

'Well, in my case you won't be looking, so if you can just steer your imagination away from the aesthetic horror of it, we will be all right.'

He isn't pleased I commented on his hairy legs. I suppose he has got hairy legs, all men do, don't they? He has a hairy chest. Not very hairy, though, just nicely hairy. Some remnant of restraint, surfacing through the effects of four glasses of wine on a nearly empty stomach stopped her complimenting Jack on the niceness of his chest. A creeping feeling of unease that perhaps this conversation was not all it should be began to steal over her.

'I think I am going to go to bed. Into bed. Under the covers.'

Jack stood up. 'Can I be of any assistance? The door is over there.'

'I know that,' she said with dignity, gathering her skirts around her and paying particular regard to her deportment. 'Good night, Mr Ryder.'

The effect of this exit was somewhat marred by a very audible hiccup.

Chapter Eight

Eva woke, far too hot and with a thunderous headache. She hadn't recalled the bedclothes being quite this thick—but then her memories of the previous evening were somewhat uncertain. She had drunk far too much, that was indisputable. She had discussed lust and beds and nightshirts with Jack in a most outrageous manner. Eva screwed her eyes tighter shut and prayed that she hadn't actually *said* anything about hairy legs. Had she? Or worse, chests. *Please, God.*

She shifted restlessly under the weight of the blankets and found that it was not layers of woollens weighing her down, but one long masculine arm thrown over her ribcage that was pinning her to the bed. At the risk of a cricked neck, she turned her head and found herself almost nose to nose with Jack.

'Good morning. Do you have a headache?'

'What are you doing!' It was a shriek that almost split her head as she uttered it. Eva closed her eyes again with a groan. Warm breath feathered her face.

'I must have turned over in the night. No inadvertent touching, though,' he pointed out with intolerable self-righteousness.

'Will you please remove your arm?'

The weight shifted. Eva opened her eyes cautiously and found that his arm might have moved, but Jack had not. They were still close enough for her to have counted his eyelashes, should she have had the inclination to do so. They were unfairly long, very dark and framed his eyes dramatically. She was also in an excellent position to note that his eyes might be grey, but there were black flecks in them. The pupils were somewhat dilated and his regard intense. She found herself unable to stop staring back, directly into them.

'One of us has got to blink,' Jack observed, 'or we may mesmerise each other and never get up.'

It seemed to Eva that someone had certainly been exerting powers of animal magnetism upon her, although she thought she had read somewhere that the effect required immersion of the subject in magnetised water. Or was it just her headache making her feel like this?

'Yes, and it will have to be you because I am completely pinned down with you lying on these covers,' she pointed out crisply. Thank goodness she still seemed able to speak with clarity and authority; she had been half-afraid she would open her mouth and mumble inanities.

'Very well.' Jack rolled away and stood up, stretching as he walked to throw open the shutters. He was dressed in a crumpled shirt and breeches, his feet bare on the boards.

'You said you were going to wear a nightshirt.' Eva sat up in bed, pushing her hair back off her face with both hands. She hadn't even plaited it last night.

'And you expressed horror at the suggestion. I believe an aversion to hairy legs came into it.' Jack turned back from the window and stood regarding her, hands on hips, a smile tugging at the corner of his mouth.

'I didn't say that, did I? Oh, Lord.' Eva buried her face in her hands. If she didn't look, then he wasn't really there, she didn't have to face the hideous embarrassment of knowing she'd been completely tipsy—no, *drunk*—and totally indiscreet. What must he think of her? She knew what she thought of herself.

'Eva.' The bed dipped beside her and a hand settled on her shoulder, large, warm, comforting.

'Stop it. Don't touch me,' she snapped. It lifted again. 'I'm sorry, I am finding this very difficult.' Silence. 'I'm not used to this intimacy with someone. I'm not used to someone being so close, so involved with what I'm doing, what I am thinking.'

She dropped her hands and looked at him, desperate to communicate how she felt. 'I do not know how to *be* with you, because this relationship we have is outside anything I've known before.' Jack's face, intent, listening, gave her no clue as to his feelings—except that he did not appear to be inclined to laugh at her.

'We are forced into this closeness and it is as if I am adrift without any chart to guide me. You are not a servant, you are not one of the family, you are not a professional man I have hired, like a doctor or a lawyer. What *are* you?'

She did not expect an answer, far less the one he gave her. 'A friend.'

'A friend?' Why did that word hurt so much? It was as though he had shone a light on the great empty loneliness at the heart of her life and forced her to confront it. 'I do not have any friends.'

'You have now.' Jack picked up her right hand as it lay lax on the counterpane. 'Eva, you have shared a dark secret fear with me, you have told me how you feel about your son, how you felt about your husband. You have got tipsy with me and you have confided your prejudices about nightshirts. We are

jointly engaged on a dangerous adventure. Today we will go
shopping together. These are all things you do with friends.'

Her hand seemed small, lost within his big brown one, the
long fingers cupping it protectively, not gripping, just cradling
it. Eva found herself studying his nails. Clean, neatly clipped
with a black line of bruising along the base of three of them,
a rough patch on the index fingernail as though it had been
abraded against a rough stone. That damage had been done
as he had climbed down the castle wall to her room. Absently
she rubbed the ball of her thumb over it, welcoming the distraction of the rasping sensation.

'Do you make friends of all your clients?' She did her best
to sound like the Grand Duchess and not Eva de Maubourg,
not disorientated, half-afraid, confused.

'You are not a client, his Majesty's Government is my
client. But, yes, I do make friends with some. Not all. Some
I do not like, many are in too much trouble to want to do
anything but see the back of me when it is all sorted out. When
we are in England I will introduce you to Max Dysart, the Earl
of Penrith, and his wife; you will like them, I think.

'But why have you no friends? Girls from your come-out
in England? The Regent, the ladies of the court…'

'Philippe is twenty-five years my senior, he is like an uncle.
Antoine, I have never trusted. The ladies of the court, as you
put it—no. Louis did not encourage me to make friends here,
or to retain them from before, and that became established. I
do not think there are any kindred spirits amongst them in any
case.' She assayed a confident smile, knowing it was a poor
effort. 'Certainly there is no one I could get drunk with, or
have an adventure with, or risk telling a weakness to.'

'Then I am the first.'

I am the first. The words Louis had used as he had undressed her on their wedding night, his green eyes heavy with desire. It had been very important to him that she was a virgin. Now, no longer an innocent, she knew it had titillated the jaded palate of a man she was to learn was one of the most energetic, and promiscuous, lovers in Europe. Theirs had not been a love match, but she could not complain that Louis had ever left her physically unsatisfied. Just emotionally empty, and yearning for affection. She had learned to be a good grand duchess, and to do without love.

'What is it?' Jack's hand closed shut around hers. 'Another nightmare?'

'No. Just a memory. Thank you, I would like to be your friend.' She looked up, relaxing, expecting to see something uncomplicated in his expression. He was smiling, but in his eyes there was something else, something she knew he was trying to mask. Heat, intensity, need. She recognised them because she felt them, too. The ordinary words she had intended to say caught in her throat. Somehow she not could pretend to herself that she did not see, or that she did not feel.

But I want… No, I cannot say it. I cannot say I want you, *because if I do the world changes for ever.*

Jack lifted her hand and pressed a kiss on her fingertips that were all that could be seen within his grasp. 'You were right, ma'am, from now on we need a considerably bigger bed and then I can sleep under the covers and safely wear a nightshirt.'

'Oh!' Eva was startled into a gasp of amusement. 'How can you make a joke about it?'

'Because laughter chases away fear and it also puts many things in perspective. Are you hungry? Because I am starving and I don't know where they are with the hot water.' Jack tugged at the bell pull and retreated behind the screen.

'I am ravenous.' And suddenly she was. And strangely

happy as though a weight had been lifted. Perhaps it was simply the cathartic effect of telling Jack how she felt. Except, of course, the fact that that she desired him. *He feels the same way.* The memory of the heat in his gaze as it had rested on her made her feel warm and fluttery inside and ridiculously girlish. Even though they had not acknowledged what that exchange of glances meant, the fact that an attractive, intelligent man found her desirable was the most wonderful boost to her confidence. *Perhaps I'm not so old and past it after all.*

There was a knock on the door and she hopped out of bed to open it, remembering at the last minute to ask who it was before she unlocked the door. Feeling wonderful was no excuse for laying them open to attack.

The chambermaid staggered in with two steaming ewers, set them both down beside the screen and went out, sped on her way by Eva's insistence on a large breakfast as soon as possible.

'Are we really going shopping?' She climbed back into bed and sat up, her arms round her knees, listening to the sounds of splashing. She had never listened to a man's morning rituals. Louis had always retreated to his own suite after visiting hers. He had never, after their wedding night, slept with her until morning.

'Of course. You need a travelling wardrobe.' There was a pause and a sound she guessed was a razor being stropped. 'They won't be the sort of shops you are used to,' he warned.

'I do not care.' Eva flopped back against the pillows. 'I don't get to see many shops, everything comes to me. It is so boring—I love window shopping and looking for bargains.' The noises from behind the screen were muffled. 'Do you hate shopping, or are you shaving?'

'Shaving.' He sounded as though he had a mouthful of

foam. She waited a few minutes, then, more clearly, 'I have very little experience of shopping with women.'

'Oh. No—what is the phrase—no barques of frailty you wish to indulge?'

'What do you know of your weaker sisters, your Serene Highness?'

'Nothing at all, except that my husband kept a great many of them, if you add them all up over the years.'

Silence. Had she shocked him? 'I am about to emerge, ma'am, if you would be so good as to close your eyes or otherwise avert your gaze.' Eva obediently closed her eyes and pressed her hands across them, as well, for good measure. Something was bubbling inside her, some ridiculously youthful feeling. There was the pad of bare feet on the boards. 'Did you mind the other women?' Jack asked from somewhere on the other side of the room. 'My back is turned, if you want to get dressed.'

'Mind? Not really. I was ridiculously shocked at first, but then, I was ridiculously young to have married a man like that.' She slid out of bed and risked a glance in Jack's direction. He was standing in front of the open window, his back to her, pulling on his shirt. The sunlight shone through, throwing the silhouette of his body against the fine fabric as he stretched his arms above his head. Eva bit back a sigh, dropped her eyes, found she was staring at the admirable tautness of his buttocks and the elegant line of his legs in the tight breeches and hastened to get behind the screen before her imagination got the better of her. *Friends,* she reminded herself fiercely. *My friend—don't spoil it.*

'You surprise me.' She followed Jack's movements about the room by ear as she washed. 'I would have expected that to have upset you greatly.'

'He never pretended to love me,' Eva explained, shaking out the remnants of her clean linen and making mental shopping lists while she talked. 'And I was too young to have formed a real attachment. It was my pride that was hurt more than anything, once I had got over my shock. Then, by the time I realised that he was not the sort of man to devote himself to one woman, I had Freddie and I was beginning to carry out my duties. It wasn't so bad, and there were some benefits to being married to one of the most accomplished lovers in Europe.'

In the crashing silence that followed this remark, Eva thought she could have heard a pin drop. The handful of underwear fell back into the trunk from her lax grip. How tactless was it possible to be? She had just intimated to a man who had kissed her—with such skill and feeling that her knees still felt weak when she thought of it—that she would have been mentally comparing his technique with the legendary erotic skills of her late husband.

Worse. This was a man who she was quite certain wanted her. Eva grimaced, wondering what she could possibly say to make things better. Nothing, probably, unless she wanted to dig the hole even deeper. To say anything acknowledged the attraction between them.

'Do you have grounds for comparison?' Jack asked coolly into the aching silence.

'Only Louis's own assessment,' she replied, then came to a decision. She could not leave this. 'Personally I have had no basis for comparison—only one kiss. On the basis of that Louis need not have been so confident.'

'Nothing? In all that time?' Jack sounded as though he was just the other side of the screen. She should step out, have this exchange face to face, but somehow Eva guessed it would be more truthful like this. 'No one?'

'No one,' she affirmed. 'No one while he was alive, no one since.'

From that, she supposed, he could conclude she was a love-starved widow, ready to turn to any personable man once she was away from the close scrutiny of the Grand Ducal court, or that she was cold and had not felt the lack of love and of loving.

'The man was a fool,' Jack said abruptly. It wasn't until she heard the snick of the latch that she realised he had walked out and left her. Eva stood for a moment, filtering the few words through her mind, listening to the emotion behind the curt statement. Her friend was angry on her behalf. Her eyes filled; no one had ever understood what it must have been like being married to Louis, and yet a man she had just tactlessly insulted grasped it immediately with warmth and empathy.

'Thank you, Jack,' she whispered to the empty room.

Shopping with a woman was a new experience. At the age of twenty-nine one did not have many of those, and certainly few that were so entertaining. If his sister, Bel, had asked him to accompany her through the fashionable lounges and shops of London, he would have pretended an attack of mumps sooner than oblige her, but Eva's delight at being let loose in the bourgeois shops of Grenoble was infectious.

In her travel-worn gown and cloak she darted from shop window to shop window, ruthlessly dragging Jack with her. 'I must have a hat,' she declared. 'I feel positively indecent without one. Which do you think? The amber straw with the ruffle or the chip straw with the satin ribbons?'

'Have both,' he suggested, ignoring the inner warning that a carriage stuffed with hatboxes was not the efficient vehicle for clandestine travel he had designed it to be.

'Really? May I?' He was still looking into the window as she glanced up at him. Something about the reflected image of himself standing there with this lovely woman on his arm, her head tilted to look up at him with delight in her eyes, hit him over the solar plexus like a blow from a fist. They looked right together, and the sight gave him an entirely unfamiliar sensation of possessiveness. Jack tried to analyse it, but Eva was still talking.

'Only I haven't bought a gown yet, and I ought to buy that first and match the hat.'

'Really? Is that how it is done?'

'I think so—when I have new ensembles made they all come together with a selection of hats and shoes and so forth. I'm not used to shopping like this.' Her nose wrinkled in doubt and Jack grinned. That was an expression far from the grand duchess he was used to.

'Come on, let's break the rules.' He pushed open the door and held it for her as the little bell tinkled, summoning the milliner. 'And you will need something in case we have to ride.'

'If we do, that will be an emergency? Yes?' Eva stopped inside the door and lowered her voice.

'Yes. We'll be picking up saddle horses a bit further north as a precaution.'

'Then I need breeches.' Jack felt his brows shoot up. 'I will explain later, but I can ride astride.' Eva turned to the shop-keeper, who was bobbing a curtsy. 'There are two hats in your window I would like to try, if you please.'

Ride astride? How in Hades had she learned that? It was certainly useful—if they had to take to horseback then it would be because they had to abandon the carriage and move both fast and unobserved. His mind strayed to wondering how one bought riding breeches for a woman off the peg in

Grenoble. Eva was tall and slender, but definitely rounded in a way that no man or youth was.

'*Jacques.*' He pulled himself away from a frankly improper contemplation of the curves hinted at by the fall of her gown and found himself confronted by a nightmare he had heard other men gibbering about. He was expected to make a judgement between two articles of clothing worn by a woman. 'Which do you think?'

Eva was wearing the chip straw, the bow tied at an angle under her jaw. The deep green of the satin ribbon did things to the colour of her eyes he could not explain, but which made him want to cover a bed with velvet in exactly that shade and lay her upon it. Naked.

'Delightful. It definitely suits you.' He remembered to talk in French just in time.

'Or this?' She replaced it with the amber straw. The brim framed her face, the colour brought out golden tones in her hair. The daydream changed to a bed strewn with amber silks. 'Delightful. Have them both.'

'Yes, but then I saw this.' She was biting her lower lip in thought. Jack closed his eyes for a moment's relief and opened them to see a pert confection he had no name for. The only word for it was *sassy* and it made his dignified grand duchess look like a seventeen-year-old, ripe for a spree.

'Wonderful. Buy them all.'

'*Jacques,* you aren't taking this seriously. You must prefer one of them, or don't you really like any?' It was exactly what friends had moaned about. Women asked you for an opinion and then were upset whatever you said.

'I think they all look marvellous on you,' he said, trying to inject sincerity into his voice. 'But I think that whatever the hat, you would look good, so it is very difficult to express a preference.'

'*Ah, monsieur.*' The milliner obviously thought this was a suitable answer. Eva cast him a roguish glance that made something deep inside respond. He knew his pulse rate was up and drew in a deep breath to steady it.

'Thank you. I think I will have the chip straw and…that one.' She pointed to the sassy little hat.

'Not all three?' Jack queried as the gratified shopkeeper hastened to pack the hats in their boxes.

'We have only just started shopping.' Jack found himself grinning back in answer to Eva's smile.

It was madness. Here he was, Jack Ryder, King's Messenger, a man who chose danger as a way of life, looking forward to hours spent exploring dress shops, haberdashers and shoemakers. If Henry found out, he would never live it down.

Chapter Nine

❧

Two hours later, laden with parcels, Jack called a halt and dragged Eva into a confectioner's. 'Enough! Can there be a single shop of interest to ladies in this town we have not explored?'

'Not one.' Eva smiled happily at him over the rim of a cup of chocolate. 'Tell me what you bought for my riding clothes.'

'Breeches, shirt, waistcoat, coat and boots. You can use one of my neckcloths.'

'But how did you know my size?' She blushed adorably, he mused, wondering how else he could provoke that reaction without overstepping the bounds of friendship he had set himself.

'I can measure your height against myself, likewise your feet.' He let his booted foot nudge against hers under the shelter of the tablecloth and lowered his voice. 'As for the rest, well, I have held you in my arms.'

'Oh.' The rose-pink colour reached her temples this time. Jack tried not to imagine how soft the skin would be there, how it would feel to nuzzle along to the delicate curve of her ear and explore the crisp moulding before nibbling his way down… 'You have a good memory.'

Confessing that he had been recalling those few minutes in vivid detail ever since they had occurred was out of the question. 'I doubt the breeches will be a good fit.' Eva looked a question. 'Any youth quite your, er…shape would be an unusual young man. They are certain to be too large in the waist.'

'Never mind. Better than too tight.' Eva put one elbow on the table and rested her chin on her palm while she nibbled at a macaroon biscuit. 'Thank you for today.'

'What, the clothes and fripperies? His Majesty's Government coffers are paying for those.' The range of items she had enjoyed browsing through had been a revelation to a man used to buying jewellery as a present for his mistress of the moment, or handing over cash for them to make their own purchases.

'No. For the holiday. For letting me take my time and relax and for pretending you enjoyed it, too.'

'I did enjoy it.' She finished her biscuit and cupped her chin in both hands, regarding him sceptically. 'It was a new experience for me. Shopping.'

'Don't men shop? Surely you do?'

'Yes, but we don't flit so much.' He ignored her *moue* of indignation at his choice of verb. 'I go to my tailor, my shirtmaker, my bootmaker, a perfumier for toiletries and so forth. But I know what I want before I set out, they are all within a very small compass of London streets, and I do it only when I need to.'

'Then what did you enjoy about today?'

Jack poured them both more hot chocolate and tried to explain. 'I enjoyed your company, I enjoyed your good taste. It was an interesting glimpse into a feminine world—and I enjoyed seeing you enjoy yourself.' And he had enjoyed just watching her, fantasising about making love to her, setting himself up for a night of disturbed sleep and physical discomfort thinking about her.

'Thank you.' The sceptical look was gone. 'I am so glad we are friends.' She put out her hand impulsively and lay it on his for a fleeting moment, then jerked it back, obviously embarrassed at doing such a thing in public. 'Jack, are we in danger here?'

'Here and now? I doubt it, unless whoever is chasing us has decided they need light refreshment. I somehow do not think this is what your brother-in-law would be expecting us to do just now. But if you mean in Grenoble, yes, certainly.' There was no point in lying to her; besides anything else, neither of them could afford to be complacent.

'It will be most dangerous from here to Dijon because there are so few alternative routes if we wish to avoid high mountains or areas that have come out strongly for Napoleon. After that, there are several possible routes.'

'And Antoine may have found out about the factory by now, and know we know about the rockets.' Jack nodded, watching her thinking. Now her guard was down with him, he found Eva's brown eyes extraordinarily expressive. 'Should we have stopped for so long? Shouldn't we travel all night? But you will tell me you know best and not to worry, I expect.' She bit her lip. 'I am not holding you up, am I? I could have managed without more clothes. Or was that an excuse to give me a rest?'

'You call that a rest? No, it was part of my plan. We could not have got more than one bag out safely, but it would draw attention to us if you are shabbily dressed.' He gestured to the waiter for their bill. 'I plan to leave early tomorrow, before sunrise. Always providing we can pack all this stuff away.'

'We can put it under the seats if there is too much for the luggage racks,' Eva suggested, gathering up the myriad of smaller packages. He was well aware that her demure expression was to hide her amusement at seeing him burdened by two hatboxes—well stuffed with lighter objects around the hats—three parcels and the unwieldy package containing the riding boots.

'No, we can't. One is full of equipment, and we may need the other one again.'

'For me.' She said it flatly and he could have kicked himself for reminding her. 'It is all right Jack. I know you will let me out.' Then she threaded her free hand through his elbow and nudged him lightly in the ribs. 'And if you are found, apparently all alone with a carriage full of female apparel, what exactly is going to be your explanation?'

'A demanding wife who expects a lot of presents,' Jack retorted promptly and was rewarded by her rich chuckle. 'Oh, and by the way, I have explained to our host that my fussy spouse finds the bed too narrow and has thrown me out, so I expect to find a truckle bed in our room when we return.'

'Did you receive much masculine sympathy?' Eva asked.

'Of course. He now regards me as intolerably henpecked, but apparently he surmised that from first seeing us.'

'Whatever made him think such a thing?' Eva demanded indignantly.

'I have no idea.' Jack sighed. 'I had thought I was bearing up so well.' This time it was not so much a nudge as a jab.

'Beast.'

'Have you any family?' Eva curled up in the corner of the carriage, her shoes reprehensibly kicked off and her feet tucked up under the skirts of her new forest-green walking dress. Jack lounged in the corner diagonally opposite, his hands thrust deep into his coat pockets, his eyes moving between her face and the road as it unwound behind them.

She thought she had never seen a man who seemed more at home in his own body. He was totally relaxed now, and yet she would wager a large sum that, if there was a crisis, he would be alert, balanced, ready for instant action. It was, she acknowledged ruefully to herself, very appealing.

'A half-brother, older than I am, and a full sister who is younger. My mother is widowed and lives out of town.'

'Not very many relatives, then?' she commiserated. It would be wonderful to have brothers and sisters and it was a deep regret that she had not been able to give Freddie any siblings.

'You asked about family.' Jack rolled his eyes. 'Relatives I have by the dozen.'

'Truly? Do you get on well with all of them? You are lucky, I wish I had lots. Any, in fact.' She sighed, smiling in case he thought she was being self-pitying.

'One aunt, three uncles and nine cousins. Plus the Scandalous Aunt we do not talk about—she may have any number of offspring, for all we know.'

'What did she do that was so shocking?' Eva asked, agog. It was so refreshing to be able to indulge in some vulgar gossip—Jack would tell her if she overstepped the mark, but his expression when he mentioned his aunt did not seem at all forbidding.

'No one will tell us *children.* Even my mama, who is considered scandalously freethinking by the others, plies her fan vigorously and blushes when questioned. All she will say is that Poor Dear Margery was wild to a fault and fell into sin. The only clue is that whatever sin she succumbed to was highly lucrative, for Mama also confided that no amount of money can wash a soul clean from moral turpitude.'

'Have you never been tempted to find out? If anyone can, I should think it is you.'

'I might at that.' Jack smiled lazily. 'I have to admit, the last time Aunt Margery was mentioned by my Wicked Cousin Theophilus, I felt a certain stirring of irritation at being designated a child at the age of twenty-eight.'

'*Theophilus?* I don't believe anyone called Theophilus could possibly be wicked.'

'He was more or less destined for either extreme virtue or vice, poor Theo. His father is a bishop and his mother the most sanctimonious creature imaginable.'

Theo sounded rather amusing. Eva wondered if there was any chance of meeting Jack's numerous relatives. 'So, you are twenty-eight?' Younger than he looked, Eva decided. She had guessed at thirty and tried to work out why. The steady, serious, watchful eyes possibly. Or the air of total competence and responsibility.

'Twenty-nine, I have just had a birthday.'

'Congratulations! And did your brother and sister and all your cousins come to your party?'

'I spent it on the road on my way south to Maubourg.' He must have seen her frown of regret, for he added, 'Birthday parties are not my sort of thing. I suppose I am not used to them. My father considered such things too frivolous for children.'

'Then you do not know what you are missing,' Eva said robustly, thinking, *Poor little boy. Not so little now, but everyone should have the memory of a happy childhood to grow up with*. Hers was always there at the back of her mind, a candle flame to warm her soul by in hard times. A man who forbade a child a birthday party was unlikely to have been a loving father in other ways.

'I give wonderful parties for all ages and you must come to Freddie's in December.' She tried to imagine Jack playing the silly party games she invented and failed. There was nothing wrong with his sense of humour, and he certainly did not stand on his dignity, but there was something lonely and distant about him in repose. She wondered if there was something else, other than a father who, she recalled, Henry had referred to as top-lofty, and felt an ache inside for him. Not that he would thank her for pitying him, for there was an armour of pride and quiet self-confidence behind his easy competence.

'I am not used to children's parties, but I would be honoured by an invitation.' Jack managed a bow that was positively courtly, despite his casual posture.

'No nieces or nephews, then?' Children would like him, she decided. He wouldn't condescend to them. Freddie must have liked him, otherwise he would never have trusted him with the secret nicknames for his uncles.

'My sister, Bel, was widowed before they had any children.'

'Your brother?' Eva prompted, curious that his eyes, which had been open and amused as they spoke, flicked back to the view from the window. His profile was unreadable. There was some secret here.

'I think it highly unlikely that Charles will ever have children,' he said, his voice so neutral that her suspicions were confirmed. In the face of that blankness, she could hardly continue to probe.

A silence fell, not cool exactly, but not comfortable, either. Perhaps the poor man was an invalid and it pained Jack to speak of it. Eva shifted to stare out of the window on her side and brooded on what else Jack had told her.

A large extended family then. A bishop for an uncle and general outrage at a sinful aunt spoke of respectability, even minor aristocracy, maybe. But then, aristocrats did not spend their time as private investigators, or King's Messengers, come to that. A puzzle, her new friend. *Friend.* That was the word she had to keep repeating in her mind. Friend. Not lover, however much she wished he was. If she thought about it, it would show in her face, Jack Ryder was no fool and he knew women, she had no doubt of that.

'Where are we staying in Lyons?' she asked, more to test his mood than for any particular anxiety to know.

'On the Presqu'île, in the business district. A modest, respectable inn patronised by silk merchants and other business men. They do an excellent dinner.'

'We can't go out, then?' The previous day's expedition had been such fun and Lyon was famous for its silks. Eva knew that more shopping was out of the question—not on borrowed money, at any rate—and the carriage was already stuffed with parcels, but she would dearly have loved to do some browsing. Despite everything the sense of being on holiday, of being let off the lead of respectability and duty, was heady.

'No. This is where it gets dangerous. Lyon came out strongly for Napoleon. Besides that, Antoine will know what we have seen, guessed at what we will have stolen. And now he has had enough time to organise the pursuit. If you are up to it, I intend that we ride to Dijon from Lyon and leave Henry to drive.'

'But that will put him in danger,' Eva protested. It no longer felt right to be curled up so casually. She sat up straight and slipped her shoes back on, as though to be ready for action.

'There will be nothing to betray him. A humble coachman carrying presents from his mistress's sister back to her in Paris. We will be taking the back roads and the plans will be with us.' He flicked her a sideways glance. 'Are you up to it?'

'Yes.' Eva nodded firmly. She had ridden all day on occasion when Louis had held one of his week-long hunting parties, although not recently. She would manage; the thought of being a burden to Jack, of slowing him down, was not to be contemplated. Everything was going so well, all according to his smooth planning, she had to do her part.

But even the most careful plans come adrift. Eva stood beside Jack in the entrance of the Belle Alliance inn and watched his face as the *patron* explained all about the fire in the kitchen. The stench of wet ash and charred timber filled the air; it had hit them as they entered, but the man assured them the bedchambers were unaffected and it was only the kitchens that were not functioning.

'There are many good places to eat along the *quais, monsieur,*' the *patron* hastened to explain. 'On either the Rhône bank or the Saône bank. You take any of the *traboules*—those are the passageways—'

'I know what they are,' Jack interrupted him. 'Very well, we will go out now, while there is still some light. I do not wish my wife to be abroad in a strange town after dark. *Henri.*' He jerked his head towards the small pile of luggage. 'You'll see these taken up to our room?'

The groom nodded. 'I'll eat over there.' That was a small, and rather greasy-looking, eating shop immediately opposite the entrance to the Belle Alliance. 'I like to keep an eye on who comes and goes.' It was only because she was looking for it that Eva caught the unspoken message between the two men. Warning, reassurance. Did Jack suspect the fire was deliberate?

She asked him directly as they made their way through one of the famous Lyonnais *traboules* that cut down to the rivers, wending their way through private courts and gardens as they went. Eva wanted to look around her at the vibrant glimpses of everyday life that they passed, the women gossiping, the looms visible through windows, merchants slapping hands on a deal, but Jack kept his hand under her elbow and walked briskly.

'No, I don't suspect that; Antoine could not possibly have found where we were going to stay and organised such a thing. But his men may start checking the lodgings and I would prefer to be inside looking out if that happens.'

'I see. Jack?'

'Yes?' He looked down at her and his eyes crinkled into a smile that seemed not so much one of reassurance but simply of pleasure to find her there on his arm.

'Are you armed?'

'To the teeth,' he assured her, the smile belying his solemn tone.

'Don't be flippant.' The tone of crisp reproof was still there when she needed it, she found. 'I cannot see any weapons.'

'I should hope not.' She narrowed her eyes at him in exasperation and he relented. 'Knives in my boots and in a chest harness. Pistols in my pockets. Hence,' he added as she glanced sideways at him, 'the dreadful cut of my coats.'

There was nothing wrong with his coats at all. This one fitted admirably over broad shoulders and snug at his waist. It was, if what he was telling her was true, exceptionally well tailored, and probably very expensive, for all its lack of fashionable flourish.

'Stop fishing for compliments,' she chided. 'You know perfectly well that coat is very smart. Why wouldn't you let me wear my cloak and hood?'

'Because that was what you were last seen in. If those officers who interrupted us in the lane have worked out who you were by now, they ought to be able to describe your clothing. 'That hat…' he flipped the brim irreverently '…is not the sort of thing a grand duchess wears. When you skim a crowd, searching, your eye stops when it sees something familiar. It is like hunting—you look for the shadowy outline of deer and ignore foxes. They search for a great lady and might miss a lovely young girl in her pert new hat.'

'Young!' Eva tried not to think about the rest of that description, but she couldn't repress a blush.

'Now who is fishing?'

'I am not, but really, Jack, I am twenty-six years old—'

'So ancient! Quite on your last prayers, obviously. I almost fell off your damnable window ledge with the shock I had when I first saw you. They did not tell me, you see, that you were both young *and* beautiful.'

'Are you flirting with me, Monsieur Ridère?' she enquired suspiciously as he steered her through the door of a respectable seeming eating house.

'Of course, Madame Ridère. A friend may, may he not? This place looks acceptable.' Eva forgot the compliments and the teasing as she watched him assessing the *bistrôt,* trying to work out what he was looking for.

'A back door, plenty of people, a table over there with a good view of who is coming in?' she suggested.

'Yes. Precisely, you are learning to get the eye. Let's hope the food is good, too.'

It was. And so was the atmosphere. Eva had never been anywhere like this. She found her elbows were on the table, that she was singing along with the group near the door who had struck up an impromptu sing-song while they waited for their order, and the simple casserole of chicken and herbs, washed down with a robust red wine, seemed perfect.

'I am enjoying this,' she confessed, as the waitress set down a platter of cheese.

'So am I.' Jack caught the hand she was gesturing with and held it. 'I enjoy seeing you relax.'

'This is so different for me,' Eva admitted. 'No one is staring. I don't have to pretend.'

'Don't you?' Jack murmured, almost as though he were asking a rhetorical question. Eva tugged her hand free, finding his warm grasp rather more disturbing than was safe and Jack let go at once, taking her by surprise. Her arm flicked back, caught the little vase of flowers set on the table and knocked it off.

'Oh, bother!' Eva jumped to her feet to retrieve it just as the door opened and a group of men walked in. She straightened up, the flowers in her hand and found herself staring, across the width of the *bistrôt,* straight into the eyes of a tall blond man with sharp blue eyes and a sensual mouth set over a strong chin.

Good-looking, arrogant, unmistakable. It was Colonel de Presteigne.

Chapter Ten

The colonel had seen her, recognised her. There was no way to avoid him. The way the hunter's smile of sheer triumph slid across his face sickened her. Eva clenched her hand around the slender vase, as she counted the men standing at his back. Three of them, all ordinary soldiers out of uniform by the look of them—there were no impressionable young officers to appeal to here.

Behind her she felt Jack slide out from behind the table, then stand, almost as if to hide behind her. But Jack was not a man to hide behind a woman—he had a plan, she knew it. He moved smoothly, so she was not surprised that the men kept their attention on her. His hand closed round her left wrist. 'When I tug, throw that vase and run with me.' The words were a breath in her ear and she nodded fractionally in response as he released her.

'*Bonsoir, madame.*' De Presteigne, feigning deference. 'Dining in style with your gallant lover, I see.' His lip curled in a sneer at the sight of Jack apparently hiding behind the shelter of her skirts. How had she ever thought the colonel charming?

Eva sensed Jack shifting his balance, her whole body

attuned to him as though they touched. Out of the corner of her eye she watched the waitress come out of the kitchen door with a steaming tureen and walk across to a table. Their escape route was clear. She shifted her balance slightly.

'Better a humble *bistrôt* than a formal dining room in the company of traitors,' she retorted, seeing the smile congeal into dark anger on his face.

'You call supporters of the Emperor traitors?' he demanded, raising his voice. People shifted in their chairs to stare, the amiable faces of the diners changing to suspicion. Lyon, she remembered, supported Bonaparte.

'You betray your Grand Duke,' she flashed back as the colonel took a stride towards her. She felt Jack's hard tug on her wrist and she threw the vase full in de Presteigne's face. Water and flowers went everywhere as the man roared in shock and clawed at his eyes.

Eva saw no more, she was running with Jack, through the door, into the kitchens towards the back door. Kitchen staff scattered. They passed a rack of knives, she snatched one, a small vegetable peeler, then they were outside in a cobbled alley, rank with the smells of food waste. A cat bolted away, hissing with fright as Jack made for the mouth of the alley. Behind them the door crashed back. Eva risked a glance over her shoulder.

'Two of them, not de Presteigne,' she gasped.

'Here's the rest.' Jack skidded out on to the street just ahead of the colonel and the other soldier, turned, reached inside his coat and threw something. With a grunt the man toppled and fell and de Presteigne went down with him, tripped beyond hope of balance.

'Run!' Jack pushed her. 'The waterfront's that way.' They took to their heels, splashing through foul puddles, leaping piles of garbage, dodging the few passers-by. The pounding feet behind them were relentless. Eva heard de Presteigne's voice cursing the men for not catching them as they erupted into a little square.

Jack made for the far exit, then recoiled. 'Dead end.' It was enough to bring their pursuers up with them. Jack pulled a pistol from his pocket and held it steady, his back almost to the wall, his left arm outstretched, urging Eva behind him.

It was as she had known instinctively: he would stand and protect her at the risk of his own life—and the odds were too great. She edged behind him, then further, out into the open, towards the alley to her right. Keeping the little knife concealed in her skirts, she waved the reticule that was somehow, against all probability, still swinging from her wrist. 'Is this what you want, Colonel? The plans? The notebooks? Don't you wonder what we took, what we know? Who we told?'

'Eva!' Jack lunged for her, but she had done what she had meant to do, split their attackers. De Presteigne shouted, 'Ducrois, with me! Foix, break his neck', and dived towards her. She spun round and ran, light-footed, impelled by the desperate urge to leave Jack with manageable odds. There was the bark of a pistol—his or Foix's? Then she was out on to the quayside. Which river? It hardly mattered, either would have boats, surely?

The edge of the quay was slippery beneath her feet. Wary of mooring ropes, she began to edge along it, half her attention on the swirling water, half on the colonel and the soldier who had come to a halt when they saw her and were now, with the caution of hunting cats with a bird in their sights, padding forward.

'Stand still, you silly bitch,' de Presteigne said irritably. 'Where the hell do you think you are going to?'

'*You* are the one going to hell,' Eva retorted. 'That is the place for traitors and turncoats.' She risked another glance down. It seemed a long way to the river's dark surface and there were no rowing boats in sight yet. *Where is Jack?* There was a shout echoing from the little square, the soldier half-turned and stopped at his officer's curse.

'Never mind them. Get her.'

Eva held her knife that had been concealed by the reticule in front of her. 'Try,' she invited.

The man rushed at her, grinning at her defiance. She slashed at him, he ducked away, slid on the slippery surface and pitched into the river with a yell of fear and a loud splash. 'Colonel?' she invited politely. The light from the lanterns hung along the fronts of the warehouses glittered off the little knife.

The tall man reached into his coat and produced a pistol. 'No. You come here, or I'll shoot you. And then, if your lover isn't dead yet, I'll shoot him.'

Slowly, trying to control the trembling in her arm, Eva held the reticule out over the river by her fingertips. It hung with convincing heaviness, thanks to the novel that she had tucked inside it that morning. 'Then you'll never get these.'

He shrugged. 'So? They'll be at the bottom of the river.' He stepped forward. 'Come on, don't be such a little fool. Back to Prince Antoine.' Eva's head spun as she tried to decide what to do. *Drop the reticule, then he won't look anywhere else... Jack...*

As she thought it he came out of the alleyway. Even at that distance she could see his bared teeth, the killing fury in every line of his body as he came, his pistol hand rising to level on the colonel. De Presteigne snatched at her as her attention wavered, caught her by the arm and held her, his own pistol swinging round towards her breast. 'Stop right there or I'll kill— Aagh!'

Eva fastened her teeth on his hand and he released her, scrabbling for balance. For a moment she was free, poised on the edge of the quay, then the momentum of her movement took her and she felt herself falling towards the river. There was the crack of a pistol, a shout immediately above her, then she hit the water and stopped thinking of anything but survival.

Despite the warmth of the summer night the cold almost knocked the breath out of her. Some corner of her brain registered that the river was fed by snowmelt as she kicked off her shoes and clawed at her bonnet strings and the fastenings of her pelisse.

I can swim, I can swim well, she told herself, fighting to calm the panicking part of her that was wanting to thrash and scream. It was a long time, but as a child she had swum naked in the river that ran through the grounds of their château. As a young woman she had swum in the private lake in the castle grounds. *I haven't forgotten, thank God...*

With her heavier outer clothing gone she was managing to stay afloat, but the current was sweeping her downstream at terrifying speed. In the darkness things loomed out of the water, swept by her before she could register them as either dangerous or a potential lifeline. A wave slapped her in the face and she gagged on foul water.

It was useless to try to swim against this current, she had to stay afloat, go with it and trust to a rope or a bridge pillar to cling to. Eva struggled to orientate herself. This must be the Rhône, rushing down to its confluence with the Saône. A vision of swirling cross-currents and whirlpools where the two rivers met almost frightened her into stopping breathing, then something struck her shoulder.

Instinctively, she reached for it, and found herself grasping a large branch, the leaves still on some of the twigs. It supported her weight just enough for her to draw in a sobbing breath and raise her head to look around. She was in midstream, the banks seeming to flicker past at nightmare speed as she pitched and rolled with the current. Ahead the right bank seemed to vanish; the confluence was almost on her.

It did not seem possible she could survive this. Even with the support of the branch her limbs were losing sensation with the cold and the effort, her head was spinning and her throat raw. Eva tried to pray—for Freddie, for Jack, for herself—and clung on.

De Presteigne went down with a shout of pain as the ball lodged in his shoulder, his own shot whistling somewhere over Jack's head. Jack did not stop to check whether the man was alive or dead as he began to run downstream, his eyes straining to search the surface of the water. Lights sparkled and flashed off the choppy surface, dazzling and confusing in some patches, leaving the river in darkness in others.

He sought mental balance, knowing that to give in to fear and panic would kill Eva as surely as walking away. If she could not swim, or catch some sort of float, she was dead already. He pushed that knowledge back and scanned the surface again. *There!* A tangle of foliage and, in the centre, a dark head, the flash of pale cloth, a raised arm. She was well ahead of him, there was no way he could reach the point where the two rivers joined before her.

People scattered in front of him as he ran, then a rider emerged from a side street, slack reined, relaxed, perhaps on his way home to his supper. Jack drew his remaining knife, reached up and dragged him from the saddle, his bared teeth and the menacing blade between them enough to have the man backing away, hands thrown up in surrender.

The animal reared, alarmed at the violent movements, the strange weight on its back, then it responded to heel and voice and they were away at a canter. With the added height he could see better, realised he had to get off the Presqu'île and on to the far bank, and dragged the horse's head round to make for the foot of the last bridge just ahead. It all wasted time, lost him distance and Eva was fast vanishing into the maelstrom of waters.

Jack blanked the thought that he was losing her from his mind, tightened his grip and kicked.

Ignoring traffic and obstacles and shouted abuse, he galloped downstream towards the place where he could recall the newly joined rivers' turbulence wearing itself out in a tangle of sandbanks and islands before resuming its long smooth passage towards the sea. If he was going to snatch her out, that was the place. If she made it so far, if he could get there first, if he was strong enough to reach her.

The stolen horse baulked and shied as he forced it through the shallows to the first sandbank. He flung the reins over the branch of a spindly willow and tore off his boots. His coat followed as he ran over the sand and shingle, vaulted a pile of driftwood and plunged into the first channel.

Even here the current was strong. He clawed his way out the far side and ran to the edge of the main stream, his eyes straining upstream for a sight of Eva. The light was surprisingly good; a glow still hung in the sky from the sunset, lights from boats and cottages laid ribbons of visibility across the water.

He did not have long to wait. The leafy branch was still afloat, the glimmer of white cloth still tangled within it as it swirled down towards him. But the figure that lay in its cradle was unmoving. Jack entered the water in a long, shallow dive and struck out to intercept it, refusing to feel the cold water biting into muscles, the enervating pull of the current, the clutch of fear at his heart.

The river was so strong it was trying to drag her out of her branch, so savage she could swear it had hands. Eva clung on, her fingers numb. She should just give in and die, this hurt so much and was so hopeless. Yet she could not— would not—surrender.

'Eva,' the river gasped in her ear. 'Eva, let go.'

'No!'

'Yes! Look at me!'

Jack's voice? Jack? With an effort that seemed to take her last ounce of strength, Eva turned her face from the rough bark it had been pressed to and saw him.

'You came for me?'

'Always.' It sounded like a vow. 'Always.' The world went black.

'Eva!' Someone was shouting at her, slapping her face, her hands.

'Stop it,' she protested feebly, then rolled on her side, retching violently as what seemed like most of the river came up.

'Good girl, that's right.' Someone was praising her for being sick? Eva let herself be lifted and found she was bundled into some strange, bulky garment far too big for her. 'Come on, up you come.' Jack. Jack was lifting her. She forced herself to full consciousness, her body unwilling to make the effort, her will screaming that she could not just leave him to cope. He must be cold, exhausted, perhaps wounded.

For a moment she indulged herself in weakness and lay against his chest. Cold, wet cloth clung to his chilled skin, his body heat fighting to warm them both. He was plodding through shingle and underbrush, she could hear. Hard going, he was stumbling slightly, but his grip did not waver.

'Put me down.' She cleared her throat and said it again, more clearly. She couldn't bear to burden him, like a sack of stones on an exhausted pack animal that somehow kept going despite everything.

'When we get to the horse.' With her ear against Jack's chest she could hear the effort to control his voice, the way he steadied it like a singer so she wouldn't hear the fatigue.

'No. Now.' She put every ounce of authority she possessed into the command.

To her amazement he gave a snort of amusement and trudged on. 'Remember what I said?' he asked. 'Do what I tell you, always, at once and without question.'

'This doesn't count.'

'Why not?' Jack stopped, she felt him brace himself, then plough on up the steep edge of the bank on to shingle.

'Because you are being a stubborn idiot! Put me down this minute before you fall down!'

'Yes, your Serene Highness.' Eva found herself set on her feet.

'There. You see? That's better.' Her legs buckled and she swayed against him, surrendering to the support of his arm around her waist. 'Oh, bl...*bother.*' They stood there, locked together and dripping. Jack must have wrapped her in his coat, she realised, trying to get her arms, and the flaps of the coat, around him. Her face was pressed into his chest and his heartbeat was slowing even as she stood there. *Very fit,* the logical part of her mind, the part she always thought of as the *Grand Duchess* observed, while the other, entirely feminine, entirely private, part just revelled in his strength and courage and wanted him. *You do chose your moments, Eva,* she thought ruefully.

'Were you wounded?'

'No. I don't think so.'

'Don't think so?' Eva arched back against Jack's arm to see his face, which was almost impossible now.

'I'm sure so,' he amended. There was a flash of white; she thought he was smiling. 'I had other things to think about. Come on, the horse I stole is just over here; if we stand still much longer we'll freeze.'

'Which would save us from being hanged for horse stealing,' Eva observed, as they picked their way back to the horse standing patiently by the willow tree. Jack boosted her up into the saddle and swung up behind her, settling her so she sat across his thighs.

'Hold tight.' The horse scrambled down into the shallow channel, then up the other side and on to the road. 'Henry can "find" it wandering tomorrow and hand it over to the authorities,' Jack added. 'I want to get you back and into a hot bath.'

'You, too.' She felt his chin pressing down on the crown of her head and let herself drift. She thought she felt him chuckle and blushed at the improper thought of them both in the same steaming bath.

'Are you asleep?' He didn't wait for her answer. 'Don't. Wake up and talk to me, it is dangerous to drift off when you are this cold.'

'Talk? What about?' Eva felt like grumbling. It was very difficult to think of conversation when you were numb from head to toe, dripping wet and perched on a horse. She wanted to sleep, to dream about making love with her fantasy of Jack, not be bossed about by the real, wet, battered hero who wanted to be her bodyguard and her friend and would let himself be nothing more. But there was something she had to say to the real man.

'Thank you. Have I said that? Thank you, Jack. You saved my

life. I cannot believe that anyone else could have done what you did.' *And if you say it is just your job, you will break my heart.*

His arms tightened, then she felt his chin move and realised he had lay his cheek against her hair for a fleeting moment. 'I thought I was going to lose you,' he said at last. 'And that didn't seem like an option I could accept.' There was a pause. Eva filled it trying to work out whether he meant that personally or professionally, and failed. Jack was just too good at keeping his emotions out of his voice. And yet, she could not forget the echo of his voice as she had slipped into unconsciousness in the river. *Always.*

Chapter Eleven

'Bloody hell, guv'nor!' The outburst of swearing was Henry's voice, Eva realised vaguely. They had stopped. She looked round, her head feeling like lead on her aching neck, and saw they were in front of the inn.

'Stubble it,' Jack growled, then, 'Help *madame* down, will you?'

'Gawd help us, you're soaked, both of you.' The groom caught Eva with as much respectfulness as was possible and set her gingerly on her feet. 'And frozen.'

'Get this animal out of sight. I've stolen it—you'll need to *find* it in the morning and return it to the authorities.'

Henry took this news with a calm that said volumes about his expectations of life with Jack, Eva thought, amused despite her weariness. It seemed impossible that she should ever stop shivering, and as Jack took her arm to steer her into the inn she felt the betraying vibration under his skin, as well.

'Upstairs, try not to be seen. If de Presteigne is in any fit state, he will start enquiries round the inns for soaking wet guests. At least we've stopped dripping.'

They went upstairs with all the caution of a pair of illicit lovers and regained their chamber with such relief that Eva found herself clutching the bed post with tears in her eyes. Jack leant back against the closed door as though he could no longer rely on his legs to hold him up. South facing and high up, the room still held the warmth of the day, but that mild air could not touch the bone-deep chill that racked her.

'Get undressed.' Jack straightened and pushed her towards the dressing screen, tugging the bell pull as he passed it. Eva began to fumble with buttons and hooks, set in swollen, sodden fabric. There was a tap at the door. 'Hot water, lots of it. And a hip bath. There's more of that if you make haste.' She heard the clink of coin and the retreating scuffle of feet.

'Here.' A large towel landed on top of the screen.

'I can't undo the fastenings,' Eva said, cursing under her breath as a softened fingernail tore. 'Oh, *damn.*' It was all too much, she just wanted to be back in Maubourg. She wanted a flock of ladies' maids and footmen, she wanted her dresser and to be warm and dry, to curl up, sleep, forget.

'Here, let me.' She gasped in shock as Jack came round the screen. He was stripped, clad only in a large linen towel slung round his narrow hips. 'You can open your eyes,' he said after a moment in a tone that hung somewhere between amusement and irritation. 'I would suggest that dying of cold and exhaustion but unsullied by a glimpse of my naked flesh is observing the proprieties too far.'

'Yes. Yes, of course.' Eva tried to sound brisk and matter of fact as she opened her eyes, trying to unfocus them at the same time. It was ridiculous to be prudish under the circumstances. Jack was her bodyguard and her friend. She had been a married woman—it was not as though she had never seen a naked man before. And, in any case, neither of them was in a fit state to do anything imprudent.

Jack began to work on the row of buttons that fastened the bodice of the dress, swore under his breath, and undid it by the simple expedient of tearing it open with both hands. Buttons pinged off in all directions. 'Jack!'

'It is ruined anyway,' he pointed out reasonably, pulling the bodice apart and dragging it down her arms.

'I..er… I can manage now.'

He ignored her, lifting the water-sodden skirts over her head and dumping the garment in a heap on the floor, then standing, hands on hips, regarding her as she shivered in stays, petticoat and chemise.

'Did you tie these with a bow or am I going to have to cut the strings?' He advanced on the neat row of lacing that secured the corset. Eva squeaked. 'A bow. Excellent woman.' The stays landed on top of the gown just as the maid knocked on the door. Eva retreated, leaving Jack to deal with the procession of inn servants with tub and steaming ewers.

She peeked through the gap in the screen, her lips curving in amusement at the sight of the maids reduced to blushing giggles by Jack's well-displayed physique. They could not be blamed, she told herself, conscious that she was admiring the view just as much as they were. The bruises had begun to turn yellow across his back and chest. She ignored them as she studied the cleanly defined musculature, the narrow hips and the well-shaped calves. Hairy, but just right, she decided, as a violent shiver shook her, reminding her just how serious their situation was. *Stop it!* she chided herself. *Ogling like one of the maids, indeed!*

The door shut and Eva hastily bent to untie her garters and roll down her stockings. Jack reappeared around the edge of the screen. 'Come on, hurry up, your teeth are chattering.'

'Go away, then! Because if you think I am taking another

thing off while you are— Jack! Put me down.' He bent, swept her up and deposited her, petticoats and all, into the deep tub the girls had brought up. 'Oooh. That's *wonderful.*' Warmth seeped through her, making her skin tingle and her frozen toes ache. But the momentary discomfort was worth it. She even began to believe that the bone-deep chill would disappear in time. 'What a huge tub.' It was big enough for her to tuck in her feet, provided she kept her knees bent up, sticking above the surface.

Jack began to scoop water up in his cupped hands and pour it over her knees and her shoulders. He paused, his hands and arms deep in the hot water for a moment, letting the warmth seep into him.

'I'll be quick, you need to get in,' Eva said hastily.

'No, you aren't warm through yet, and your hair needs washing.' Jack picked up one of the ewers. 'Close your eyes.' He poured the water through her tangled hair, then found the scented soap and began to work up a lather and rub it in. 'Sit still, don't wriggle or you will get soap in your eyes.' He seemed quite at home doing it. Eva wondered vaguely if he bathed his mistress. *Mistresses, more like,* she reflected, moving her head languidly to the pressure of his hands. She could not believe that this man would find much attraction in celibacy.

'You're purring.' His chuckle was close to her ear. 'Keep your eyes closed, I'm going to rinse it.' The warm torrent drowned her protest that of course she was doing no such thing, then she found her head swathed in a towel and realised he was rubbing it dry. It was so easy to let go and allow him to do it. Eva's eyes stayed closed, even when the towel was lifted away and she heard Jack moving across the room. He came back almost at once, lifted some of the damp weight of her hair and began to comb it.

'Jack, don't bother with that, you'll get chilled, I must get out.' Eva opened her eyes and found he was very close, his fingers working carefully through the tangles.

'No, I'm warm, here in the steam, I promise. Relax while I comb this.' The grey eyes that could be so hard and cold were gentle as he watched her, the lines of his face relaxed out of their habitual vigilance as she had never seen them before, even in laughter.

Her eyes drifted shut again. The memory of being cold, of being afraid, seeped away under the strokes of his hands. 'Lean forward.' She found herself resting against his chest, her forehead on his shoulder as he reached round her, plaiting her hair into a thick tail. Then he coiled it on her head, fastening it with a pin he must have found with her comb.

The heavy weight of it made it difficult to lift her head up off his shoulder, or so she told herself. Against the skin of her forehead she could feel the hard line of his collarbone, smell the scent of him through the soap-scented steam. River water, chilled flesh, man. Jack. Her lips moved, touching lightly on the flat plane of his chest and he shifted, his hands slipping down from her hair to hold her against his body as he knelt there beside the tub.

'You are cold,' she murmured against his skin.

'Warm me, then.'

Awkward, her wet petticoats tangled round her legs, Eva shifted in the tub until she was kneeling up, breast to breast with Jack. Her hands slid, palms flat, up his back, holding him close to her, pressing herself to the length of his torso so her heat soaked into him. Her nipples peaked, hard under the soaked petticoat, rubbing against the subtle friction of wet linen as she buried her face in the angle of his neck, feeling the thud of his pulse close to her ear.

Jack's breath was hot on the side of her face, feathering her ear so that she caught her own breath, the almost-forgotten heavy heat of arousal settling low in her belly. She expected him to touch her ear, perhaps run the tip of his tongue around the curl of its moulding; instead his hands moved down to cup her buttocks.

The sensation of the two palms, cooler than her own hot flesh, the gentle grasp of the long, clever fingers, had her pressing closer so that when, without warning, Jack stood up, she was lifted with him in one smooth motion. He shifted, taking her off balance so that she clutched at him, then he was standing in the hot water with her.

They were so close that she could feel the hem of the towel he wore around his waist pressing against her knees, the roughness of wet hair where one of his legs pressed between hers. The sodden fabric she was wearing might as well not have been there as her body melted into his, the touch of hard nipples against her breast, the unmistakable heat and pressure of his arousal against her stomach.

Eva lifted her face from the shelter of his neck, his hair spiky with wet as it brushed her cheek. 'Go,' he said huskily.

'What?' she whispered. His eyes were closed, the lashes as wet on his cheeks as though he had wept, but the skin below was dry.

'Go. Get into bed.' Still blind, his mouth curved into a smile that had her longing to touch her lips to the corner of his. 'I think you have warmed me as much as a friend might be expected to.'

Jack stood motionless, following Eva's retreat behind the screen by sound. When he heard the flap of a towel from the direction of the screen he opened his eyes, poured in the remaining ewers of hot water and, discarding the towel, took her place in the tub.

The heat took him into its embrace like a lover and he leaned back against the high back of the tub, his knees hooked over the other side and his feet dangling. It was possible, he thought hazily, that he would just lie there all night, luxuriating.

If only he did not have to think. To plan. To try to get some sort of perspective on what had happened just now. The warmth was doing absolutely nothing to subdue the evidence of just how much the sensation of holding Eva in his arms had aroused him.

What had gone wrong? Cold, battered, exhausted, all he had intended was to get her tucked up in bed, warm and safe. If he had been asked, he would have laughed at the thought that he could have summoned either the strength or the inclination to think about sex. It seemed he did not know his own body as well as he thought.

There was a discreet cough and he closed his eyes as Eva's footsteps padded past, wondering if she was looking at him, wondering, for the first time, what she thought of the man she saw.

Arrogant devil, he chided himself, as he fished blindly over the edge of the tub for the soap. What she saw was an adventurer, a man she could rely on for violence, low cunning and an insolent disregard of her status and position. She saw a man who promised to be her friend and who had damn nearly taken her there and then, dripping wet, on the floor beside this tub.

But he hadn't. Why not? Jack began to scrub the smell of the river water and mud off his skin, grimacing as he realised he'd picked up Eva's soap and not his own. He would reek fragrantly of gardenias as a result, but he felt too relaxed to get out and find something else. He hadn't even kissed her, hadn't bent his head to sweep his tongue over those taut nipples he had felt fretting against his own chest, hadn't let his hands take the sweet weight of her breasts in their palms.

Because I want to make love to her, not just have sex with her. And make love when she is fully awake and aware of what she is doing, he thought grimly, *not clinging to me because she is exhausted, frightened and I have saved her life—just.*

And what the hell am I thinking? Jack demanded of himself savagely as he slid down so his head went under the water. He emerged, streaming, and scrubbed his hands through his hair with intentional force.

That was a grand duchess in that bed, not some game pullet, not even a sprightly matron who was interested in showing her gratitude for a well-executed commission in ways that went beyond paying his bill. That happened now and again. He never sought it, sometimes took steps to evade it and sometimes found it a mutually satisfying, if short-lived, encounter.

This was different. The Grand Duchess Evaline was different. There was an innocence about her that was at odds with her marriage to one of the most hardened roués in Europe, a softness under that imperious manner that she could adopt at the blink of her long-lashed eyes. The memory of those lashes against his skin sent a stab of lust lancing into his already aching groin.

It was going to be a long night. He might want to make love to her, she might, in her vulnerability and disorientation, turn to him, but Jack knew full well that he could not let it happen. She was chaste, he could tell that almost at a glance, and she would have had countless opportunities discreetly to be otherwise. The fact that she had not meant that this was something that was important to her, to what she was as a woman, and he could not destroy that.

He opened his eyes, saw nothing but a mound under the white covers to show where Eva was, and began to scrub at the soles of his feet which seemed irrevocably black. Had she spurned de Presteigne at some point? His instinct told him that she had. The man would take that as an insult, would nurse it in his breast as a slight to be repaid. It made him even more dangerous—if he still lived.

Jack climbed out of the tub, registering dispassionately the muscles that ached, the ones that felt least responsive. Weaknesses he could not afford, gaps in his training to be worked on. Tomorrow he wanted to ride, if Eva was up to it. Two of their pursuers were dead, he had made sure of that. But there remained de Presteigne—wounded certainly, and if alive no doubt as furious as a scalded cat—and the soldier who had fallen in the river who might have been able to swim.

Pursuit was either still on their heels, or as far away as Prince Antoine, waiting impatiently in the brooding castle of Maubourg for news of the hunt. Ahead was safety. He rested one foot on the edge of the tub as he scrubbed the leg dry and reconsidered that thought. Safety unless Antoine had had the sense to send agents on ahead of de Presteigne in the hope that the colonel would act as the ferret down the rabbit hole and drive them headlong into his hands.

Without ever having met Eva's brother-in-law, Jack felt a deep dislike of the man, a traitor both to his own family and his country and the attempted murderer of his nephew and the boy's mother. But that did not make him a fool, and to misjudge him could be fatal.

Dry and warm at last, he padded over to the bedside and looked down at Eva. The thick plait had come loose from his inexpert attempt at pinning it up and lay on the covers, making her look heart-wrenchingly young. He thought about just falling into bed, then spent several minutes extricating the long bolster without waking her, and setting it down the middle of the bed. He might be resolved now to fight her sensual spell, but he would not have wagered so much as a groat on his body paying any heed to that if he touched her as he slept.

The soft mattress took him like a cloud as he finally slid between the sheets and sleep swept over him even before he could pull the covers up to his shoulders.

The tattoo of knocking on the bedchamber door had Jack out of bed with his pistol in his hand before he was even conscious of moving. The sun was streaming in through the window, the old clock in the corner registering eight. He took a steadying breath and called, *'Oui?'*

'C'est Henri, monsieur.' It must be, no one could imitate the groom's atrocious accent.

Jack turned the key in the lock and let the man in. 'Thought I'd better check, seeing the time's getting on.' He glanced round the room and added reprovingly, 'You know, guv'nor, you shouldn't be walking about like that, stark naked with your wedding tackle on show. There's a lady to consider, and not just any lady. She's a grand duchess, when all's said and done.'

He looked defiant as Jack glared at him, but the retort came, not from him, but icy—if somewhat muffled—from the bed. 'The Grand Duchess in question is right here, Henry, and the reason I am stuck under these very hot covers is to spare myself the sight you so graphically describe. If you *gentlemen* would be kind enough to remove yourselves, dressed or undressed, I would like to get up now.'

Jack dragged on his breeches and shirt, scooped up the rest of his things and strode out of the room. 'We will be in the private parlour, *ma'am*. Please be so good as to lock the door behind us.'

The lock clicked before they were three steps along the landing. Jack dropped his shoes, swore mildly, and kicked them ahead of himself into the parlour. 'You don't half whiff, guv'nor. Like a flaming lily,' Henry observed.

'Gardenias,' Jack corrected, dragging off his clothes again so he could put on his drawers and stockings. 'Better than smelling like the banks of the Rhône, believe me.'

'Can believe that.' The groom hitched one hip on the window ledge and regarded Jack critically as he dressed. 'You hurt any? You look banged about.'

'Nothing that won't heal soon enough.' He felt as though he had been stretched on the rack, then beaten with broom handles, but admitting to that would only lead to Henry offering one of his brutal massages.

'Good enough.' The groom looked uncomfortable. 'Look, guv'nor, you really shouldn't be getting involved with her Highness like this.'

'Like what?' Jack demanded.

'No, don't you go pokering up on me, guv'nor, you look like your late unlamented father when you do that, and it's enough to give a man the colic, with all due respect…'

'The chance of some due respect would be welcome, but I suppose you are going to have your say,' Jack retorted grimly. To an outsider the liberties he allowed the groom would have been inexplicable, but Jack was prepared to listen to a man whose loyalty and courage had been proven over and over again, even if his tendency to embarrassing frankness was legendary.

'I am that. She's a real lady, that one, and royalty, almost. You shouldn't be—'

'I'm not.'

'Yes, that's all very well for you to say, but when you come hopping out of her bed in a state of Abram, who's going to believe that?'

'You are, if I tell you so, you suspicious old devil. There's a bolster down the middle of the bed every night—stop laughing, will you!'

'Are you two going to indulge in whatever crude conversation is amusing you for much longer?' a frosty, disapproving voice enquired from the doorway. 'Because I want my breakfast.'

Jack saw Henry's jaw drop and turned slowly. The figure standing on the threshold was clad in breeches, boots, a snug-fitting waistcoat and white shirt. Her hair was bundled into a net at her nape and a neckcloth dangled from her hand. 'Can one of you show me how to tie this?' Eva enquired calmly, her eyes defying them to comment on her attire. 'I must say, I had no idea how difficult it is to get into men's clothes.'

The unfortunate turn of phrase was too much for Henry, who collapsed in hoots of laughter. Eva went scarlet. 'You should meet Mr Brummell,' Jack said, attempting to save her blushes by pretending not to notice the *double entendre*. He kept his face straight with an effort that hurt and aimed a kick at the groom's ankle. 'He would assure you it takes two hours at the very least.'

Chapter Twelve

Embarrassment and her own sense of the ridiculous fought inside Eva and humour won. Her lips curled in a reluctant smile. 'I am not used to using my English every day,' she admitted. 'Thank you, Jack, it was, as you kindly assumed, the difficulties of dressing as a man I was referring to. You,' she said with calm reproof to Henry, who was still spluttering gently, 'have a dirty mind.'

'Me! Now, that's unfair, ma'am, I was only this minute lecturing the guv'nor on proper behaviour.'

'Hmm.' She handed the cravat to Jack. 'Please?'

'Fold it like this, then wrap it round once, and again and then… The devil—I can't explain. Sit down, please.' Eva sat obediently while Jack went to stand behind her and took the ends of the cravat in each hand. The warmth of his body was pleasant, although she could almost feel the tension in him as he tried to avoid pressing close to her. 'Then under here, spread it out, tuck it in… Let me see.' He came round to the front and regarded her, hands on hips. 'Not bad.'

'Thank you,' Eva responded demurely. Jack was different this morning, she concluded sadly. He was pleasant, apparently cheerful, yet there was a reserve underlying his words and his eyes were impossible to read when she managed to catch them directly—which was not easy.

Last night, of course, that was what was concerning him. They had almost—what? Made love? But he had made no move to caress her, to seduce her, only to hold her. The fact that she had found the entire experience utterly arousing would, she suspected, surprise him. He seemed not to have any vanity about the effect he must surely have on any woman who had the slightest interest in the opposite sex.

She let herself be concealed behind a screen while the maids laid the table and brought breakfast in, hardly listening to Jack's explanation that she must not be seen in men's clothes by the inn staff in case they were questioned later. It must be, she concluded, that he saw the problem as his own desire for her—and she had too much experience of the instinctive masculine response to any halfway attractive woman to be greatly flattered by that—and did not have any concept of how much she was coming to want him.

Eva could feel the bedrock of her preconceptions, of the limits she had set on her life, her rules of conduct, begin to shift subtly. It was disturbing, like sensing that the ground you were on might slip, yet not being able to see any fissures yet. Was it just that she was too weak to resist temptation? Or that something had changed?

'Safe to come out now,' Jack called, and she emerged, frowning, to take her seat.

'What is it?' Jack put out a hand as though to smooth the line she could feel between her own brows, then turned the gesture by pulling out her chair. 'Are you very tired after yesterday?'

'I am well, a little stiff, but that is all. It is nothing. No, perhaps not nothing after all. Something I need to think over and perhaps talk to you about later.' When she had some idea if she was just overwrought and adrift, or whether she really did need to think again about her life and how she lived it. 'Where are the horses?'

'At a livery stables on the Lyon road. We will travel that far with Henry, and then you and I will leave him to the post road and we will take to the minor roads that parallel it.' Jack cut a healthy slice off a beefsteak and bit into it with the appetite of a man who had exercised hard.

Eva toyed with the preserves spoon. 'And we meet at the inn tonight?'

'No. We travel separately, with rendezvous points we have already agreed. It will be easier then to spot danger, see if we are followed.'

Henry finished chewing his mouthful of ham. 'I called on our agent here first thing this morning. Word is that Bonaparte's moving troops towards the frontier. Thought you said they aren't expected until July, guv'nor.'

'Well, Wellington certainly wasn't expecting the French until then,' Jack said, frowning at his coffee cup. 'That timing was what persuaded us to plan for this route, otherwise I would have organised some convenient English smugglers at Calais.'

Eva supposed she should be anxious about this news, but somehow she couldn't manage it. She trusted Jack to get her back, and after last night she was half-convinced he could work miracles. In any case, she felt too strange to worry.

He put down his fork and eyed the slice of bread and butter she was nibbling. 'Eat! That is not enough to keep a sparrow alive. Eggs, ham, black pudding.' Jack pushed the platter towards her. 'Goodness knows when we will get our next square meal.'

Obediently Eva helped herself, piling the food on her plate

until Jack nodded approval. Jack was the expert—if he said eat, she would eat, even though she had little appetite. Possibly it was the water she had swallowed last night, or perhaps it was the unsettling, hot, ache inside her that had started last night and now would not leave her. When she looked at him it got worse.

Desire. *I should be ashamed.* But where, exactly, was the shame? she pondered, dutifully chewing her ham like a small child told to eat up. She set her own standards, it was herself she was letting down if she fell short of them, and it was her own conscience she must consult.

But there were two people in this equation. Eva looked down and saw her plate was empty. Suddenly finding her appetite restored, she reached for the bread and butter and spread a slice with honey. There were Jack's standards to consider, as well, his conscience. She gave herself a little shake. They would ride, it would clear her mind. Then they would talk. Frankly.

The horses Jack had hired were fine animals, strong, sound and looked fit enough to carry them to the frontier, provided they kept to a steady pace. Eva stayed with the carriage until they were some distance from the stables, then Jack, leading her saddle horse and a laden pack animal, caught up with them and she was able to shed her cloak and mount.

'Oh, you lovely thing.' She ran her hand down the arching, satiny neck of the bay gelding, settling herself in the saddle while Jack checked the girth and adjusted the length of the stirrup leathers for her. 'It seems so long since I was able to ride anything so big and powerful. Since Louis died I have been expected to ride side-saddle at ceremonies, or on gentle hacks around the vicinity of the castle on a nice, quiet mare.'

'You can mange him, then?' Jack swung up on the black horse, a good sixteen hands, with a wicked glint in its eye. 'I hoped perhaps you could, because of the distances we need to cover, but I did have one in reserve.' He grinned suddenly. 'A gentle, solid little mare.'

'An armchair ride?' Eva enquired indignantly. 'Certainly not.' She did feel an inner qualm that perhaps she was so out of practice that she might not manage, or that she would slow him down. Jack's high expectations of her reinforced her determination to live up to them, gave her courage, even while part of her wondered sceptically if this was just good management of the forces under his command. She decided to test him. 'Why do you think now that I can ride this horse?'

'Because you've got guts, determination and a certain natural athleticism,' he said matter of factly, neck-reining one handed to turn his horse towards the track that led away from the post road. Eva stared at his retreating back. 'Come on.' Jack twisted in the saddle. 'Don't you believe me? When have I ever flattered you or been less than honest with you?'

'Never.' Eva dig her heels into the horse's flanks and cantered up alongside him. 'I don't think so. Thank you.'

'Thank me later, when your muscles are remembering that they have not worked like this in months—'

'Years,' she said ruefully.

'Years, then. You will be convinced your posterior is one big blister and your shoulders will ache like the devil and then it will all be my fault.'

'I'll just have to look forward to a good deep hot bath,' Eva said without thinking, then went red to her ear tips at the rec-ollection of last night's bath.

But Jack was already forging ahead, up the slope. 'I

wouldn't count on it,' she thought he said. But that could not be right—any inn would be able to provide a tub.

The pace Jack set was steady but fast, wending their way between the small ponds, thickets and fields on the east side of the wide river. They would canter, then drop to a walk to spell the horses, then canter again. From time to time he would check a compass, glance at the sun or stop to study the black notebook he kept in his pocket. He took half an hour at noon to eat from the packages of food that were stowed in their saddlebags, then watered the horses and walked, leading them for half an hour before mounting again.

They spoke little, although Eva was aware of Jack's eyes on her from time to time. Something strange was happening to her as the lush countryside unrolled beneath their horses' hooves, as the wildfowl rose in honking panic from the pools or the cattle raised their heads and watched them pass with great liquid brown eyes.

The wind was in her hair, the air was sweet in her lungs and it was as though she was stripping off some heavy, uncomfortable robe, freeing her limbs so she could run and laugh. Reality narrowed down to the landscape around them, the feel of the horse beneath her, her awareness of the man by her side.

Slowly, very slowly, the realisation came to her that she was herself again, not the girl who had left England, a wide-eyed bride, not the Grand Duchess with the weight of a tiny country on her shoulders, but herself, the Eva who had always been inside. For years she had looked out through her own eyes as though viewing the world from behind a mask, and in time she had become to believe that that was who she was.

I was beginning to think I was middle-aged, she thought in amazement as she followed Jack's lead and popped the gelding over a low post and rail and whooped in delight at the sensation of flying. *I was a mother, a widow, a Duchess. They are all important, but they are not me, not all of me. I'm me and Freddie's mother. Me! Eva, having an adventure. Last night I nearly died and now I feel more alive than I ever have in my life.*

Jack reined in and pointed upwards and she squinted into the blue sky at the pair of kites wheeling above them. Free. She was free. What did she want? What was important for her, inside? Inside, where she was a woman…

Despite her euphoria she was beginning to flag, to think longingly of the inn ahead. As the sun dropped low over the hills of the Beaujolais to the west, Jack reined in. 'This will do, I don't want to press on past Châlon tonight.'

'What? Where?' Eva stood in her stirrups and looked around. There was no sign of so much as a farmhouse, let alone the snug inn she was imagining. 'Are we going back down to the post road?'

Jack, she saw suspiciously, had the air that seemed to be shared by every male with a guilty secret from small boy to King's Messenger. He was trying to look innocent—and failing.

'Well?' she demanded.

'We are camping out,' he admitted, cornered.

'Out here? What about my bath?' Now they had stopped she was painfully aware of her sore bottom and the fact that she was going to have to unbend her legs and stand.

'I did warn you. Look, there's a nice grove of trees and a stream.'

Nice grove, indeed! Eva considered grumbling. Complaining loudly even. She wanted a hot bath, she wanted a good dinner and she wanted a soft bed. She wanted her major-domo, her footmen, her Swiss chef and her maids. She wanted clean, soft linen. She sat on the tired gelding, absently rubbing her hand along his neck and watched Jack, who had swung down off his horse and was exploring the glade.

It *was* rather nice, now that she came to look at it. The trees whispered softly in the warm evening breeze, there was fine grass and the stream ran busily over glinting pebbles. And there was the man in the middle of it, stretching mightily, his hat tossed on the ground. As she watched he stripped off his coat and threw that down, too, then turned and smiled at her. And Eva smiled back, her aching muscles, her grumbles, her empty stomach forgotten. He was why she felt so free, so *new*. And she was going to have to decide what to do about that.

'It is lovely,' she called, and sensed, rather than saw, the way he relaxed. Had he expected her to be difficult? 'I don't think I can get down by myself, you will have to help me.'

It was part calculation on her part, a feminine wile to get his hands on her, and partly the absolute truth. Jack strolled across and held up his hands. 'Throw your leg over the pommel and slide,' he suggested.

'I don't think I can throw a shoe, let alone an entire limb,' she joked, slipping her foot out of the stirrup and creakily lifting the leg over. The horse, impatient to get at the water and soft grass, shifted and she slid, with more speed than elegance, into Jack's waiting embrace.

He caught her around her waist and held her for a second, feet dangling, then he let her slide down, sandwiched between his body and the horse. She was aware of every inch of his body, and of hers. As her feet touched the ground she realised she was holding her breath and raised her eyes to search his face.

It was expressionless, those searching eyes shuttered and uncommunicative. Jack opened his hands and stepped away. 'I'll gather firewood. Can you water the horses?'

'Yes, of course.' So, the door was still firmly closed. If she wanted him, she was going to have to be very explicit, not rely on hints or flirtation. Eva unsaddled the riding horses, removed their bridles and led them to the stream, then tied them on long leading reins to a sturdy branch. The pack horse stood patiently while she fiddled with straps and buckles, but soon he too was free of his burden and cropping the grass with the others.

'I did not expect you to do that.' Jack was back with an armful of wood. He crouched in the middle of the glade where travellers had obviously lit fires before and began to methodically stack the wood, sliding twigs and dried grass in at the base.

'Why not? I am perfectly capable of it.' Eva searched in the unloaded packs and found food, then bedrolls, which she shook out by the fireside. 'Can we eat all of this tonight? I am starving.'

'So long as we have something left for breakfast.' Jack finished lighting the fire and stood, studying his surroundings, shading his eyes against the setting sun as he watched the track and the fields that lay between them and the river. He looked back at the fire, apparently satisfied with the almost invisible trickle of smoke from the dry wood.

Eva busied herself setting out the meal, then went to scoop water from the stream. 'Shall we make coffee?'

'Why not?' Jack folded himself down on to one of the bedrolls with enviable ease for a man who had been in the saddle all day. 'Do you know how?'

'Er…no.' Eva passed the packet of coffee across and began to slice and butter bread. Somehow, in the last few minutes she had made up her mind what she was going to say to Jack, how she wanted to resolve the conflicts inside her.

'That was good,' Jack said at length, pushing away his empty plate and flopping down on his back. 'Are you warm enough?'

'Yes, thank you. It is going to be a very warm night.' *Now, while I have the courage…* 'Jack, I did not thank you. For last night.'

'For what? Fishing you out of the river? Yes, you did. When we were on the horse.' He was flat out on his back, one knee raised, the other foot balanced casually on it.

'No. I know I thanked you for that. I meant for later, in our room.' Eva took a deep breath and plunged. 'You could have seduced me with no effort at all and I think you know that very well.' The foot that had been describing lazy circles stopped. She had his full attention now. 'I was exhausted, vulnerable and I had been very frightened and I want to thank you for not taking advantage of that. In the morning I would have felt regret, whatever the night had been like.'

'I know.' Jack's voice was neutral, but she knew him well enough by now to hear the tension in it.

'I am not exhausted, vulnerable or frightened now,' Eva said deliberately. And waited.

His reaction seemed to take for ever. He put both feet on the ground, then levered himself up on his elbows and finally sat up, looking at her. The sunset painted gold and rose across his face. 'What are you saying, Eva?'

'That I feel myself now. More myself than I have for nine years and I can see clearly what I need and what is important to me. I have been chaste since my husband—'

'I know. I could tell almost by looking at you. Eva, you do not have to—'

'Let me finish.' She smiled at him, smiled at the serious expression in the grey eyes.

'Here, I am not the Grand Duchess. I am not a widow, I am not a mother. I am just Eva. And I am alone in a beautiful place with a man I desire and I trust and I like.' Jack moved abruptly, as though he was going to stand, and Eva held out a hand to still him. 'I am just a woman, asking a man if he would like to make love to me. If you say *no,* if I am wrong about what I see in your eyes, what I feel when you are close to me, then I apologise. If you lie to me, I will know and that will hurt far more than you explaining that you do not want to do this.'

'Not want? I have wanted you since I first set eyes on you.' The breath, so painfully held, left her lungs in a soundless sigh of relief. Jack pushed himself up so he knelt on one knee, the movement bringing him close enough to take her hand. 'I desire you so much it hurts, but I fear hurting you far more than I fear that pain. Eva, have you thought about this?'

'Idiot man,' she said roughly, tears forming behind her eyes. 'I have thought of very little else since I turned and saw you in my bedchamber, brought there by magic.'

'I don't believe that,' Jack said. *Oh, thank God, he is smiling…*

'Well, I admit I think a lot about Freddie, and Philippe and the Duchy and how we are going to get back safely and whether I have a blister on my behind. But in all the gaps between I think of you and how I want to be in your arms and feel your mouth on me.'

'Do you want to sleep on it?' He was still regarding her with questioning eyes.

'No,' she declared roundly. 'I want to sleep *with* you.'

Chapter Thirteen

Jack searched the wide brown eyes looking so candidly into his. She meant what she said, and he could believe that she had been thinking about it, seriously, all day. Something like this, for Eva, was not to be taken lightly. And for him, after an adult life treating such encounters as either a matter of amicable business, or simply a fleeting moment of mutual pleasure, the responsibility of what she was offering felt as heavy as the duty laid upon him to keep her life safe. She, for some bone-deep reason he could not understand, and was afraid to analyse, was different from all the women before.

'Well, that was definite enough.' He smiled at her decisive declaration, fascinated by the play of colour under her creamy skin. She was shocking herself, he could tell, seeing the soft pink ebb and flow in her cheeks. But she was enjoying that sensation at the same time. 'Eva, we are out of our real worlds here, for as long as this journey lasts. What happens when we get back to England?'

'I do not know,' she said frankly. 'I do not care.' She shook her head. 'No, I do know—it must stop then, I cannot risk the scandal. But we may never get there, for all your skill and courage. I do not want to add losing this to the list of my regrets.'

'Come, then.' Jack stood up with a sensation that he had cast the dice, laid his bet and that his life would change for ever with the fall of those fickle white cubes. Which was madness. She was right; this liaison, whatever it was, could last only as long as it took to feel the swell of the English Channel under their boat's keel. How could that change his life?

He held out his hand to Eva and she took it, with a certain formality, and got to her feet. 'Let me put these together.' He shook out the two bedrolls to their widest, laying one upon the other and raked the fire, adding a thick log. He did not want her becoming chilled; he sensed she was nervous enough, despite the strength of her declaration.

When he turned, she was balanced on one foot, tugging at her boot. 'I'll do that,' he promised, 'and you can help me with mine. Let's start at the top.' The neckcloth he had tied for her that morning was still firmly in its knot. Jack untied it, unwrapped it from around her neck and folded it carefully in his hands before raising it to his face and inhaling. He held her startled gaze as he filled his senses with the fragrance of her skin.

'But I didn't wear any scent this morning,' she murmured.

'I know.' Jack put the neckcloth into his pocket. 'I can smell gardenia perfume any time I want. I cannot bottle the scent of you.'

Eva reached up and began to untie his neckcloth, her face serious as she fiddled with the knot. He ached for her to hurry, desperate to ignore clothes and simply pull her to the ground and take her here, now, while he still felt he had any control left. But this was Eva, and for her this night was not something to be taken lightly, and for him his whole focus and pleasure must be her delight.

She had managed the knot and was untangling the neckcloth, pulling it free and bunching it in her hands, burying her nose in it in imitation of his gesture. 'Man, warm cloth, bay soap—Jack.' She folded it and put it in her own pocket. 'For nights when I may need courage to sleep,' she said simply, starting on his waistcoat buttons, her lower lip caught between her teeth in an agony of concentration. Jack imagined her applying the same intensity to touching his body and shifted, uncomfortably aware of the constriction of well-fitting breeches.

To hasten matters he threaded his arms through hers and began work on her waistcoat. The effect as their release allowed her bosom to swell free was far more interesting than the equivalent result in his case, he was certain.

'This feels very odd,' he observed, his fingers grazing against fine suiting cloth. 'No ribbons or bows, it's like undressing myself.'

'Indeed? Her eyebrows went up in mock-outrage, then, as though teasing was too dangerous a step into intimacy, she slid her hands up hurriedly and pushed his coat from his shoulders, then his waistcoat. The warm air was delicious through the fine linen of his shirt. Jack felt his eyelids grow heavy as he contemplated the effect of that breeze on bare skin. His, hers.

Jack copied her actions, pushing off her coat and waistcoat, and studied the result. The breeches, which he had chosen with some care, moulded her rounded hips and thighs, but were inevitably too big in the waist. She had cinched it in hard with a leather belt and her hands were hovering, uncertain, over the buckle.

Jack reached out, brushing her fingers away and undid it. He had to stand closer to do so, no longer able to see the whole of her, but close enough now to observe how her pupils had dilated, and trace the flickering pulse under the fine skin at her throat. His own pulse was thundering in his ears as though he had run full tilt up a flight of stairs as he drew the length of plaited leather slowly through the belt loops. It dropped away, a warm snake in his hands.

With a snap of his wrist he flipped it around her again, this time lower, around her buttocks, catching the free end in his left hand and using it to pull her in against him. With both hands holding the leather he could not hold her, but she leaned in of her own accord, her face tipped up for his kiss.

He took a deep breath, drawing in not just the familiar scent of her but the sweet musk of arousal that seemed to perfume her skin, just on the edge of his ability to sense it. Could she detect that on his skin yet? Soon, very soon, he knew their urgent bodies would be sending that thrilling signal unmistakably; now it was as tentative and shy as Eva felt against him.

But this wasn't a virgin trembling so close that the tips of her breast brushed in agonising unpredictability against his chest. This was a woman who had been married, even if she had been alone for a long time.

There were some benefits to being married to one of the most accomplished lovers in Europe.

Hell and damnation. He had tried so hard not to remember those words, not to dwell on them, to tell himself that, just as he never thought of one of his former lovers when with a new one, she would not remember Louis when she was in his arms. That was all very well when the thought of making love to her was just a fantasy to keep him painfully awake at night, or to distract himself with while he should have been thinking of practical matters. Now he was about to put that theory to the test and he knew, perfectly well, that while he could dismiss any number of lightly undertaken affairs, Eva's memories of lovemaking were going to be clear, specific and important to her.

Well, Jack, he told himself ruefully, *you had better do your very best.* And he lowered his head, took her soft mouth with his and found that rational thought fled before the sensual shock of her yielding.

At last! She had dreamed of his mouth on hers again ever since that fierce, intense kiss in the alleyway, dreamed how it would be, wondered if it would be as overwhelming the second time. He was so gentle, yet so certain, in the way he kissed her. He did not even use his hands to hold her; he did not need to. His mouth angled over her lips, seeking, tasting, the flicker of his tongue teasing at the seam until she opened to him with a little gasp of surrender.

Eva found her hands were locked around his neck, her interlinked fingers brushed by the thick black hair at his nape where the strong tendons braced against the pull of her urgency. He explored her mouth slowly, as though seeking to understand something, tasting perhaps, as she tasted him, coffee, the freshness of the celery he had crunched and a taste that just had to be him. Jack.

Louis hardly had ever kissed her like this, taking his time, caressing. It almost seemed that for Jack this was enough, an end in itself, not a hasty part of a rush to consummation. Perhaps she could be more active… Eva let her tongue tangle with Jack's then, greatly daring, thrust it into his mouth, almost gasping at the intensity of the experience. Something slithered across her bottom; he had dropped the belt, catching her in his arms and straining her against him in a blatant gesture that pressed her intimately against the hard ridge in his breeches.

Eva burrowed closer, twining herself wantonly against

him, rubbing like a cat urgent for stroking, the hot ache low down where their bodies throbbed together, crying out for him to assuage it.

Jack left her mouth and began to lick and nuzzle at her neck, bending her back over his strong arm so that she arched like a bow in the hands of an archer while he followed the curve of her throat to where her breasts, unconfined by corset or waistcoat, swelled in the vee of her shirt.

'You are so beautiful.' His voice was husky, the words murmured against the aching curves as he lowered her on to her back on the blankets. He followed her down with a control that spoke of his strength and his care of her and lay against her flank, propped up on one elbow as he slowly opened the buttons to reveal her. 'It is like pushing back the petals of a rose to find the fragrant, golden centre.'

As the sides of the shirt fell open, he made no move to caress her, only lay there, watching her, his warm hand lax on her ribs. As she breathed in and out she was conscious of the roughness of a rider's calluses on his palm, the slight friction of his nails as his curved fingers touched her.

The intensity of his gaze shook her confidence. What was he looking at? What was he seeing? Surely she could never match up to his mistresses who thought of nothing else but how to make their lithe young bodies and smooth faces attractive to men. Her certainty wavered.

'What is it, sweet? He sensed her mood instantly, his hand coming up to cup her cheek. 'Are you cold?'

'No.' She shook her head, her lashes falling to hide the embarrassment she knew must show in her eyes. 'Jack, I'm not a girl any more…'

'No,' he agreed instantly, his voice a sensual growl. 'I can see that.'

'I'm nearer thirty than twenty, I've had a child…' He cut off her stumbling words by pressing his hand over her lips as he sat up. The other hand caressed over the fullness of her breasts, stroking and cupping the weight of them, his thumb flicking from one nipple to another until she bowed up, moaning against his palm.

'You are a woman, Eva,' he said huskily. 'A beautiful, sensual woman. I am a man and what I want—what I *need*—is a woman. Not a girl, and not a woman pretending to be one, either. A real woman. You.'

She heard him, believed him, but she could not reply, for he was kissing her breasts now, suckling her pebble-hard nipples until she thought she was going to climax from that alone. Her fingers dug into his shirt; she felt the fine cloth tear and, reckless, ripped it more so that she could feel the skin of his back, hot satin, under her fingertips.

Jack's hands were at the waist of her breeches, fighting with the fastenings, dragging them down over her hips, taking her drawers with them. He reached her boots, swore and spun round on his knees to drag them off, then sat down, pulling his own off with equal force. By the time he turned back to her she had kicked the tangle of cloth away. The heat of his gaze on her naked body stilled her and she crouched there, her eyes wide on his face as she absorbed the look in his eyes. Desire, heat—and something so fragile, so tender, it took her breath. This hard man, this adventurer felt like that about her. *Her*.

'Jack,' she whispered. 'Jack, love me.'

'Yes.' He sounded as though his teeth were gritted in pain. 'Eva—'

Her hands were on the fall of his breeches, slipping under the cloth to caress hot flesh as she found the buttons and pulled, breeches and underthings with them, freeing him in all his awesome state of arousal. 'Oh. *Oh.*' She should be fearful—how long was it since her body had known a man? Would it be like losing her virginity all over again? She did not care; all she knew was that she wanted this magnificent man inside her, joined with her.

Coherent thought, even about her wants and needs, fled as Jack came down over her, his knee pushing hers apart, his long, clever fingers slipping between them to caress her intimately. 'Oh, so sweet, such honey.' He teased and explored, inciting her and opening her ready for him.

As he thrust, one long stroke of mastery and possession, Eva wrapped her legs around his waist and pulled him close, so close against her that she could feel their pubic bones together. He filled her, completed her and she pulled his head down to her lips as he began to thrust. Both of them were desperate for this, neither had any desire to temper the pace of their passion.

She felt his ardour building, meeting her, driving her and she knew only that she screamed as he took her over into dizzying oblivion and that the sound mingled with his shout as he left her body. And then the little grove fell silent.

The moon was riding high when they finally fell apart, lying side by side, fingers entwined, bathing in the silver light.

So this is what it can be, Eva thought in wonder. *This intense, this tender, this fierce.* It was as though she had found the counterpoint to herself, she marvelled. They had hardly spoken—single words, gasps of pleasure, murmurs of delight—yet he had known how to drive her in to ecstasy, time and again, and some sure instinct had steered her hands, her mouth to bring him there, too.

'Jack.'

'Mmm?'

'Just *Jack.*'

He chuckled and sat up, propped on one rigid arm, running his free hand down over her. 'Cold?' Without waiting for an answer, he stood and began to make up the fire. Eva found her shirt and pulled it on, leaving it loose. With the warm night air and the glow of the fire it was all she needed. *Warm inside,* she thought, wrapping her arms round her knees and sitting watching Jack.

In the moonlight, lit by the fire, he seemed like primeval man—naked, unselfconscious, beautifully made. The light slid over matte skin, highlighted muscle, threw intriguing shadows. She wished passionately that she could draw, could capture him, just as he was now.

He came and lay down again on his back with the relaxed, unselfconscious grace of a big cat. Eva lay, too, propped on her elbows at right angles to him. She rested her chin in one cupped hand and began to run the other over Jack's torso.

'What are you about?' he asked lazily, his mouth twisting as she inadvertently tickled him.

'Exploring.' She let her fingertips trail down the line of hair below his navel, then drifted them lower to thread into the dark tangle of curls.

'There is nothing there but standard male equipment having a rest.' Jack sounded amused as she caressed him. 'And if you are hoping to provoke me into further activity, I give you fair warning, it will take a little while.'

'No, I'm not,' Eva assured him, meeting his eyes with a smile of fulfilled satisfaction. 'It is just that I've never been able to do this before, you see. As I said, I'm exploring.'

'What?' Jack levered himself up on his elbows, looking down the length of his torso to where she was cupping his testicles, gently weighing them in her palm.

'This. Louis would always leave my bed as soon as we had finished making love. I have never been able to examine a naked man like this, so closely. Your body is fascinating,' she explained seriously, then leaned forward and blew lightly as an experiment, intrigued by the way the skin contracted. 'This is all very sensitive, isn't it?'

'Very,' Jack said emphatically as she teased him with the back of one pointed nail. 'Why would your husband always retreat like that?'

'I don't know.' Eva pondered it, realising it had never struck her as odd before. But then, she had no basis for comparison. 'I think perhaps he would see it as a sign of weakness to be naked and vulnerable, and not at his most potent. Louis would always want to be rampant—like the lion on the Maubourg coat of arms. But I think it is more a sign of strength to be able to trust, like this.' On impulse she leaned even further and dropped a kiss onto the half-hidden flesh.

'Come here.' Jack sat up, pulling her almost roughly into his embrace, then lay back with her against him. Under her cheek the sound of his heartbeat was reassuring, his skin was warm, slightly rough from his chest hair. 'It must be trust for two people to do what we have just done, together. We made love *together*. That is new for me, that feeling of partnership.'

'I know,' she said sleepily burrowing into his shoulder. 'I felt it, too: counterpoint.'

'Music, yes,' she heard him agree as she drifted off, feeling him draw the blanket over her, cocooning her safe against his body.

Eva woke to warmth and to the drift of hands over her breasts and stomach. Sleepily, eyes closed against the daylight, she snuggled back into the hard body she was curled against.

'Good morning,' Jack whispered in her ear, and slid into her with one slow thrust. She gasped, shifting to accommodate this new position, then relaxing as he continued to move gently within her, his hands the perfect complement as they caressed with a total lack of urgency, focused only on pleasuring her.

It was bliss, but she could not touch him, could not kiss him. Except one way. Eva tightened her muscles around him, playing with the effect it had both on her and, from the gasp as she did it, on Jack.

It was blissful, languorous, sensual beyond belief. Eva had no idea how long they lay curved together, only that when it came she lost herself entirely in the peak of sensation he brought her to, shuddering with delight in his arms.

She must have dozed again, for when she opened her eyes she was alone in the nest of blankets, water was heating on the fire and Jack was standing knee deep in the stream, washing. Eva got up and took herself off into the bushes, treading cautiously in bare feet. When she got back Jack was just rinsing off by the simple expedient of lying flat in the water. He emerged, shaking himself like a wet dog, and saw her.

'It's cold. Come in,' he invited.

Was she ever going to get used to looking at him? Get used to the way he looked and the effect it had on her? It wasn't simply the lines of his face, or that he was beautifully made and superbly fit. It was the fact that he did not appear conscious of those things that was so attractive. And that a man so self-contained, so disciplined, should let down his guard so totally with her still filled her with awe.

'Only if you get out first. Or we'll get…distracted again.' Eva kept the shirt firmly wrapped round her body.

'All right.' He splashed to the bank and climbed out, pausing beside her. 'I could become very easily…distracted.'

What if we never go back? What if we stayed here for ever? Eva tossed her shirt to one side and stepped off the bank. The cold water was enough to recall her to the real world—danger, duty and a small boy who needed his mother.

Chapter Fourteen

They rode on again all that day, up through the rich and gentle landscape of the Côte d'Or, halting at noon for their rendezvous with Henry in an inn in the little wine-growing village of Auxey Duresse, just south of Beaune.

Jack watched Eva as they rode. She was easy in the saddle now, apparently unaffected either by her ordeal in the river or their lovemaking. The memory of her supple body answering his, following where he led—sometimes, as her confidence grew, leading him—had him hard, the thought that tonight she would be even less inhibited, even more unreserved, had him aching with longing to hold her again.

From time to time, apparently prompted by some thought, she would turn in the saddle, her eyes warm and happy as she smiled at him. No one had ever looked at him like that, he realised, impossibly flattered when she reached out her hand and touched him fleetingly on the knee, as though it gave her pleasure just to know he was there.

Henry was at the inn already when they arrived. He had made himself thoroughly at home as usual, Jack noticed, sitting on a bench under a spreading tree, a tankard on the table in front of him and a serving girl with a twinkle in her eye flirting as she talked to him.

'Here they are now. You be off inside, *mam'selle,* and bring out the luncheon, just like I ordered it.'

'Found an admirer?' Jack asked in French, swinging down from his gelding and keeping half an eye on Eva. It wouldn't do to draw attention to her sex by making too much of a fuss, but she dismounted easily, handed him the reins and went to sit beside Henry at the shadowy end of the bench.

'Huh.' Henry sniffed at the teasing, but smiled at Eva. *'Bonjour, madame.'*

'Are you all right? No adventures along the road?' she asked anxiously as Jack walked the horses round to the stable yard.

She looked serious when he returned, but the girl setting a laden tray on the table and laying out tankards and plates kept him silent until they were alone. 'Quietly, and in French,' he warned. 'Trouble Henry?'

'I think I've set eyes upon *madame*'s brother-in-law.'

'Antoine?' Eva went pale and Jack put his hand over hers. She sent him a flickering smile of reassurance and freed herself. Embarrassed at the show of affection in front of the groom, Jack guessed.

'If he's a sharp-nosed streak of misery?' Henry asked. 'Brown hair, Maubourg uniform with enough silver braid for a general?'

'That's Antoine,' Eva nodded. 'But in uniform?'

'With a mounted troop behind his carriage, all pale blue and silver.'

'That is our uniform, but this is France. We're a neutral country, he cannot bring troops across the frontier like that, for goodness' sake!'

'You can if Maubourg is now allied to the Emperor,' Jack pointed out, then snatched his hand off the table as Eva slammed her knife, point down, into the wood. Henry jumped. Both men regarded her furious face with guarded interest; Jack had not seen her lose her temper since that first glimpse through the castle window.

'The bastard!' She glared as Jack tried to shush her. 'Oh, very well, I know, becoming angry does no good. But he has no right to take us to war with half Europe, the maniac—only Philippe can do that. How many men had he?'

'About fifty,' Henry estimated. 'Hard to see, they made so much dust.'

'Excuse me.' Eva slid off the bench. 'I cannot eat while I am this furious. I will be back in a minute.'

They watched her while she strode off towards the little river that vanished beneath the mill.

'They had outriders checking every vehicle going north,' Henry added, tearing a lump of bread off and spreading it liberally with pâté. 'Cantered up alongside, peered in, then off. Here, guv'nor, try this.' He pushed the pâté towards Jack, who took it and began spreading his own piece of bread, his attention half on Eva, who was standing, hands thrust into her breeches pockets, staring at the water.

'You didn't take any notice of what I said back at the inn, did you? Knew you wouldn't,' Henry said gloomily. 'You shouldn't have done it, you know, guv'nor, for all that she's a nice lady, and lonely with it.' He ignored Jack's glare. 'Look at her, she's all of a glow. Lovely to see, that is, but what about when you get to England?'

'Damn your impudence.' Jack grabbed the tankard and half-drained it. 'Of course she's glowing—she's furious.'

'No, before then. I could see when you arrived. She was all sort of soft and…glowing. And have you had a look in a mirror yourself lately?'

'If you tell me I'm all soft and glowing, I'll darken your daylights for you,' Jack warned ominously.

'You look happier than I've seen you look since I've known you, and that's since you were a lad,' Henry said frankly. 'I just hope you can stay that way. You don't want it all ending in tears.'

'Damn it, man, we're in the middle of a mission, this is no time for your romantic tarradiddles.'

But the impudent old devil's words struck home. So that was what it was he was feeling: happiness. An odd sensation he seemed to recall from a long time ago. Different from satisfaction, gratification, relaxation, contentment. Something deeper. Something that threatened to make him weak. Damn it, he was sitting here, eating pâté and listening to his groom, however trusted, however much of a friend, lecture him on how to behave with the woman he—

Jack's thoughts juddered to a halt. No. He was not going there, he was not going to think about Eva beyond the pleasure of making love to her between now and their return to England. He was not going to analyse this strange, warm, profound sensation and he was certainly not going to speculate on how he would feel when he handed her over in London.

'Jack?' She was there by his side, a rueful smile on her lips. 'I've sworn at a poor innocent moorhen, kicked pebbles at an inoffensive water lily and I feel better now.'

'Good.' He moved so she could sit down on the bench again. 'Eat up, this is good food.'

'No doubt tested on your way south.' She was tucking in with a healthy appetite, he was glad to see. The elegant toying with her food had vanished; this was a healthy young woman getting a lot of exercise in the fresh air. He caught himself grinning, recalling exactly what sort of exercise might have contributed to the appetite, and got his face straight before Henry noticed.

'Yes,' he acknowledged. 'And the wine is good, too. Henry will be collecting a number of cases before he leaves.'

'Wine?' Eva stared at him, then burst out laughing. 'You English! Such sangfroid. Here we are in the middle of Continental upheaval, the return of Napoleon, you are on a dangerous mission and you stop to taste wine? I had forgotten the English aristocrats' way of behaving as though nothing is a crisis, everything is a bit of a bore.'

'It makes us look like ordinary travellers, *madame*,' Henry supplied, then, with his regrettable tendency to over-explain, added earnestly, 'No aristocrats here.'

Her gaze slid sideways to Jack's face. There was speculation behind the amused brown eyes. 'Indeed?'

'Saving your presence, *madame*.'

'Hmm. So Jack, do we travel with the wine or are we taking to the back roads again?'

'We ride.' He had been intending to resume travelling by coach, but Henry's encounter made him wary. Prince Antoine could be taking those troops to Paris as a very visible pledge of his allegiance to the Emperor, or he could be intending to throw a cordon across the roads further north. Or both. 'Henry, we'll meet at the rendezvous near the frontier. If we aren't there by the seventeenth, or if you run into trouble, push on to Brussels. Have you supplies for us?'

'Aye, enough for a week if you get your fresh stuff in the villages. That'll get you there so long as you don't have to go making any big detours. There's bacon, some hard cheese, sausage, coffee and sugar. I reckoned you'd want to stay on the back roads when I told you about Monsieur Antoine and his little army. What'll you do if it rains?'

'Find some small inn off the beaten track.' The idea of making love to Eva on a goose-feather bed was powerfully attractive. Not that the prospect of another night under the stars was any less so. He caught her eye and saw she was having the same thoughts. She blushed and hastily reached for the cheese. Henry rolled his eyes.

Eva sat watching the carriage roll away down the dusty road towards Beaune. 'He knows about us, doesn't he? Did you tell him?' Jack was checking the pack horse's girth and she was amused to see the flush on his cheekbones at her question.

'Of course not. It is not something I would ever speak of—to anyone. But he has known me a long time, the insolent old devil. He says I look happy and that you are glowing.'

'Oh.' Eva was so taken by this unexpectedly romantic side to Henry that she had to urge her mount to a trot to catch up with Jack. 'I think that's lovely. But I expect you bit his head off.'

'I did. You don't need to worry that he would ever gossip.' Eva shook her head—no, she wouldn't imagine Henry ever doing anything that was against his master's interests. 'I'm not at all sure I like being so transparent, even if it is him.'

'You have a good gambler's face, I would guess.' Any excuse to gaze at Jack as they rode along was welcome—she had the urge just to sit and stare at him all day.

'I have. At least, I had thought I could bluff anyone. It seems I am wrong. You are a bad influence on me, Eva.'

'I am?' Eva's amusement fizzled out, leaving a hollow feeling inside. Jack had enviable focus and concentration—was she undermining that, distracting him? Even weakening him? Was that what Henry was anxious about? She had put his disapproval down to moral objections to a liaison, now she wondered.

Mortified, she rode in silence, picking up pace when Jack spurred on, wrapped in examining her conscience. Jack was a professional. He might have been attracted to her, but he had been keeping that attraction well in check. She had stormed straight through that armour.

He could always have said 'no', she told herself defensively. Or perhaps she was not doing any damage and was being over-sensitive. *Just because I have fallen in love, it doesn't mean that he…*

Eva swallowed hard. *Just because I have fallen in love. Oh, my God, I have done just that.* She thought she simply wanted comfort—physical comfort and the emotional relief of being close to someone who seemed to care about her. But she loved him. And it was impossible. She was a Grand Duchess, he was a King's Messenger at his most respectable, an adventurer at worst, even if he was the younger son of a good family, which she guessed he must be.

I can't ever tell him. She stared at Jack's broad shoulders, relaxed almost into a slouch as he rode at an easy hand canter. He even managed to be elegant when he was slouching. But it was not his physical beauty that made her feel like this, even if that had been a powerful attraction to begin with. She loved the man under that hard, cool, competent exterior. And she must not let him guess.

She had said that this could only be while they were out of England and he had agreed. Now she knew she must persuade him otherwise, without betraying her innermost feelings for him. She could not lose him so soon, it was too cruel.

'Eva?' He reined in and circled back to come alongside her. Eva realised with a start that she had come to a halt and was sitting gazing blankly into space. Hurting. 'Are you all right?'

'Yes. Yes, of course, I am sorry I was just thinking… about England.'

Jack reached over and touched her cheek fleetingly. 'You

miss Freddie, I know. I'll try and get you back as soon as is safe. Come on, let's get past Beaune before we stop again.'

Guilt washed through Eva as she followed the black gelding along the vineyard terrace path. Freddie. His reaction to this had never crossed her mind. He must never know his mother had taken a lover, and she could not hope to keep it a secret in England under the close scrutiny of court and society. If Henry could see it, then others could, too. She had told Jack she would have no regrets if they were to become lovers, and she must never let him guess how she felt, how she had broken her implied word not to become involved.

Some people are never able to consummate their love, she told herself fiercely. *I have been fortunate, I have him for this little span of time. It must be enough. It must.*

Four days later they were across the border, the River Sambre just behind them after the bridge at Thuin. The days had been hot, the nights dry and they had not had to take refuge in an inn yet. Somehow Eva managed to push her knowledge of her love for Jack away to the back of her mind, not to think about it, only to feel—and in that way hide her feeling from him.

Or she tried. 'What is it, sweet?' he would ask, capturing her face between his big hands and staring deep into her eyes. 'Tell me what is hurting you.'

'Nothing,' she said every time. 'Just worries.' And she would stand on tiptoe and kiss him until he forgot whatever betraying expression had crossed her face. Until the next time.

By the fourteenth they had begun to hear cannon fire. At first it was so distant and irregular that she thought it was thunder out of a clear blue sky, but Jack shook his head. 'There's fighting up ahead, border skirmishes as they all sort themselves out, I expect. Now we begin to take great care.'

Dodging small groups of French troops became routine. Jack seemed to know the uniforms, jotting notes whenever they sighted them. Sometimes they were seen themselves, but Jack would let the horses walk, wandering along, doing nothing to raise suspicions that they were anything but innocent local riders. No one challenged them.

Making love by starlight in owl-haunted woods, or in meadows so soft and sweet you could almost taste the goodness of them, became completely natural. They had never made love inside, on a bed, and somehow that did not seem a loss to her, so it was a surprise when Jack sat studying the sky in the late afternoon.

'It is going to rain,' he said, taking the notebook out of his pocket and studying one of his meticulous maps.

'Is it?' Eva looked round, puzzled. 'I am no weather expert, but it looks just the same as yesterday afternoon to me.'

'No. It will rain.' Jack gathered up the reins and turned his horse's head down the fork in the track through the woods. Ahead, across fields, a church spire punctuated the low hills. 'Or there will be a heavy dew in the morning. Or a thunderstorm.'

'Or a plague of locusts?' Eva enquired, beginning to see where this was going. 'You are looking for an excuse to find an inn. Why not say so? Do you think I am going to accuse you of becoming soft because you want to bathe in a tub instead of a cold stream?'

'I think you might be alarmed if you guess the things I would like to do when I get you alone in the Poisson d'Or's best bedchamber with its big goose-feather bed.' Jack grinned, managing to look nearer twenty than thirty.

'Indeed?' Eva attempted a severe expression. She appeared to have forgotten how. 'What a very depraved imagination you have, Mr Ryder.'

'I am shocked you can know of such things,' he teased back. 'Tell me, what would *you* like to do in that big feather bed?'

'Ooh…' Eva pouted provocatively. 'I would like to take all my clothes off—very, very slowly. Then I'd brush out my hair, bathe in a deep hot tub with scented soap, climb out, dripping wet…' Jack's eyes were glazing in a very satisfactory manner. 'Dry myself, then climb into bed. And—go to sleep.'

Laughing at his expression, she urged her horse on, cantering down the track. It curved, perhaps fifty feet above the main road that cut across the country between them and the village. Some instinct made her glance to her left. Dust was rising above the scrub and spindly trees that covered the slope. Eva reined in, holding up her hand to halt Jack, who was rapidly catching her up. They moved into the shelter of a coppice and waited.

'Soldiers,' Jack breathed as the sound of tramping feet reached them, drowning out the song of skylarks over the wheat field. 'French soldiers heading towards Charleroi. A lot of them—this is different from what we have seen so far. I thought our luck would not last much longer.'

'Are we in danger from them?' Eva shaded her eyes and tried to make out uniforms, but her knowledge was not good enough.

'No, probably not. There is nothing about a pair of apparently unarmed riders to cause them any concern, provided we merely cross their path and do not appear to be shadowing them.'

He sat watching the slowly vanishing column of infantry through narrowed eyes. 'Wellington is assembling an Anglo-German army around Brussels, but our agents along the way so far have not known what the weight of troops were on either side, and they were very vague about where Bonaparte is heading. That is Fontaine l'Eveque ahead. I'm going to strike north-east tomorrow and aim for Nivelles.'

'You haven't been talking to me about all this,' Eva accused. 'I should have worked it out for myself—my brain must be turning to porridge. I suppose I have just been so focused on our own adventure I haven't been thinking about the wide world. Of course Bonaparte isn't just going to sit there in Paris, sending out a few scouting parties, and the Allies certainly aren't going to let him.'

'No.' Jack was scrutinising the plain. 'You know, that cannon fire is a fair way off to the north and east, but it is almost continuous now. I think there is a battle going on.'

'And by making for Brussels we are riding right into the middle of it.'

'Maybe. If we do not take care.'

'Jack,' Eva asked with a calm she was far from feeling, 'have you been keeping quiet about this so as not to worry me?'

'Yes,' he admitted ruefully, surprising her by his frankness. 'My orders were to bring you back overland to Brussels; it seemed faster and safer than risking the sea route. It probably still is the right thing to be doing; we just need to avoid wandering into Napoleon's HQ or the no man's land between the two front lines by mistake.'

He dug his heels in and sent the black gelding and the pack-horse trotting down to cross the main road. 'After today we ride hard and fast for Brussels and skirt round any trouble we see. I'll dump the pack and we can rotate between the three horses—it will keep them fresher. We'll do it in the day that way.'

'Have we been going too slowly up to now?' Eva asked, suddenly feeling guilty again. 'Have I been holding you up?'

'No, and, no you haven't.' Jack reined back to a walk. 'We were right to take to the horses—Henry's encounter with Antoine proved that. And I could see no merit in flogging the horses at such a speed that we would have had to be changing them as we went. It draws attention to us, and it was no part of my instructions to deliver you bruised and exhausted. We can make it to Brussels tomorrow, even if we arrive after dark.'

'So tonight is our last night on the road.' The last one alone with Jack. Things would be different in Brussels, she would become the Grand Duchess again then. Even if Jack was still her escort, that was all he could be. Did he realise? Had he thought about that? Probably not—he had a job to do and personal considerations would always come second. 'What is the date?' she asked, wanting to fix this night in her memory for ever.

'June 16th,' Jack said. 'Look, there is the Poisson d'Or.'

'What about my clothes?' she asked, suddenly recalling the way she looked. 'It hasn't been a problem because I have not been close to anyone yet, but I cannot hope to fool people close up.'

Jack seemed unconcerned. 'I will speak quite frankly to the landlord, and anyone else who stares, and say that I do not like my wife riding about the countryside with all these troops about. Of course, if we did not have to hurry to the bedside of your ailing grandmother in Celles it wouldn't arise, but you insisted, so here we are.'

Eva nodded—that was a good tactic, to confront the issue, not to try to keep her sex a secret and arouse suspicion. Jack rubbed his chin, rasping the stubble as though in anticipation of a shave in ample hot water. 'We will have a good dinner to celebrate our last night on French soil. Shall I order champagne so we can drink to the confusion of our enemies?'

'Of course,' Eva flattered herself that the smile she managed was perfectly natural. *To the confusion of our enemies and to the last night in Jack's arms.*

Chapter Fifteen

'To victory,' Jack said quietly in French, touching the rim of his glass to Eva's.

'To victory,' she echoed. There was no private parlour at the Poisson d'Or, but there was a low-beamed room with tables set around. The noise level from the other diners was high enough for them to talk quietly without fear of being overheard, but they kept to French so there would be no unfamiliar rhythms of speech to draw attention to them.

Outside, the rumble of the distant guns continued. Inside everyone pretended not to notice it. Yet there was a febrile excitement in the air, an unease, a whisper of rumour. Did these people really want their emperor back? Eva wondered.

Where were the Maubourg troops? Following where Antoine led them into the midst of a battle or reluctantly marching north and not yet in danger? Were they convinced of the rightness of joining the Imperial cause, or was it simple obedience that kept them with him? If she had been in the carriage when they had stopped it, could she have won them round, convinced them to go back to the Duchy, their families and safety? Eva gave herself a mental shake; thinking *what if* and *maybe* was futile, but when they reached Brussels she would do what she could to ensure the men were found and treated well.

Up ahead was bloody battle, men dying and being wounded and there was nothing they could do. Wellington would win, of course he would, she assured herself. Anything else was unthinkable.

'To victory, and to us,' she added to the toast, touching the painful subject like someone with toothache who cannot resist worrying at the sore tooth. 'It has been good, Jack, these last few days, has it not?'

'It has.' He watched her over the rim of his glass as he took a mouthful of wine before setting it down. 'And it is not over yet.' There was a familiar heat in his gaze, a heat that made her feel hot inside, roused the fluttering pulse of arousal so that she shifted on her chair. The anticipation of a night spent in that big soft bed made her mouth dry and she was uncomfortably aware of her nipples peaking against the restriction of her waistcoat.

'One more night,' she agreed, lightly. One more night and day while he was still hers and hers alone. One more set of memories to live on.

'And then Brussels, and the journey back to England.' Jack stopped speaking as the maid brought bread and a pitcher of water. He dropped his broad hand over hers and squeezed reassuringly. 'Fréderic will be beside himself to see you again.'

'If he remembers me,' Eva said. It seemed to be her evening for probing all her worries.

'He does!' Jack lifted her hand in his and kissed her fingers, earning himself a sentimental smile from a plump *bourgeoise* sitting opposite with her family. 'He told me so—not in so many words, but with what he said, what he mentioned of

Maubourg and you. He has no doubts—lads of that age don't. He knows he will see you again, he knows you are there waiting for him, and he feels quite safe. It is you who has suffered, knowing that you have missed those years of him growing, knowing you have had to trust him to the safekeeping of others.'

'Thank you.' Eva blinked back tears, dropping her cheek momentarily to rest against his raised hand. He smiled at her, then she saw his eyes focus beyond her, the laughter lines creasing attractively. 'And who are you flirting with, might I ask?'

'Behind us. A most respectable dame who obviously thinks we make a pretty couple.'

'We do.' Eva dimpled a smile. 'Look, see the mirror to your right, you can see us in it.' Jack glanced across. She was right—on the wall was an ancient mirror, probably something that had found its way from one of the great houses of the district during the Terror, for it was too fine for this workaday place

The old glass was soft and kind, framing them as a portrait of lovers, hands clasped, heads close. Eva, so feminine despite her severe man's clothing, with her dark plait lying heavy on her shoulder. Him, just a man… Jack stared. That *was* him, it couldn't be anyone else, but somehow the reflection looked different. Younger, more—he fought for the word—more complete. Which was nonsense. It had to be the flattering effect of the mirror. But Henry had said he had changed, and he felt different.

He stared deep into his own eyes, deep into the eyes of a man in love. *Hell!* Jack shut his eyes on the betraying image, turned his head sharply and released Eva's hand. No, that was not going to happen, he could not let it, it was impossible and there was nothing there for him but misery.

But the trouble was, he knew it was too late. That warm centre of contentment, that feeling of completeness that threaded through the desire he felt for Eva, that stab of black misery that hit the pit of his stomach when he thought of leaving her—he had never felt those things before.

The bustle of the inn dining room faded around him as he sat there. He had fallen in love, the one thing he had sworn he would never do. And he had fallen in love with the most inappropriate, most unobtainable woman he could have chosen, short of one of the royal princesses. He felt his lips part without conscious volition and tried to control his instinct to say the words, here, now, at once.

'Jack? What is it?' Eva was staring at him, her lovely mouth curving into a smile that was half-amusement, half-concern. He must be gawping at her like the village idiot, that fatal declaration trembling on his lips.

'Nothing.' *Everything. My heart. My world. My soul.* 'Nothing at all important, just a thought that struck me. This chicken is good, is it not?'

'It is pork.' The smile became a teasing grin as he clenched his hands around knife and fork to stop himself reaching across the table and pulling her to him. 'Does champagne always have this effect on you?'

No, you do. 'No. It is not the champagne, it is pure, unadulterated desire.' He made himself match her bantering tone and found himself smiling as the ready colour stained her cheeks. She was so deliciously modest and reserved, yet when they touched she was utterly abandoned in her lovemaking. It was like her whole character. Outwardly she could be aloof, autocratic, reserved; inwardly she was warm, vulnerable, loving. 'We will take another bottle upstairs—I have wicked thoughts about what we can do with the contents.'

The brown eyes watching him opened wide with speculation that was both shocked and titillated. Jack called up
reserves of self-control he had never had to apply to his own
feelings before and made himself focus only on the here and
now. This meal, this tension between them and the sound of
cannon fire which was becoming fainter and less frequent as
the darkness drew in, became the whole of the world. Jack felt
the urgency draining out of him, to be replaced by a sense of
anticipation that was thrumming through his body with almost
orgasmic intensity.

He was going to make love to Eva tonight, and when he
did it would be astonishing, even better than all the times
before, and yet that was not all he wanted any more. He
wanted—no, he *needed*—to watch her, see her in minute
detail. He needed to learn the way she wrinkled her nose at a
flavour she did not like, how she smiled when she thanked the
maid for some small attention, how the colour of her eyes
changed in the candlelight, how the tiny mole at the corner of
her left eye moved when she frowned at him in mock-anger
at a teasing word.

He packed away the pictures of her at every moment, the
sound of her voice when she chuckled, the throaty laugh of
real, uninhibited amusement, the sudden, serious, expression
that kept transforming her face and which he could not
persuade her to explain. All of these impressions he saved,
learned, as he would a map of enemy territory or a complex
brief from a client, storing them away for the time when they
would be all he had of her. All he could ever have.

Eva pushed away her plate with a little sigh of repletion.
He poured the last drops of the champagne into their glasses
and gestured to the maid for another bottle. 'Shall we go up?'

Their chamber had been cleared of bath tub and shaving

water. The puffy white eiderdown on the big wooden bed had been turned down invitingly and candles burned on the dresser and beside the bed. On the washstand a bunch of June roses made a blotch of warm colour in the pale room.

'Eva.' Jack reached for her.

'No.' She held up a hand, halting him. 'No, tonight I want to make love to you.'

'What have we been doing up to now?' he asked, conscious of the straining ache of arousal that had been building all evening towards this moment.

'You have been making love to me, we have been making love together,' she explained. 'Tonight I would like to…to lead.'

Had he the strength, the willpower, to let her set the pace? Jack swallowed, realising he wanted this, badly, and that his imagination was already threatening to tip him over the edge. Unable to speak, he nodded.

'Good.' She was blushing, but determined. 'Undress for me.'

He could not unlock his eyes from hers. By touch Jack pulled off his neckcloth, unbuttoned his waistcoat, shed it with his coat, careless of where they fell. He had hardly any recall of how his shirt got off, or his shoes, but he found himself standing there in bare feet, clad only in the light trousers he had changed into when they arrived.

'Everything,' she said huskily, releasing his eyes as her own gaze slid down his torso.

He was so hard his fingers fumbled momentarily on the fall of his trousers, then he was pushing them down, feeling the relief as his erection was freed from the constriction, hearing her gasp as she saw him. 'You have me excited almost beyond bearing,' he confessed.

'Do not apologise,' Eva murmured, apparently transfixed.

Her intent regard made him swell harder, larger, as if that were possible. 'Lie on the bed. On your back, please.'

Intrigued, Jack did as she ordered. This was a new experience. What was she going to do now?

What she did was to proceed to torture him by slowly removing each article of her own clothing with deliberate intent to send him insane. She took off her coat and waistcoat with prim care, hanging them carefully on a chair while he admired the tight fit of her breeches over her buttocks and the slender length of her thighs.

She eased off her boots, sliding each down her leg in turn in a way that made him fantasise about sliding in and out of her body. Her neckcloth came next. She stood by the bed untying it, shaking her head reprovingly as he reached for her and only moving again when he lay back. Then she used it to trail down his body, the featherlight touch of the muslin wafting the subtle scent of her heat to him as it teased his nipples into hard knots, then slithered over his groin.

'Have some mercy!' He grabbed for it, only for her to whisk it away, leaving him aching. Jack fought the urge to take himself in hand to gain some relief from this torment.

Eva began to unfasten her shirt, then turned her back on him as she slowly slid it over her shoulders, giving him the view of her slim, white back, and the merest hint of the curve of her breast as she moved. Jack locked his hands into fists in the sheet as the leather belt fell to the floor and she eased the breeches down over her hips, taking her linen underwear with them.

She was a Venus standing there, white and smooth and exquisite. But it was not a marble statue that looked over its shoulder at him but a warm, soft, curving female. How had she learned to be this provocative, this alluring? He sensed this had not been the way she had behaved with her husband. Eva was doing this for him and because of him. Unable to bear the throbbing need any longer, he curled his fingers round the hard flesh that was tormenting him.

'No,' she whispered, coming close, reaching down and unclasping his hand. 'No, I forbid it.' Her heavy plait fell forward, swinging down lie a soft pendulum above his groin, the very tip touching his swollen erection. He was going to disgrace himself, lose all control in a moment. Jack gritted his teeth as Eva loosened the ribbon and slowly, still letting the hair brush him like tiny lashes of fire, unplaited it until it swung, a silken curtain between them.

He was hanging on to his self-control by his fingertips, Eva realised, watching Jack's set jaw muscles, the clenched fists, the magnificent, straining evidence of his desire for her. Enough teasing—she hardly thought she could bear any more herself.

The bed was yielding as she climbed on to it, knelt up and straddled Jack's body, keeping herself raised above him as she bent her head and let her hair fall in a cloud over his chest. His hands came up to cup her breasts, taking their weight as she hung over him. Her nipples, already sensitive, stiffened into aching nubs as his fingers found them. She put her hands on his shoulders and leaned further, giving herself up to his caresses, using her hair to caress in return.

Between her thighs she could feel his hips lifting, straining to rise enough to take her. Aching for him, she lowered herself to meet him, gasping as the hard flesh touched her, wriggling to take him into her, sighing with the exquisite sense of fullness as their bodies interlocked, sinking down until she could go no more and he was fully lodged in the core of her.

She had never done this before, but the feeling of power

and control was intoxicating as she began to ride him, rising and falling, slowly drawing upwards, then, as he bucked beneath her, moving rapidly so that his head fell back and he grasped her hips with fingers like iron.

Her body was aflame, she could feel her control slipping, knew her rhythm was becoming ragged even as Jack took control, reared up and turned her over so he was on top. She knew he was close, knew he was holding on to take her with him and bowed up to meet him, feeling the swirling ecstasy possess her as he freed himself, cried out, hung rigid above her for a moment, then fell down to crush her into his embrace.

'What had you meant to with the champagne?' Eva murmured later, against Jack's shoulder. The candles were low, he had drawn the covers up over their entwined bodies and they had dozed lightly, occasionally stirring to murmur against each other's skin or trail the lazy kisses of lovers who had exhausted themselves, but not their desire to touch.

'Mmm? I wondered what it would taste like if I licked it off your body.' Jack lifted himself on one elbow to look down at her from under hooded lids. He looked tousled, sleepily replete, yet that fire was still there, banked down perhaps, but enough to warm her deep inside.

'Really?' Eva pondered this. 'That sounds nice.'

'That's what I thought. But it is a pity to waste it when we are both too tired to really concentrate on wine tasting. We'll take it with us.'

'To Brussels? But can we… I mean, where will we be staying?'

'I am sure that, wherever it is, your bodyguard will find it necessary to spend the night in your dressing room.'

'Armed to the teeth?' Happiness bubbled up inside her

like the champagne they had drunk earlier. This was not to be the last night after all.

'Well, certainly fully armed,' Jack said with a certain male smugness, settling down again and pulling her into his arms. 'And ready to give you his undivided and close personal attention.'

'There was a battle at Ligny yesterday, that was what we could hear,' Jack told her as Eva came out to the stables. The inn had been in hubbub that morning, the staff distracted and the breakfast service haphazard. They had eaten up and stayed quiet, trying to overhear what was going on, but making sense of it was impossible. Jack had left Eva to settle their account while he went out to saddle up, hoping to get a more coherent account from the stable hands.

'Ligny.' Eva frowned, trying to place it. Jack opened a much folded map from his pocketbook.

'Here,' he pointed. 'And at Quatre Bras to the north-west of it.'

'Who won?' Jack was maintaining his usual neutral expression, but Eva could tell it was not good news.

'Napoleon, by all accounts. Wellington has pulled back towards Brussels. Quatre Bras is a key crossroads,' he added, folding the map away.

They mounted up and rode north in sombre mood until they were out of sight of the village. Then Jack halted and stripped the packs off the led horse, dumping out everything except weapons, water and some of the food. 'Will this fit in your saddle bag?' He flipped open the flap to push in a small loaf of bread. 'The champagne? Eva, what's that doing in there? We are supposed to be travelling light!'

'For tonight,' she insisted. 'You promised.'

'For tonight,' he agreed.

With the led horse free of its burden they made better speed, riding at a canter, constantly scanning the land ahead as they rode through the fields and along the dusty tracks. They saw nothing, for the local peasants seemed to have kept close at home for fear of what might be out there in the aftermath of the battle, but there was sporadic gunfire from their right.

Jack kept away from the main roads, crossing the rivers by little pack mule bridges, or splashing across fords. 'We're not far south of Nivelles,' he told her as they pulled up to a walk to rest the horses.

The edge of a wood curved ahead of them and they hugged it close, grateful for the shade. The sun was scorching now, the sky a queer brazen colour forewarning of thunderstorms to come. They rounded the curve and there, right in front of them, were the first troops they had seen all day.

A dozen men slumped on the ground or hunkered down around the pile of their packs. Weary horses stood, heads down, barely able to flick their tails to keep the flies away. The men were filthy, bandaged, and their uniforms were torn, disfiguring the familiar light blue cloth and the silver trimmings.

'Jack! They are the Maubourg troops!' Eva was riding forward even as she spoke, ignoring Jack's sharp order to come back. There were so few of them, perhaps half of the troop Henry had seen, but they were here, her men, and these, at least, were alive.

At the sound of the hooves they raised their heads, hands reached for weapons and a man strode out from behind the screen of horses, a pistol in his hand.

The long muzzle lifted, the tiny black eye unwavering on her breast as she pulled the horse to a slithering standstill. 'Antoine!'

Chapter Sixteen

'Fleeing the Duchy with your lover, my dear sister-in-law?' Antoine enquired. The pistol did not move. Behind her she could hear Jack's horse, stamping in impatience as he reined it in. The rest of the men got to their feet, staring.

'I am the Grand Duchess Eva de Maubourg,' she said, ignoring Antoine and raising her voice to reach the troopers. 'Prince Antoine has no right to lead you to war, no right to break our neutrality.'

'This woman is a whore, a traitor who has fled with her lover,' Antoine countered, drawing their attention back to him. 'Seize their horses, bring them here to me.'

Some of the men started forward. 'No! Remember who I am! I am the mother of your Grand Duke and I am on my way to him now.' But their faces showed nothing but exhaustion and dull shock. Would they even recognise this woman in man's clothing from the images that they would have seen of her, or the glimpses caught from a distance at parades?

What was Jack doing? Nothing, probably; seeing the aim that Antoine was taking, there was little he could do without risking her being shot. Then she heard him, his voice pitched just for her ears, in English. 'Faint. Now, to the left.'

With a little gasp she slumped sideways, keeping a grip of the pommel just sufficient to break her fall. As she hit the ground, her horse between her body and the men, she saw the led horse gallop riderless through the gap, sending the troopers scattering. There was a sharp report—the pistol—she thought hazily, and then Jack was there, the big black gelding a wall between Antoine and herself.

Had he a pistol? Eva ducked down, peering under the belly of the two horses. Antoine was scrabbling in a holster for a loaded weapon, his horse backing away, frightened by the firing; three hefty troopers were hurling themselves towards Jack.

Eva swung back on to her horse, groping in the saddlebags in the hope that Jack had stashed a weapon there, but all her frantic hand met was the neck of the champagne bottle. She dragged it out, hefted it in her hand and kicked the animal into an explosive canter. They rounded the knot of troopers Jack was holding at bay with a long knife and bore down on Antoine. His second pistol was in his hand now, aimed at Jack. Eva dragged on the reins and swung the bottle. As her horse crashed into the prince's, the champagne cracked over his head and he slumped, unconscious, beneath her hooves.

'Jack!' She pulled up the bay on his haunches as the big black horse erupted towards her through the group of troopers.

'Ride!' His hand came down on the bay's rump and both animals flew along the track at a gallop. 'Keep down!' Eva flattened herself over the withers, expecting the crack of musket fire behind at any moment, but nothing came. Jack kept up the pace, zigzagging through the trees until they reached the far edge of the wood. Even there, he only slowed to a canter, twisting in the saddle to check behind them for pursuit.

'Jack,' Eva called across to him. 'I must go back—those are my troops, my men, I cannot leave them.'

'You can and you will.' The face he turned towards her was implacable. 'Philippe may be dead. If that is so, who will rule Maubourg for Fréderic? You. I cannot risk Antoine being in a fit state to rally them, and I cannot risk your life for the sake of a handful of men who made the wrong choice.'

'No,' she protested, but even as she said it, she knew he was right. It was her duty. The very fact that Antoine had dared bring the men north to the Emperor made her fear that Philippe was indeed dead, that the moral influence of his position, even in sickness, had gone, leaving his brother free to do his worst. If anything happened to her, then who would be there for Freddie, alone in a foreign country, however benevolent?

'Are you hurt?' Jack slowed the pace.

'No. Just shaken.'

'We'll ride on, then, but steadily—we have only the two horses now, we cannot keep this pace up.'

It was then that her bay put his foot in the rabbit hole. Eva was flat on her back on the grass before she knew what had happened, the breath knocked out of her. She sat up, whooping painfully, to find Jack kneeling beside her. 'I'll try that question again.' He smiled reassuringly. 'Are you hurt?'

'No.' She shook her head as he helped her to her feet. The bay gelding was standing, head down, his offside fore dangling.

'Hell and damnation.' Jack strode across to his mount, pulled the long-muzzled pistol from the holster and began to reload. 'Don't look.'

'This really is not our day,' Eva said shakily as she wrapped her arms round Jack's waist and tried to get a comfortable seat behind him as the black horse walked stolidly north under its double burden. The track was uneven, which made keeping her balance even harder.

'You could say that.' She could hear the rueful smile in his voice. 'I could try buying a horse, although I doubt we'll find one. This is going to be a long day.'

They had ridden, then walked, then ridden again, for perhaps three miles, before Jack was confident they had bypassed Nivelles to the west. 'Another seven miles or so to Mont St Jean, then, surely, we will be close enough to Brussels to risk the main road.'

The journey seemed to take for ever on the tired horse. Gradually Eva felt herself flagging, leaning against Jack's straight back, her cheek pressed between his shoulder blades. It should have been uncomfortable and flashes of memory of Antoine's face, the muzzle of his pistol, the sound as she had hit him, kept jolting her with fear, but the solid warmth gradually filled her with a sense of safety and she slipped into sleep.

'Eva, wake up.' It was Jack, twisting in the saddle. 'It's started to rain—we need to get under cover.'

Sleepily she shook herself awake and looked round, surprised to find how dark it had become. The sky was black and heavy drops of rain were hitting the dusty track. 'Where are we?'

Jack threw his leg over the pommel and slid down, holding up his arms for her. Eva almost fell into them. 'Nearly at Mont St Jean, just over that rise, but I don't want to go blundering into a village in the middle of a rainstorm when I can't see what's going on. It could be full of French troops. There's a barn over there.'

Barn was a somewhat optimistic description—leaky hovel was closer to it—but Eva was not about to start complaining, not when the rain started hitting the thatch like lead shot. Jack brought the gelding in and unsaddled it, tethering the animal near a pile of hay. It lipped at it suspiciously, but when he lugged in a bucket of water from the well outside it drank deeply.

'Eva, come and lie down and get some sleep.' She stumbled obediently to where Jack had laid his coat on some straw, then stopped, the memory flashes coming back to almost blind her.

'Have I killed him?' she blurted out, suddenly realising what was causing that cold lump in her stomach.

'I don't know,' Jack said with the honesty he had always shown her. She certainly would never feel patronised with him, she thought with a glimmer of rueful humour. He put down the saddle bag he was sorting through and came to take her in his arms. She leaned in to him with a sigh that seemed to come up from her boots: *Jack will make it all right.* But he couldn't, not if she had killed her own brother-in-law. 'He was trying to kill us, Eva. Whatever has happened to him, it was self-defence. If you had not ridden into him, one of us would probably be dead. You saved my life, as well as your own.'

'He's Freddie's uncle,' she whispered. 'What do I tell him?'

'That his uncle was misguided, that he took some troops to join the Emperor and that he was killed on the battlefield. If Antoine survives, he'll be on the losing side and in no position to make accusations about two people he tried to kill.' Jack was rubbing his hand gently up and down her back; it filled her with peace and a sense of his strength.

Comforted, she tipped her head back to look up into his face and caught her breath at the unguarded expression of tenderness she caught there. Then it was gone and he was back to normal: calm, practical, austere. But the wicked glint she had learned to look for was missing from the grey eyes and in its place was something akin to sadness.

'Jack?'

'We're both tired.' His lids came down, hiding his expression from her. 'We'll sleep while this rain lasts; it is so heavy that no one is going to be moving troops around in it.'

'All right.' Eva nodded. She was too tired and bemused to try to read what had changed in Jack. He was here, with her, and for the moment that was all that mattered.

Jack woke cold, and lay still with his eyes closed, trying to work out what had roused him. It was safer, he had found from experience, to check out his surroundings before revealing that he was awake. There was a slanting scar over his ribs to remind him of that on a daily basis.

His internal clock told him it was early, not long after dawn perhaps. His ears could detect nothing amiss. The rain had stopped, birds were singing, the horse was mouthing hay. Against his chest he could hear the soft, regular breathing of the woman who slept in his arms. His mouth curved in an involuntary smile. Nothing alarming there to have awakened him. He inhaled deeply. Eva: gardenias and warm, sleepy female. Horse. Damp thatch and dusty hay. The comfortingly domestic smell of bacon.

Bacon? The very faintest hint of frying ham was threading its way through the chill, damp air. Jack shook Eva gently. 'Wake up, sweet.'

'What is it?' She sat up, pushing back the stray hair that had escaped her plait in the night. Her eyes were wide and soft with sleep and his heart lurched painfully. *My love.*

'Someone is frying bacon.'

'Oh, good. Breakfast.' She rubbed her eyes, then, suddenly completely awake, stared at him. *'What?'*

'Stay here.' He got to his feet, checking the knife was still in his boot top and picking up the pistol that had lain by the makeshift pillow all night.

Outside the day was sodden and chill. The ground was soaked, the heavy clay turned to mud by the torrential downpours of the night before. Jack scanned the field in front of him, but it was empty, the wisps of misty steam already rising as the faint early sun, struggling through the grey clouds, struck the moisture.

He slid round the corner of the barn and made his way up the slope. Beyond the hedge that formed the northern boundary the land rose for perhaps fifty yards, then dropped away. What lay beyond was invisible, but smoke rose in a myriad of thin trickles. Camp fires. The breeze shifted, bringing with it the smell of cooking again and, faintly, the sound of many voices and of barked orders. Troops.

'What is it? The French?' Eva, was at his elbow.

'I don't know, I can't see. And I told you to stay put.'

'I needed to find a bush, so I had to come out,' she said with dignity. 'Are we going to find out who it is, then?'

Ordering her to remain behind was probably futile. How he had ever imagined he could compel any obedience from this woman he had no idea. 'Watch my back from here.' Jack put the pistol into her hand. 'Don't use that unless it is absolutely necessary or we will have two armies down on our heads.'

'I can do that better if I follow you,' she said stubbornly, taking the pistol.

'You will be safer here. Will you do as I tell you? Please!' He felt his voice rising and lowered it hurriedly.

'I know it is your job to keep me in cotton wool, but, Jack, don't you see—'

Something snapped. He yanked her into his arms without conscious thought, heedless of the pistol that ended up pressed against his ribs. 'I *see* that I almost lost you in that damn river,' he snarled, heedless of her white-faced shock. 'I see that I almost lost you yesterday. Can't *you* see, you pig-headed, in-dependent, bloody-minded woman, that I—' Some sense returned, from somewhere, God knew where. 'Can you not see,' he finished more moderately, 'that you are more than a *job* to me? And if I get you killed or captured, I will punish myself for it for the rest of my life?'

Those soft, red lips parted in a little gasp, but the colour was coming back into her face. Jack tightened his grip on her upper arms and lifted her bodily against him, his mouth taking hers in an uncompromising kiss. His tongue plunged into the warm sweet moistness: mastery, ownership, desperation. Then he set her down roughly on her feet again. 'Now, damn well stay here.'

'Yes, Jack.' Her shocked whisper just reached him as he ducked through a gap in the hedge and, crouching, made his way up the slope. Training and discipline kept him focused on what he was doing and not on who he had left behind, or what he had almost told her. Heedless of the mud, he dropped to the ground and squirmed forward on elbows and knees until he could see down the slope in front of him.

Dark blue uniforms covered the ground below and to the right of the continuation of the road they had left the night before. In the bottom of the valley he could see a crossroads and beyond it a small farm-like château with red coats around it. Beyond that, on the crest that he knew hid the hamlet of Mont St Jean, he could see more red coats.

So, the French were between them and the Allied army and the road to Brussels. Jack slid further forward. There was ar-tillery below and to his left, the guns trained out over the Allied flank, but most of the troops were to the right. It was a scene of an anthill from this distance: hundreds of tiny figures, some grouped around campfires, some with horses, others moving guns or clustering around officers.

The light was good, despite the cloud. Why then, he wondered, had the fighting not begun? He realised why not as he watched a horse team struggling to move a gun limber stuck in the mud. Bonaparte needed to manoeuvre his artillery and he couldn't do it in these conditions. How long would it take for the ground to drain?

Long enough, if they started now, for them to get to the Allied lines before the firing began. Jack studied the slope to the left, then eased back from the edge and ran back down to the barn.

Eva had found a spot where she could watch both the field and the road. 'I've seen no one,' she reported. He saw her take in his mud-soaked clothes, but she did not comment, nor did she make any reference to how they had just parted. He should apologise, he knew, but not now.

'The French are drawn up below us, all along this scarp. The Allies are on the opposite ridge, and they are also holding a farm, half a mile below in the valley. If we can get down there, we can make our way up through the lines to the Brussels road.'

'Right.' He saw her throat move convulsively as she swallowed, but Eva showed no fear, only determination. 'What do we do?'

Fifteen minutes later they were trotting steadily to the west, away from the French, the Allied flank still visible on the ridge to their right. Eva clung on grimly, determined not to complain at the jolting.

'Ah!' At Jack's sigh of satisfaction she leaned round the side of him and saw what he had been looking for. Ahead was a small farm and a track led down from it into the valley. 'See—' Jack pointed '—we can cross the road down there and take the track into that farm in the valley with the Allied troops around it.'

'More of a small château,' Eva said, squinting in an effort to make out detail. 'I can see why the Allies want to hold it, it gives a good command of the valley floor.'

Jack turned the gelding's head downhill and, screened by a thick hedge, they made their way to the valley bottom. 'Get down, Eva.' He helped her slide down, then, to her surprise, stayed where he was, reaching down for her. 'Come on, up in front of me.'

Puzzled, she let herself be pulled up, swung a leg over the horse's neck and found herself settled on Jack's lap. Then, as he urged the gelding forwards again, pulling her back tight against himself, she realised what he was doing. If there was a sniper with them in his sights, it was now Jack's broad back that would take the bullet.

'Have you got anything white we can wave as we approach?' Jack wrapped his arms round her waist and sorted the reins out.

'Only my shirt,' she retorted tartly, 'And if you imagine I am going to go cantering up to companies of soldiers half-naked, you have another think coming, Mr Ryder.' They were cantering, and she was still fuming before she realised what they were doing and then it was too late to be scared. 'You wretch,' she shouted, above the sound of the hooves. 'You are trying to distract me.'

'True.' He sounded smug. 'It worked, too.'

'Can we gallop now, please?' she demanded, trying to keep the shake out of her voice.

'No, I want to give the troops ahead a chance to see who we are.'

'Jack, I do not want you to get shot.' *Of all the daft things to say,* she chided herself. *As if he can help it if some sniper is sighting down his rifle barrel even now. He doesn't need me wittering nervously at him.*

'Neither do I.' Now he sounded amused, almost as though he was enjoying himself. Men were very strange creatures and being married to one, giving birth to one and having another as a lover did nothing to make them any more comprehensible. 'Look, the piquet have seen us.'

They were closing with the white, buttressed walls of what looked like a large barn forming the western boundary of the château. Jack did not slacken their pace as they closed with the line of soldiers who were training their weapons on them.

'Wave!'

Eva waved, then shouted, 'English! English!' as the black gelding finally skidded to a halt in front of the troops.

'Who the devil are you?' The Guards officer who strode forward stared up at them. 'Good God! Raven—'

'Jack Ryder, Captain Evelyn. We met in London last year at Brook's, if you recall.'

'Ryder? Yes, of course, forgot. What are you doing here of all places?' The other man seemed ready to settle down to a thoroughgoing gossip. Eva stirred restlessly. She could almost feel the imaginary sniper's hot breath as he sighted at the middle of Jack's back.

'Can we go inside? I am escorting a lady and I doubt she wishes to sit under the eye of our friends up on the ridge much longer.'

'Yes, of course.' The captain recollected himself. 'There, through that gate. Swann, escort them. Oh, and Ryder, the Duke's here.'

'What did he call you?' Eva demanded, trying to twist

round as they rode through the narrow gate and into the barn. 'Raven? Is that a nickname?'

'A mistake, he has a poor memory. Do you want to meet the Duke?'

'You know him, I suppose?' Eva gave up for the moment; now was not the time to try to probe Jack's reticence.

'We have spoken.' Jack sounded amused. 'At least, I should say, he has barked at me on occasion.'

Their escort led them out of the other side of the barn into a courtyard. It was indeed a château they had arrived at, but a small one, more of a glorified farm than anything. Through another gate and they saw a group of horsemen. The figure in the cocked hat and black cloak could only, if the nose was anything to go by, be the great man himself. He was surrounded by a group of officers, all in earnest talk. Jack rode across and four faces turned to view them.

Eva saw eyebrows rising as they took in the fact that she was a woman, then the Duke doffed his hat. 'Madam. From the fact that you are with this gentleman, I assume you are not sightseeing on the battlefield?'

'Ma'am,' Jack said, without a quiver in his voice, 'may I introduce his Grace the Duke of Wellington, Commander of Allied forces?' Eva bowed, as best she could given her position. 'Your Grace, I am escorting this lady to England. I regret that at the moment I am unable to effect a proper introduction.'

The Duke doffed his hat and the others followed suit. 'I presume that Rav…Ryder is taking you to Brussels?'

'Yes, your Grace. I must not distract you from the task in hand, forgive me.' Another *mistake* with Jack's name. What was going on?

'We will ride back together, ma'am, and find you a mount. Allow me to present General Baron von Muffling, Prussian liaison, and Major the Viscount Dereham.' He rose slightly in his stirrups and the other officers who had been standing further out moved forward attentively. 'Lieutenant Colonel McDonnell, gentlemen—you have your orders, this place is to be held to the last extremity, I have every confidence.'

Chapter Seventeen

The Duke and the Prussian general rode off ahead, through the orchard gate and into a sunken lane that led up towards the crest. The younger officer drew up alongside and grinned cheerfully across at them. 'You have chosen a hot day to visit us, ma'am.'

Eva smiled back, trying to make her mind work; it was beginning to feel decidedly bruised, as though it had been hit by little hammers for hours. *Pull yourself together, you can do this.* What was his name? Ah, yes, Dereham, and he was a viscount and a major. 'You must all be very wet and uncomfortable after last night, Major.'

Dereham shrugged. 'I can think of better ways to recuperate between battles, but I have no doubt we'll all have our minds taken off our wet feet before much longer.'

Eva liked him on sight—with his blond hair, blue eyes and devil-may-care expression he was the opposite of Jack's dark, serious, hawk-like looks. 'I hope you have managed to get a good breakfast this morning. The French are frying ham.'

'Stale bread and cheese, ma'am, washed down with rainwater. I'll tell the men about the ham, it'll make them even madder to get at the French.'

'I should imagine they would follow you anywhere, ham or not,' Eva said, meaning it. Under his cheerful exterior the major looked like a man who would inspire loyalty and trust.

'Stop flirting,' Jack murmured in her ear. 'I do not want to be fighting duels over you in the middle of Allied lines.'

'Nonsense,' she murmured back. 'Flirting, indeed!'

They breasted the crest as she spoke and the teasing words dried on her lips. In front of them were the massed ranks of Allied troops, muddy, damp, many of them bandaged or weary looking. She could see individual faces as they rode past, read the suppressed fear, the determination, the sheer professional spirit of the men and her heart contracted. How many of them would walk away from this place by evening?

Their eyes followed as she rode past; one or two raised a hand, or called a greeting to the major. Eva was just about to ask him what troops he commanded when there was a sharp crackle of gunfire from the valley below. Dereham swung his horse round and stared down the way they had come.

'They're attacking Hougoumont at last. The Duke put some backbone into the troops in the wood when we were down there, I just hope they stand firm now.' He spurred his horse on, 'Let's get you a mount, ma'am—the sooner you're away from here, the better.'

In the event, when Jack saw the raw-boned, hard-mouthed troop horses that were all that were available, he slid off the gelding and gave her the reins. 'He's tired, but I know he's reliable. I'm not having you carted halfway to the French lines on this brute.' He swung up on to a massive grey and hauled its head round away from the lines. 'Come on, you lump, I'm doing you a favour today, taking you off to Brussels and a nice quiet stable.'

'God's speed.' Dereham touched his hat to Eva and

stretched out a hand to Jack. 'Perhaps we'll meet at a party in Brussels tomorrow night. I deserve one—I missed the Duchess's ball, after all.'

'Ball?' Eva queried as they left him and wove their way through the last of the lines and into the baggage train.

'Duchess of Richmond, I'd guess,' Jack said. 'Brussels was *en fête* when I came through. The whole mob of diplomats and their wives had arrived from the Congress—picnics, parties, you name it. A ball on the eve of battle would be no surprise.'

Behind them there was the boom of artillery as the guns began to fire. Eva looked back over her shoulder, knowing she was taking a last look at history being made.

'Come on.' Jack kicked the reluctant troop horse into a canter. 'I want you well away from those shells.'

'Your Serene Highness, welcome.' A bowing butler, curtsying housekeeper, an expanse of polished marble flooring and a sweep of staircase. She was back. Back in the real world of status and duty and loneliness.

Eva smiled, stiffened her spine, said the right things and searched Jack's face for any expression whatsoever. She found none. A respectful half-dozen steps to her left, hat in hand, he waited while their host went through his ceremonious greeting.

'Would your Serene Highness care to go to her suite?' She dragged her attention back to what Mr Hatterick—no, Mr Catterick—was saying. A wealthy banker, he was apparently part of the network of contacts, agents and safe houses that Jack and his masters maintained across the continent.

Just at the moment Mr Catterick was struggling to keep up the pretence that the Grand Duchess standing in his hallway was not dressed as a man and thoroughly grubby and dishevelled into the bargain. His question translated, she knew full well, into *Please go and make yourself respectable so I know what I am dealing with.*

'Thank you, Mr Catterick.' Eva produced her most gracious smile, then felt it turn into an involuntary grin as Henry emerged from the baize door at the back of the hall. 'Henry, you are all right! I was worried about you!'

'Yes, I'm safe and sound, thank you, ma'am, and all the better for seeing you and the guv'nor here. Did you know there's a battle going on out there?'

'Thank you, Henry,' Jack said repressively, the first words he had spoken since introducing her to their host. 'We had noticed. Are her Serene Highness's bags in her room?'

'Aye.' The groom's bushy eyebrows rose at the tone, but he took the hint and effaced himself into a corner.

'I will go up now,' Eva announced. The housekeeper hastened to her side and gestured towards the stairs. 'Thank you, Mrs—?'

'Greaves, your Serene Highness.'

'Ma'am will do nicely, Mrs Greaves. Have you been in Brussels long?' Eva maintained a flow of gracious small talk aimed at putting the nervous woman at ease. It carried them up to the bedchamber and she felt her shoulders relax as the turn of the stair took her out of Jack's sight. She could feel the brand of his eyes on her back as clearly as if he had pressed his hand there.

The room, an over-decorated chamber that was doubtless the best in the house, was a bustle of maids unpacking baggage and pouring water into the tub she could glimpse behind an ornate screen. Eva almost sent them all away, then stopped herself. She was a Grand Duchess, she must behave like one and try to put the dream that had been the last few days behind her.

Sipping hot chocolate while lying in a tub of hot water while twittering maidservants flitted about with piles of towels, soap, a back brush and enquiries about gowns and stockings made such a contrast to how she had spent the morning that it would have been easy to convince herself that she had been in a fever and had only just awakened.

'There only seems to be one suitable day gown, ma'am,' Mrs Greaves said dubiously from the other side of the screen. 'Most of your luggage must be missing.'

That gown was one she had bought in Grenoble with Jack; it was not, Eva thought defensively, anything to be ashamed of, however simple in cut and construction. She remembered him in the milliner's, his expression desperate as he tried to find the right words to answer her queries—the only time she had ever seen him at a disadvantage. Her eyes swam with moisture for a moment and she pressed a towel to them, pretending soap had made them teary.

'Indeed?' she said languidly. 'Never mind, that one will do for now, although I regret I will not be able to dress for dinner. I trust Mr Catterick will not be offended.' Mr Catterick, she was sure, would not be offended if she chose to turn up for dinner in masquerade costume, he was so thrilled at her presence.

Clean, dressed and refreshed by a cold collation, Eva drifted downstairs, maintaining an outward calm she was far from feeling. The sound of gunfire was constant, the scene in the street when she had looked from the window was chaotic, the servants were barely concealing their agitation at the closeness of the French, and out there, in country she could picture vividly, the men she had seen this morning, the officers who had been so pleasant, were fighting for their lives in mud, blood and smoke and a hellish din.

Bonaparte had won, so they said, at Quatre Bras. Was he going to triumph again here at Mont St Jean?

And where was Jack? The butler, materialising just as her feet reached the marble of the hall floor, informed her that Mr Catterick and Mr…er…Ryder were in the study, making preparations for her onward journey to England. Could he assist her Serene Highness with anything?

Mr…er…Ryder, indeed! 'Yes, thank you. I wish to consult an English *Peerage* if there is one in the house.'

'Certainly, ma'am. If you would care to step into the library, ma'am, I would beg to suggest you will be comfortable in here while I fetch the volume down.'

Eva sat at a velvet-draped table and waited until the red leather volume was laid before her. 'Thank you. That will be all.'

Ryder. *Rycroft…Riddle…Ribblesthorpe.* She made herself stop thumbing rapidly and began to work through carefully. There. Lord Charles Ryder, Earl of Felbrigge, deceased. Married… Children… Lady Amelia Ryder married his Grace, Francis Edgerton Ravenhurst, the third Duke of Allington. 'Hmm. Dukes might be considered to be top-lofty,' she mused out loud, recalling Henry's vivid description of Jack's father. But surely…

She searched again, this time for Allington. The current duke was Charles, definitely too old to be Jack, and *his* mother was not Lady Amelia and had died years ago. Ah, there it was, married the second time to Lady Amelia, the previous duke had fathered two more children. Sebastian John Ryder Ravenhurst and Belinda Ravenhurst, now Lady Cambourn.

Jack, she seemed to recall from her days in England, was a familiar form of John. So, Jack was, in fact, Lord… Eva frowned in concentration as she worked out the proper form of address for the younger son of an English duke. Ah, yes, first names. Lord Sebastian, and his wife, rather strangely she had always thought, would be Lady Sebastian.

Only of course he did not have a wife. And he was, by all accounts, at odds with his family. No, that was not quite right. He had spoken with somewhat wry affection of his numerous relatives. It was his father he appeared to have had the strained relationship with. That, and his own position as an English aristocrat.

He was not living this adventurer's life for lack of money, nor, from the way Wellington had spoken to him, because of any disgrace. He just seemed to enjoy it.

Her lover, she mused, was a lord. A duke's son. A very respectable position for a lover, in fact. Only she did not care tuppence whether he was a lord or a labourer, she just loved him. And he was no longer her lover. He might come to her tonight, if it could be done without risk of scandal, but it would not be the same. Out there, anonymous fugitives, they had been free, simply Eva and Jack, with only Henry's sniff of disapproval to remind them of what the real world would say.

Now, when she thought of him, looked at him, she had to guard her expression every second. When she was close to him she must be constantly vigilant in case she reached to touch him. When they were alone they were in peril every moment of being spied upon or overheard. In constant danger of having something that was heartfelt and honest and beautiful turned in to a squalid scandal for the gossip columns to hint and snigger at.

Eva closed the heavy volume and stood up, weighing it in her hands. Then she took it over to the bookcase it belonged in, pulling over the library steps so she could reach the shelf. It slid back easily into its rightful place, but she stayed where she was, seized with inertia.

They had been travelling to such purpose; now they had stopped, if only for a while, and it all seemed strange and purposeless. She had no control, she was simply the queen on the chessboard being moved about by invisible players. Should she even be here now—or should she be in Maubourg? What if Philippe had succumbed to his illness, or Antoine had made his way back? Or perhaps there was no one there in control. She wanted to be with Freddie so much it hurt, but the anxiety over what was the right thing to do nagged painfully.

'What are you dreaming about?' Jack was so close beside her that she jumped and almost overbalanced on the steps. He reached up his hands, and, heedless of all her mental warnings to herself, she let him lift her down, sliding down the length of his body, aware that he was finding that contact as instantly arousing as she was.

'Those trousers are too snug for this sort of thing,' she remarked, letting her eyes linger on the very visible evidence as she stepped away. 'I was thinking about chess,' she added.

'Indeed. And you are quite right, I had best stay in here studying something dull while you remove yourself.' He seemed serious under the flash of humour, turning to study the rows of books.

'No…actually I was thinking that perhaps I should go back to Maubourg, now. What if Philippe has died? Or Antoine has got back there? What if King Louis discovers our troops came across the frontier and invades? The French would love an excuse.'

Jack turned slowly on his heel and regarded her. 'Are you saying you want to turn round now and go all that way back, into God knows what and with Bonaparte still on the loose?'

'I think perhaps I should.' Eva found she was twisting her hands together in her skirt and made herself stop.

'And your son?'

She shook her head, helplessly. 'I know what I want, to be with him, but is it *right?* How can I tell what my duty is?'

'To hell with your duty,' Jack said explosively. 'I do not know, and I do not care, about the Grand Duchy of Maubourg, but I do know what *my* duty is—and that is to get you back to England and reunite you with a small boy who needs his mother.'

'Do you think that isn't what I want?' she demanded. 'Do you think I want to meddle in politics rather than be with Freddie?'

'I don't know—do you?'

'No! Oh, for goodness' sake, can't you see I love my son more than anything? But Maubourg is his inheritance.'

'If he loses his mother, that is irretrievable. If something happens to the Duchy, then the Allies will sort it out.'

'Possibly they will—some time, when all the big, important things have been done. Or they'll find a good use for it and we'll be helpless.' Eva found she had marched down the room in a swirl of skirts and swung round, infuriated by Jack's lack of understanding. 'Jack, I think I should go back. I'll write to Freddie, let him know I will join him as soon as I can.'

She paused, catching her breath on a sob as she thought of Freddie reading such a note, expecting Jack to answer with a solution that would make it all right, but he was silent, watching her. As she glared he folded his arms, casually, as though waiting for her tantrum to blow itself out.

'Do not stand there like that!' Goaded, Eva jabbed one long finger at him. 'Say you'll take me back'

'And do not do that,' Jack retorted, unmoving. 'I am not your footman to be hectored. I will not take you back, and if you try to arrange it yourself I will take you back to England by force.' For the first time she saw the full power of his anger turned on her. It was not in his voice, or his tone—both were calm and polite—but it was in his eyes, hard flint that were sparking fire.

'Oh!' Exasperated, frightened by what she read in those eyes, Eva acted without conscious intent. The flat of her hand swung for his right cheek, even as she realised what she was doing and that Jack had not even troubled to move to avoid the blow. His hand came up with almost insulting ease and caught her wrist and they stared at each other, so close that the angry rise and fall of her breasts almost touched his shirt front.

Then both her wrists were held tight, she was pulled against his chest, and, as he had in that field above Hougoumont, he punished her with a kiss. But then, as she had known full well at the time, it was a reaction to his fear for her safety, a plea to her to obey and stay safe. This, she realised with the part of her mind that was still capable of rational thought, was pure temper and her own rose to meet it.

Her fingers flexed into claws in his grip, her body arched against his, struggling to be free, yet wantonly provoking his reaction. Her lips opened under the assault of his and his tongue claimed her, thrusting arrogantly in a quite blatant demonstration of intent. Everything in her responded, love and fury and anxiety mingling into molten heat that pooled in her belly, driving her almost wild with desire.

Eva jerked both wrists down, surprising Jack just enough to free herself, then she had fastened her arms around his neck and was kissing him back with all the passion she was capable of, her body burning against his, her hips urging her tight into the hard, aroused masculinity she craved. She rocked, rubbing herself against him in blatant invitation until she was rewarded by the sound of his growl, low in his throat.

Somehow he had pushed her against the bookshelves; hard leather spines pressed into her shoulders and buttocks as his knee worked between her thighs, opening her as flagrantly as if she was wearing not a stitch. And still, neither could break the kiss, the furious, all-devouring, heated exchange that threatened to topple her into utter abandon.

What would have happened if there had not been the knock on the door Eva had no idea. Possibly they would have stripped each other naked and made angry, brazen, heated love on the library's rich Turkey carpet.

She wrenched herself away, her hands flying to her hair, her décolletage, her skirts. 'Get out,' she hissed. 'Just get out!' Without a second glance at Jack she ran across to the pair of globes which stood by the desk, turned her back on the door and called, 'Come in!'

'Ma'am, Mr Catterick wondered if you would care to join him for tea?' It was the butler. Eva looked back over her shoulder. Jack was apparently engrossed in a vast folio of maps on a stand that effectively hid whatever state of dishevelment he was in.

'Certainly. Please tell Mr Catterick I will join him in a few moments.'

'Ma'am. And Mr Ryder?'

'I am going out, I have arrangements to make,' Jack said curtly. 'I will be back for dinner.' He looked directly at Eva. 'Henry will remain here.' It was a warning not to try to leave.

'Certainly, sir.' The butler bowed himself out. Eva stepped across to the over-mantel mirror and surveyed her flushed face and wide eyes. At least the day was becoming uncomfortably hot, that at least might be taken as some excuse.

Grand Duchesses, she reminded herself desperately, do not plump down in the middle of the floor in the library and burst into tears of frustration, they get themselves under control and make small talk over the teacups. She gathered her skirts and swept out without so much as glance towards the atlases. She had foreseen this *affaire* ending in heartbreak—she had not expected it to fizzle out amidst bad temper and macaroons in a Brussels merchant's house.

Chapter Eighteen

Eva could not recall shedding a tear since the day Louis bore Freddie off to school in England, leaving her frantically weeping in the schoolroom, his slate clutched in her hands. Weeping was undisciplined, an unseemly weakness she had learned to do without.

Now, in her bed, the maids finally departed, a single candle on the nightstand, she leaned her head back on the pillows and let the tears trickle down her cheeks. From the street came the hubbub of laughter and shouts and cheering. The news had been coming in since about half past eight that the French were beaten. The early rumours became hard fact, as more and more messengers arrived. The Prussians were pressing hard from the east, the Foot Guards were advancing and then the French were in full retreat, the Old Guard alone standing firm to the last to allow the Emperor to escape the field.

Dinner had become a celebration of toasts, of speculation, of vast relief. She tried to tell herself Maubourg would be safe now, whatever fate had befallen her brothers-in-law. Someone was going to have to explain to King Louis XVIII why his neutral neighbour had invaded with a small troop of men, but at least the monarch had more pressing things on his mind just now.

And throughout the meal Jack had been distant, correct, formal. It was exactly how he should have been of course, and she thought her heart was breaking. Would he have been like this anyway, once they reached Brussels, or had her attack of nerves and indecision, her demands, alienated him?

She scrubbed at her cheeks, angry at herself for being so weak. There was so much to be happy about. Jack had at least taken the choice away from her, she must do what she wanted so passionately to do. In a few days she would see Freddie, hold her son in her arms. She could get news of the Duchy, hopefully of Philippe's recovery, Europe was saved from more years of war…and all she could think about was Jack's face, the feel of his mouth, hot and angry on hers, the knowledge that something magical had gone for ever.

The clocks began to strike, past one. The noise in the streets was dying down, or perhaps people were moving to the Grand Place to celebrate. Wearily Eva blew out the candle and closed her eyes. Tomorrow they would be travelling again; she had to get some sleep.

She opened her eyes on to pitch darkness, to chill, musty air, to a sense that the walls were closing in around her. Then she knew where she was: in the tomb, in the vaults. The terror coursed through her; she threw up her hands, desperately pushing against the unyielding stone. It did not move one inch.

Defeated, quivering with fear, she fell back, feeling the grave clothes shifting around her, her unbound hair slipping about her shoulders. Into the silence, broken only by her rasping breath, came the sound of the stone gritting above her. Louis. Louis had come for her. Somewhere, glinting in the black fog of panic, she glimpsed another thought and grasped it. Jack. Not Louis, Jack. He had said it would be him who would come, he had promised to rescue her. The stone lid slid further, she saw fingers gripping it as light flooded in.

'Jack!' He smiled down at her, reassurance, strength. 'You came.'

Without speaking, he reached in and lifted her against his chest and she buried her face in his shoulder so as not to see as he carried her back through the vaults, past the tombs, out to the stairs and the air and freedom. With a sigh Eva closed her eyes against the white linen of his shirt and let herself drift into peace.

When she opened her eyes again there was a candle burning on the night stand, her cheek was pressed to damp white linen and she was held against a warm, male body. 'Jack?' Disorientated, Eva twisted so she could look up at him. 'I was sleeping—dreaming. I had that nightmare, but you came into it, just as you promised. But that was a dream.' What was he doing here? He was angry with her, yet here he was, cradling her in his arms.

Jack looked down into the sleep-soft eyes and felt a wave of tenderness swamp every other confused emotion he had brought with him into her bedchamber. When he had curled up on the bed next to her he had kissed her cheek and tasted salt. He had made her cry.

He loved her, nothing could change that; he feared nothing ever would. There was a puzzled furrow between her brows and he bent his head to kiss it away. 'Don't frown. I came to say sorry. You were asleep, so I stayed.'

'But…'

'Your reputation is quite safe. Everyone thinks we are being somewhat over-protective of you, given that the battle has been won, but Henry is asleep in an armchair on the landing and I, as you will have realised, am sitting in your dressing room with a shotgun.'

That made Eva laugh, as he hoped it would. 'That was not what I meant.' She wriggled out of his arms and sat up, half-turned so she could watch him. 'I should apologise, not you; I was foolish to waver now, when I had agreed to go to England, and I did not mean to try to make you go against your orders. To *hector* you.' Jack grimaced. Was that what he had said to her?

'You weren't. I was angry and I overreacted.' How to explain, when he hardly understood the violence of his reaction himself? This was probably all to do with falling in love, against all sense and reason. No wonder he did not understand himself any more. Eva was waiting; that damned furrow was back again, making him feel guilty for upsetting her. Hell, he *never* felt guilty!

'The thought of you in danger makes me afraid,' he admitted at last. 'I am not used to being afraid, it makes me irritable.'

She wrinkled her nose in what he could see was an effort not to laugh at him. 'Irritable? Is that what you call it?' Those frank brown eyes were looking so deep inside him he was afraid she could see his love for her written there. 'Are you truly never afraid? Isn't that rather dangerous?'

'Yes. I am. Of course I am, often. I meant afraid for someone else, afraid and not able to do anything about it.'

'Oh, I see.' Her face lit up. 'You mean, like I am afraid for Freddie? I try and be brave for myself, but even if it is irrational, I worry so about him. But…he is my son. I love him.' That little furrow of puzzlement was back as she looked at him, her head tipped slightly to one side

It was almost a question. Almost *the* question. He could answer it truthfully, and have her turn away, embarrassed by such an inappropriate declaration, or he could think damn fast, and learn not to get into intimate conversations about feelings in the small hours.

'I get like that about clients,' Jack said lightly. 'Very protective.'

'Oh.' The puzzlement had gone, replaced by a slight haughtiness. 'And you become the lover of many of them?'

'Only the women.' He tried to make a joke of it.

'What?' she demanded, bristling.

'One or two,' Jack admitted, knowing he was burning his boats. But this liaison, which was all it could ever be for her, had to end soon and it was best a line was drawn under it.

'I see. You mean, I am the latest in a long line?'

'Eva, I never pretended to be a virgin,' Jack began, feeling the conversation slipping wildly out of control. Then she buried her face in her hands and her shoulders began to quiver and it was as though he could feel the salt of her tears in his mouth all over again. 'Hell! Eva, sweet, don't cry. I didn't mean that. There isn't a long line, just a… Damn it, I'm not a saint.'

The quivering got worse, then she looked up, her eyes brimming with tears. Of laughter. 'Pretending to be a virgin?' she gurgled. 'You know, Jack, I don't think you would have deceived me for a moment.' She rubbed the sleeve of her nightgown over her eyes. 'Don't worry, I am not such a hypocrite that I expected you to have been saving yourself for me. In fact,' she added, a decidedly wicked twinkle in her eyes, 'I'm glad you didn't.'

Jack reached for her. 'Get back under the covers and go to sleep. It is late and tomorrow we are going to Ostend. I want you on a ship before half the English army decides to head home.'

'Won't you stay?' Something of his feelings must have shown, for she added hastily, 'I mean just sleep.'

'While you drop off, then,' he said, resigning himself to the bittersweet pain of having her so close, perhaps for the last time.

'That's what I used to say to Freddie,' she murmured, wriggling down between the sheets, then turning on her side so she could wrap an arm across his chest.

'I'm not singing you a lullaby.'

'No?' She sounded almost asleep already.

'No.' Jack settled her more comfortably against his chest and lay back. He had never understood the need women seemed to have for cuddling, until now. You made love and then you slept, he had thought. But now, as always with Eva relaxed in his embrace, he felt a calm soaking into his bones, despite the lurking knowledge that he might never experience this again. This was love, damn it. Love.

'Is this the road to Eton?' Eva demanded, trying to read signposts as the post chaise bounded up the road from the coast.

'No. London.'

'But I don't want to go to London, I want to go to Eton to see Freddie.' She twisted round on the plush upholstery to glare at Jack indignantly. 'You know I do.'

'And my instructions are to take you to London.' Eva opened her mouth to protest, but Jack shook his head before she could get the words out. 'We have a charming house for you in the heart of fashionable London. I am taking you there, then I will check with the Foreign Office and, if you still want to, we will go to Eton tomorrow, after you are rested.'

'But I don't want to rest! I've tossed about on that wretched boat for twenty-four hours—without getting seasick—and now I shall be stuck in this bounding carriage for hours.

Compared to days in the saddle and sleeping under the stars, I am perfectly rested.'

And no lovemaking to make her feel languid and lazily inclined to do nothing but curl up in Jack's arms until one or other of them began those irresistible caresses that ended, inevitably, in ecstasy and exhaustion. She ached for him, but ever since they had set foot on the sloop he had waiting at Ostend, Jack had behaved with total circumspection.

It made her restless and impatient now, and, when she let herself brood, miserable for the future. The thought of seeing Freddie had been buoying her up; now that treat had been snatched away and she knew she was reacting like a child told to wait until tomorrow for her sweetmeats. Well, she was not going to stand for it…

'Don't even think about it.' The corner of Jack's mouth twitched, betraying his awareness of her rebellious thoughts.

'What?'

'Getting on your high horse and ordering me to take you to Eton, your Serene Highness.'

'Surely you are not frightened of a lot of Whitehall clerks, are you?' She opened her eyes wide and was rewarded by his grin at her tactics. Wheedling was not going to do it.

'I thought you understood the concept of duty,' Jack said mildly.

'I do. But would it matter so much if I were one day late arriving in London?'

'Yes.' Jack produced a travelling chess set. 'This will wile away the time.'

'No, thank you, I have no desire to play chess. Please? Take me to my son, Lord Sebastian.' That got his attention. Jack placed the box deliberately on the seat next to him and leaned back into the corner of the chaise.

'So that was what you were doing up a ladder in Mr Cat-terick's library.' Eva nodded. 'I do not use my title when I am working.'

'Why not?'

'Because it makes me more of a target, less invisible. I am two different people, Eva. You have not met Lord Sebastian Ravenhurst, and I doubt you will.'

'Why not?' she demanded again, kicking off her shoes im-patiently and curling up on the seat facing him.

'Lord Sebastian is a rake and a gamester and does not mix in the sort of society that grand duchesses, even on unofficial visits, frequent.'

'Is that why you fell out with your father?' That would explain it, an estrangement between the duke and his wild-living son.

'Actually, no. My father rebuffed my efforts to be a dutiful younger son, learn about the estate, make myself useful in that way. He supplied me with money beyond the most extrava-gant demands I might make and sent me off to London to become, in his words, *a rakehell and a libertine.*'

'But why? I do not understand.' Jack's face was shuttered. Eva leaned across the space that separated them and put her hand on his knee. 'Tell me, I would like to understand.'

'I think because he was disappointed in Charles, my elder brother, and he did not want to admit it. I am very like my father, probably very like what he expected Charles to be. But Charles was—is—quiet, reclusive, gentle. My father main-tained he was perfect in every way and dismissed me so he would not see the contrast proving him wrong at every turn.

'By the time I was ten—and my brother twenty—I was careering round the estate on horseback, ignoring falls and broken bones. I was pestering him to teach me to fence, to shoot. Charles was stuck in his study, reading poetry. By the time I was sixteen I was in trouble with all the local light-heeled girls, Charles had to be dragged to balls and virtually forced to converse with a woman. And so it went on. Eventually the contrast was too extreme, but my father's sense of duty to the family name, the importance of primogeniture, was too strong. He could not admit he loved me more, so he had to pretend the opposite. I had to go.'

'How awful,' Eva said compassionately. What a mess people got themselves into with their expectations and their pressures. Why could they not accept each other for what they were? 'Did you miss your family and your home very much?'

Jack shrugged. 'I was eighteen, the age when you want to get out and kick your heels up. He didn't show me the door, I still came home, saw Charles, my mother, Bel, my sister. But for a few days, every now and again. And my father got the constant comfort of people comparing his sober, quiet, dignified elder son with the wild younger one.'

'Then why aren't you drunk in some gaming hell now?' she asked tartly, to cover up the fact that she felt so sad about the young man he was describing. In nine years Freddie would be that age.

'Nothing was expected of me,' Jack went on, gazing out of the window as though he were looking back ten years at his younger self. 'Nothing except to spend money and to decorate society events. I did my best. I can spend money quite effectively, I scrub up quite well, I can do the pretty at parties—but I was bored. Then I found myself helping a friend whose former valet was blackmailing him over indiscreet love letters. One thing led to another and I found that I liked Jack Ryder far more than I did Lord Sebastian Ravenhurst.'

'Aren't they now the same person, just with two different

names?' Eva asked. 'Hasn't Lord Sebastian grown up with Jack Ryder?'

'Perhaps.' He shifted back from the window to regard her from under level brows. 'It makes no difference to you and me. The Grand Duchess Eva de Maubourg does not have an *affaire* with a younger son any more than she does with a King's Messenger.'

'That was not why I wanted to know.' *Oh, yes, it was, you liar. It was curiosity, certainly, but something was telling you that this man was an aristocrat and that would make it all right.* 'It was curiosity, pure and simple. I dislike secrets and mysteries.' She said it lightly, willing him to believe her.

The way the shadow behind his eyes lifted both relieved her and hurt her. He did not want their *affaire* to continue. Why not? She thought he would be as sad as she at its ending. But then, by his own admission, he was a rake. Loving and leaving must be as familiar as the chase and the seduction. Only he had neither chased nor seduced her, when he very well could have done.

'What do I call you, now we are back in England?' she asked. 'Mr Ryder, or Lord Sebastian?'

'I am Jack Ryder. As I said, you will not meet my *alter ego.*'

'You are not invited to the best parties?'

'Duke's sons are invited everywhere, even if fond mamas warn their sons against playing cards with them or their daughters against flirting. I do not chose to accept, it is as simple as that.' He looked out of the window again. 'And here is Greenwich. Another hour and you will be almost at your London house.'

Eva sighed. Even if she could persuade him, it was too late to set out to Eton now—there was the whole of London to traverse before she could be on the road to Windsor.

'Don't sigh—it is a very nice house.'

'How do you know?' Eva sat up straight and found her shoes. Time to start thinking and behaving like the representative of the Duchy in a foreign country, not an anxious mother or a sore-hearted lover.

'I chose it.'

'Really? You were very busy before you left.'

'I mean, I had bought it, for myself. I was finding my chambers in Albany a touch small these days. But I am in no hurry to move in. The staff are all highly trustworthy, employed by the Foreign Office for just such eventualities.'

'So you have never lived there?'

'No.'

That, at least, was a mercy. The thought of living in the midst of Jack's furnishings, the evidence of his taste, of his everyday life, was disturbing. Eva set herself to talk of trivia, of London gossip, and the last hour of the journey passed pleasantly enough. It was as though, she thought fancifully, they were skating serenely on a frozen sea, while beneath them, just visible through the ice, swam sharks.

'Here we are.' Jack opened the chaise door and jumped down, flipping out the steps for her before the postilions could dismount. She lay her hand on his proffered arm and walked up to the front door, gleaming dark green in the late afternoon sunshine. Jack lifted his hand to the heavy brass knocker, but the door swung open before he could let it fall.

'Your Serene Highness, welcome.' An imposing butler, with, she was startled to see, the face of a prize fighter, ushered them into the hall, then stood aside.

Facing her across the black-and-white chequers was a boy, sturdy, long-legged, with a mop of unruly dark hair. Hazel eyes met hers and for a moment she was frozen, unable to believe what she was seeing. Then Eva flew across the hall and fell to her knees, her arms tight around her son. 'Oh, Freddie, you're here!'

Chapter Nineteen

'Mama!' The pressure of his arms around her almost took her breath away. This was not the little boy she had last seen—he was so grown she could glimpse the young man he would become. And they would not be separated like that again, never, that she vowed. Disentangling herself with an effort, Eva sat back on her heels and stared happily at her son.

'You've grown,' she managed to say. 'How you have grown!'

'Well, the food's pretty grim,' he confided, startling her with his perfect English accent. 'But I stock up in the shops in the High—Uncle Bruin keeps me well supplied with the readies, you know.' He stared at her, his eyes solemn. 'You look just as I remember, Mama.'

'Good,' Eva said, fighting to keep the shake out of her voice. 'You have been very good at answering all my letters.'

'I missed you.' He was biting his lower lip, the desperate need to maintain his grown-up dignity fighting with the urge to hug his mother and never let him go. 'Are you going away again soon?'

'We are both going back to Maubourg together, just as soon as the situation in France is calm and we can travel safely.' She hesitated. 'You know Uncle Philippe has been ill?' He nodded. 'I don't know if he is better yet, or worse. And I am afraid that Uncle Antoine might have been…hurt in all the confusion with Bonaparte invading.'

Too much information. She was pouring it out, kneeling here on the hard floor, her hands tight around his upper arms, terrified of letting him go in case he proved to be a dream after all.

Awkwardly Eva made herself loosen her grip and tried to stand. Her legs felt shaky. Two hands reached for her and she placed her own, one in each. 'Thank you, Freddie, Ja…Mr Ryder.' For a long moment they stood there, linked. Like a family group, she thought wildly, releasing Jack's hand as though it were hot. Then Freddie let go, as well, and held out his hand to Jack.

'Mr Ryder. Welcome back. Thank you for looking after my mama.'

Jack shook hands solemnly. 'Your Serene Highness. It was a pleasure. I am glad to see you so well. You were a trifle green when we last met.'

'Mushrooms, Mama,' Freddie explained.

'I know. Mr Ryder kindly told me all the horrid details.'

Her son chuckled. 'I was very sick. Did you know this is Mr Ryder's house?'

'Yes. It is very kind of him to lend it to us.' She looked around. The pugilistic butler was still standing, statue-like, in the corner. A pair of equally large footmen were at attention at the foot of the stairs and a small covey of female domestics were gathered behind them. 'Have you been here long?'

'Long enough to know everyone; I arrived yesterday morning,' Freddie said importantly. 'This is Grimstone, our butler.' *It suits him,* Eva thought. 'And Wellings and O'Toole, the footmen. And Mrs Cutler is a spiffingly good cook. And Fettersham is your dresser.'

A tall woman dressed in impeccable black came forward and curtsied. 'Shall I show you to your room, your Serene Highness?'

'Ma'am will do nicely,' Eva said automatically. 'Yes, I will just take off my bonnet and mantle and I'll be right back down, Freddie. Then we'll have tea.' *And talk and talk and talk...* 'You will look after Mr Ryder, won't you?'

She almost tripped over the stairs because she keep looking back to make sure he was still there, her son. Just as the turn of the stairs took them out of sight, she saw Freddie slip a hand into Jack's and tug him towards what she assumed must be the salon. They looked so right together, the tall, lean man and the eager boy.

'Are you quite well, ma'am?' Her new dresser was regarding her anxiously. 'You went quite pale a moment ago.'

'Quite well, thank you, Fettersham. It was a wearing journey.'

In the event it took her longer to return downstairs than she had intended. Her gown proved sadly salt-stained, her hair was tangled, Fettersham found it hard to locate a full change of linen in her limited baggage and a mix-up in the scullery resulted in cold water being sent up, not hot.

Half an hour later, leaving a wrathful dresser descending upon the kitchen quarters to complain, Eva went downstairs to find Freddie sitting alone on one side of a tea table laden with cakes and biscuits, which he was eyeing greedily. He stood up punctiliously.

'I am ready for the tea now, thank you, Grimstone.' The butler bowed himself off. 'Where is Mr Ryder?' Eva sat down opposite her son.

'Gone. May I have a scone, Mama?' She nodded absently,

shifting slightly to give the footmen room to deposit the teapot and cream jug on the table beside her.

'Gone where? Thank you, that will be all.' She did not want to discuss Jack in front of the domestic staff.

'I don't know, Mama. Oh, and he said would I please make his excuses to you, and…' Freddie frowned in concentration '…he said I must take care to get this right—he said to say goodbye, and that it was better that he went now, as his job was done and he did not want to make complications. And that you were to remember him if you ever have a bad dream.' A mammoth mouthful of scone vanished and Freddie chewed valiantly. 'Mama, do you think that means he isn't coming back at all? I didn't think anything of it at the time, but—'

'Don't talk with your mouth full,' Eva said automatically. 'Yes. I think that means Mr Ryder is not coming back.' He had walked away, without a word, without a kiss. There was just the memory of the pressure of his hand when the three of them had stood together in the hall and the knowledge that she would love him and miss him and want him for the rest of her days.

'That's a pity.' Freddie picked up a slice of cake, looked at it and put it down. When his eyes met Eva's, they glistened with a shimmer of tears. 'I like him. I'll miss him.'

'You hardly know him,' Eva said bracingly. What was upsetting Freddie so much?

'Yes, I do. He came to see me three times at Eton, and we had long talks. He wanted to know all about the castle and my uncles and you. I said I didn't remember very much, but he said I was intelligent, so if I put my mind to it, I would recall lots—and I did. It was really exciting. He said I was briefing him for his mission, and he would send me coded dispatches, and he did.'

'He did? How?' And why hadn't Jack told her so she could have sent messages, too?

'They went through his agents to the Foreign Office. And when the first one arrived, they sent Grimstone with it to stay with me. *They* said he was just a butler, but I think he's a body-guard, don't you, Mama? Because the first message from Mr Ryder said there was danger and I had to take great care and Grimstone started going everywhere with me. I got ragged a bit, but then the chaps shut up, because Grimstone showed everyone how to box.'

'How dare he worry you like that?' Eva banged down the teapot, disregarding the splash of hot liquid from the spout. 'And if I'd known he was writing to you, I would have sent a message.'

'Mr Ryder said the messages had to be short and you wouldn't like me to be worried, so you'd fuss. But Mr Ryder said I was old enough to understand and start taking care of myself. Are you *growling,* Mama?'

'Yes, I am!'

'But he was right, wasn't he? Things *were* dangerous. I don't expect Uncle Bruin's really just ill, I expect someone's tried to poison him, like they did me with those mushrooms.'

'Freddie!'

'It's Uncle Rat, isn't it? He's a Bonapartist.' Freddie's clear hazel eyes regarded her solemnly over yet another piece of cake.

'Yes. Freddie, I wasn't going to tell you all this, all at once. But I'm afraid Antoine has been very…foolish. He may be…hurt.'

'Mr Ryder said he was trying to develop rockets for the Emperor, and he was trying to kill both of us and he took Maubourg troops into France—so I expect I'm going to have to write to King Louis and say sorry, aren't I?—and he may have been killed, but we can't be certain.'

Eva picked up her cup with a hand that shook and took a gulp of tea. It did not help much. 'When did he tell you all this?'

'Just now, before he left. He said it's called a de-brief and he had to tell me because you probably wouldn't, because of mothers worrying. May I have a macaroon?'

'You'll make yourself sick,' Eva said distractedly.

'And he said you were a heroine, and found out about the rockets and helped him raid the factory, and fought off Uncle Rat's agents and probably saved his life.' The macaroon vanished and Freddie sank back with a happy sigh of reple-tion. 'And he said I wasn't to worry if you seemed a bit upset about things, because you had had a very difficult time, and finding I was all right would actually make you more upset, because that's the way shock and relief work.'

'Did he?' Eva took a macaroon and ate it rather desperately. Sugar was supposed to be good for shock, was it not?

'I like him a lot,' Freddie said again. 'And I think he likes me. And I thought perhaps, when I saw him looking at you, that he likes you, too. And now he has gone away.' He scuffed a toe in the Aubusson carpet. 'He's just the sort of person a chap would like for a friend, don't you think?'

'Yes. He would be a very good friend,' Eva agreed, filling up her son's teacup. Jack appeared to have handled breaking the news of all this to Freddie much better than she would have. She was angry with him, of course she was…but it was all part of the role he had assumed when he undertook to bring her back to England. *Do as I say, when I say it.* When Jack was with her, she knew he would look after her. Totally.

She would have resisted him telling Freddie about the danger, but her son was so much more grown up and percep-tive than she had realised. He would have spotted the new bodyguard for what he was, and, in the absence of information, would have worried. Jack had involved him in the adventure, treated him like an intelligent young man so it became understandable and exciting. *What a wonderful father he would make for Freddie.*

'Mama! You are spilling your tea.'

'So I am.' Eva put down her cup, and dabbed at her skirt. A father for Freddie. *I am thinking of marrying him,* she realised. *And that's impossible, of course, Dowager Grand Duchesses do not marry King's Messengers. Only he's a duke's son…*

'What are you thinking about, Mama?'

'I am having a very silly daydream about something that cannot possibly happen,' Eva said briskly. 'Now, let's go and sit down, kick off our shoes, and we can talk until we are hoarse.'

It took three days before the invitations began to arrive. Three days during which Eva and Freddie did indeed talk themselves hoarse, she shopped exhaustively for a new wardrobe and they explored the house until it became like a second home and the staff familiar faces.

It was not just Grimstone who was a bodyguard, she soon realised. The pair of large footmen were never far from the door of any room she and her son were in. They stuck to her like burrs whenever she went outside the house, politely refusing to wait in the carriage whenever she entered a shop. Eventually she tackled the butler. 'We are here and safe, Grimstone. Surely there is no risk now? Prince A… The source of danger may not even be alive.'

'But his agents will be, ma'am,' the butler pointed out in his gravelly voice. 'This has just come for you from the guv'nor, ma'am.'

'Mr Ryder?' Eva snatched the letter off the silver salver

before she could school herself into an appearance of indifference. She broke the seal and read the three lines it contained. The handwriting was black, sprawling, undisciplined, a complete contrast to Jack's methods of operation. Or was this Lord Sebastian writing? she wondered.

The absent troops returned home with the body of A. It has a bullet wound in the back. From very close range. P. improves daily. Show this to Grimstone and assume A.'s agents are still at large and may not yet know of his death. It was signed with a J., a slashing flourish across the bottom of the page.

Wordlessly Eva handed the letter to the butler, who read it through with pursed lips, then gave it back. 'Own men shot him by all accounts,' he commented. 'Didn't like being made traitors of, especially in view of what happened. P. will be the Regent, ma'am?'

'Yes, my brother-in-law, Prince Philippe.' Eva folded the paper and slipped it into her reticule. It was the only thing of Jack's she had. 'I will go and tell Master Freddie the good news.'

Master Freddie, as the entire staff called him, was in his favourite place, the kitchen, charming sweetmeats out of Cook. Eva tried to imagine him back in the castle. It was not hard—within the week he would have even the tyrant of the kitchens his devoted servant, the footmen would all be polishing armour for him to play with and he would no doubt be attempting to introduce cricket to the bemused inhabitants.

'Freddie, good news from Maubourg. Uncle Philippe is on the mend.'

'Can we go back soon, then?' He scrambled off the table, eyes wide, mouth ringed with raspberry jam.

'As soon as the Foreign Office tells me it is safe to travel. Shall we go and write to Uncle?'

She followed that letter up with one to the Foreign Office,

asking about travel and received, not a response on that subject, but the first, and most imposing, of a flood of invitations. The Prince Regent, Freddie's godfather, begged the honour of her company at a reception in her honour at Carlton House in two days' time.

'Oh, Lord,' she lamented to Fettersham. 'I suppose that means feathers?'

'Yes, ma'am.' The dresser was agog with the thought of court dress. 'Hoops are no longer worn, though,' she added with a tinge of disappointment. 'The full-dress *ensemble* you ordered yesterday will be most appropriate.'

'Well, thank goodness for that. It is difficult enough walking about with those wretched feathers in one's coiffure without worrying about hoops flattening every small table in sight every time one moves!'

The gown arrived from the modiste on the morning of the reception along with the hastily purchased set of ostrich plumes. 'My goodness, waistlines are up,' Eva complained as Fettersham fastened the gown. 'There is very little room for my bosom in this!'

'I think that's the point, ma'am,' the dresser observed, tweaking the narrow shoulders so they sat securely. 'It's a very good thing you have such excellent shoulders, ma'am, otherwise I don't know how this style is expected to stay decent.'

They regarded the effect in the long mirror. The gown, in palest almond green, fell from under Eva's bosom to exactly the ankle bone. She was not convinced about the decency of showing so much ankle, either, although she was prepared to admit the fuller skirts were charming. The hem was banded with satin ribbon, of exactly the same shade, the texture making it show up subtly against the silk, and the whole lower half of the skirt was heavily embroidered in wreaths of flowers. The pattern was repeated on the puffed sleeves and the deep vee of the neckline was dressed in lace, which went some way to preserving the decencies.

'Very striking, ma'am,' Fettersham pronounced.

'Very dashing,' Eva amended. 'I do not recall it seeming so at the fitting!'

Long kid gloves with lace at the top to match the bodice, simple slippers, a gauze scarf at the elbows and the nodding weight of the feathers completed the ensemble. It was certainly striking enough for the occasion, Eva decided, wondering wistfully what Jack would make of it. She was managing very well, she congratulated herself. She thought of him only a dozen times an hour during the day. It was the nights that were so hard, when all she could do was toss and turn, aching for the sound of his voice, the caress of his hands, the heat of his mouth.

Fettersham produced the diamond eardrops, necklace and cuffs borrowed from Rundell and Bridges, the jewellers who had proved only too willing to oblige the Grand Duchess, in return for her tacit agreement to them making as much capital out of the fact as they wished.

'Mama?' It was Freddie, knocking at the door. 'May I see?'

'Wow!' he said as the dresser let him in. 'How do you dance in those feathers, Mama?'

'I do not have to,' she explained, stooping to kiss him. She was loving rediscovering her son, getting to know him again, not as the little boy she had left, but this new, much more independent and lively nine-year-old. 'Now, you will be good and go to bed when Hoffmeister tells you?'

'Yes, Mama.' She gave him high marks for refraining from rolling his eyes. The arrival of his private secretary-cum-tutor from the Eton lodgings had restarted the rivalry between the

German and the butler. Freddie played one off against the other with what Eva tried to tell herself was precocious statesmanship, but she had to uphold Hoffmeister's authority when it came to bedtime and study periods.

Carlton House was just as she had seen in pictures, and even more stiflingly hot, crowded and elaborately ornate than she could ever have imagined. The Regent was gracious, over-familiar to the point of discomfort and determined she would enjoy herself. He insisted on escorting Eva around the crowded reception rooms, introducing her to one person after another until her head spun. She searched the rooms as they went, but there were no tall, elegant, dangerous men with grey eyes and a wicked smile.

'I am quite out of practice with this sort of thing,' she confessed to Lord Alveney. 'My brother-in-law Prince Philippe has been unwell for several months, so our court has been extremely quiet. Please, sir…' she turned and smiled prettily at the Regent '…I beg you not to neglect your other guests for me, I have so much enjoyed seeing these wonderful rooms in your company, but I can see I will be very unpopular if I monopolise you.'

The Regent beamed, blustered a little, then took himself off with a pat on her arm and a promise to show her the Conservatory later.

'Nicely done, ma'am,' Alveney said with a lazy smile. Eva was spared from replying to this sally by the arrival of a tall young woman who bumped into her and knocked her feathers all askew.

'Oh, my goodness!' I am so sorry! And you are the Grand Duchess and I haven't even been presented to you and I do this! Oh, dear! Oh, look, there is a retiring room, please, your

Serene Highness, if we just go in there I am sure they can be pinned back…'

Eva sent Alveney an apologetic smile and allowed herself to be swept off into the retiring room, which was empty save for a maidservant with a sewing basket, smelling salts and a bottle of cordial. *Every eventuality covered.* Eva was thinking with amusement when the young woman snapped, 'Out, now,' to the maid. The key turned in the lock and the stranger was standing with her back to the door, eyeing Eva with angry grey eyes.

Antoine's agent? Here, in the Regent's own house? Eva edged towards the dressing table, hoping to find scissors or a long nail file. 'What do you want?' She spoke calmly, as though to someone mentally disturbed. The words she had spoken the last time she had been in this predicament—*So, you have not come to kill me?*—did not seem appropriate now. This young woman looked as if she intended to do just that, for all her lack of an obvious weapon, and asking the question seemed likely to inflame her further.

But even if her defiant words to Jack when he had appeared like magic in her room were not the ones to use now, she could not help but feel a strong sense of *déjà vu.* Why? Because she was cornered and in fear for her life? Or because…

Eva stared at the other woman. She was like a feminine, younger version of Jack. The tall, elegant figure, the dark hair, the clear, intelligent grey eyes with their flecks of black. She found her voice.

'What do you want?'

'I want to know what you are doing to my brother—and I want you to stop it. Now.'

Chapter Twenty

'Your brother? You are Jack's sister?'

'Sebastian.' The flurried and apologetic young woman was gone, replaced by a determined, poised and angry one.

'I know him as Jack.'

'Oh, it is the same thing! I don't care how you—'

'It is not the same thing,' Eva said firmly. 'And I am doing nothing to your brother, and have done nothing to justify your behaviour now.'

'You have broken his heart,' the other retorted.

'Nonsense! Why, that is complete nonsense. Your brother left my house without a word to me a week ago. There had been no disagreement, I had not dismissed him. Broken heart, indeed, what melodrama. If Jack Ryder has anything to say to me, he knows where I am.' *Broken heart? I know whose heart is broken—but I did not leave him.*

'You were lovers.' It was a flat statement. 'No, do not bother to deny it. He has said nothing about you, all I knew was that he had been in France, on a mission. Then when he came to see me, he had changed—something inside was hurt.'

Eva discovered that her head was beginning to ache, and

so were her feet in their new slippers. 'Oh, sit down, please, for goodness' sake. What is your name?'

'Belinda. Lady Belinda Cambourn. I am a widow.' Eva nodded—Jack had mentioned Bel. 'I shouldn't be here, am still in mourning. But I love my brother very much, and I know him very well. And he is hurting. Deeply.'

'But—'

Bel waved a hand, silencing her. 'No one else would be able to tell, except possibly you.' She shot Eva a look of positive dislike. 'When he is on missions—when he is Jack— he is cool and calm and quiet, but there is still that wicked enjoyment of life behind those eyes of his. When he is Sebastian, he is the warmest, kindest brother you can imagine.' Bel directed another withering look at Eva. 'But now something has gone—the laughter has gone, the warmth inside has gone. He came to see me; he was very sweet, just as he always is. I asked him what was wrong and he laughed and said nothing, just a tiring mission in France.'

'There you are, then,' Eva said briskly.

'So I asked Henry,' Bel pushed on, as though she had not spoken. 'And he said that the guv'nor had got himself entangled with you. He said the pair of you were smelling like April and May and—' She saw Eva's blank expression. 'Like lovers, like people in love,' she supplied irritably. 'And he had warned Jack that no good would come of it.'

'If your brother does not choose to tell you about his personal life, I am certainly not going to.' Like April and May…like people in love. She loved him. But Jack… Surely if he loved her he would never leave her like that?

'Don't you care about him? Henry says he saved your life.'

'Yes. He did.' Suddenly it was too much, she had to speak of him, about him, and this angry young woman with Jack's eyes at least cared enough about him to virtually kidnap her in the middle of a Carlton House reception.

'And, yes, we were lovers. And I have never had one before, in case you think I sleep with every good-looking man who comes my way,' she added militantly. 'And I had to ask him, because he was being so damnably gallant and gentlemanlike. We knew it could only last while we were in France—I cannot risk the scandal. We both knew that.'

Bel was watching her in wide-eyed silence now. At least she had stopped glaring. 'I fell in love with him. I didn't mean to, I really did not mean to. But I couldn't help it. I love him so much.'

'Then—?' Bel was thinking hard, her brow furrowed. 'Of course, you thought he was just a King's Messenger, a glorified bodyguard. No wonder you dismissed him when you got to England.'

'I knew he was more than that. And in Brussels I found him in the *Peerage*. But what difference does that make? I'd love him if he was a fishmonger's son. I told you—I did not dismiss him, he left me. He does not want me, or he would never have gone like that, without a word, just with a message to my son.'

Bel was biting her lip thoughtfully. 'Was it worth it?' she blurted out. 'Was having him as a lover worth all this heartache?'

'Yes! Yes,' Eva added more softly. 'But he never pretended it was anything more than an *affaire*.'

'He never *said* it was anything more, you mean,' Bel retorted. 'Did you tell him you love him?'

'No, of course not. Can you imagine telling a man you love him when you know he does not love you? How humiliating to see the pity in his face, the tact he will have to use to extricate himself.'

'Not if he loves you, too—how can you be sure he doesn't?

I do not know about love, I was not in love with my husband and I have taken no lover. But I know my brother, and he is hurting. He is missing you.'

'Then why did he leave me like that?' Eva demanded. 'That hurt *me*.'

'I expect he thought a clean break was kindest for you. I imagine it must have been difficult to talk intimately in a houseful of servants and with your son there,' Bel said thoughtfully. 'Do you want to marry him?'

'Yes.' The word was out of her mouth before she could think. Yes, of course she did.

'And he can hardly ask the Dowager Grand Duchess, can he? I don't expect it is etiquette. You will have to tell him you love him and ask.'

'But…what if he says no?' Eva shut her eyes at the thought of it, every cell in her body cringing. She could almost hear that cool, deep voice, carefully and kindly masking his amusement at such a preposterous idea.

'What if he says yes?' Bel countered. 'You'll never know until you try, because, believe me, Sebastian is far too proud to plead with a woman who has been making it clear she wants no entanglements. And you have, haven't you?'

'Of course! I would never have got him to agree if he had thought I was going to fall in love with him. What are you smiling about?' she added indignantly. Bel's mouth was curving into an unmistakable grin.

'The thought of my rake of a brother having to be asked if he wanted to make love to a beautiful woman,' she explained frankly.

'Is he a rake, then?' He had said as much, but somehow she had let herself think about gaming and clothes and racehorses, not mistresses and lightskirts.

'Shocking,' his loving sister confirmed. 'But somehow I doubt if he is seeking solace elsewhere this time.'

'Oh.'

'And, ma'am…'

'Eva. Please call me Eva.' Somehow this stranger had become someone she wanted for a friend.

'Eva. There is something Sebastian would never tell you, but if I am going to trust you with one of my brothers, I may as well trust you with both. Our half-brother—'

'The duke?'

'Yes. Charles. He is never going to marry. Possibly one day Sebastian will succeed him—he is ten years the younger, after all. But if you have a son together, the boy most certainly will.'

'The duke is unwell? Disabled in some way? Er…disturbed?'

'The duke does not find women attractive. Not sexually attractive. Do you understand me?'

'Oh. Yes.' One came across it, of course, although Louis had had to explain it to her. 'But is that not illegal?'

'Yes. You see how I trust you.'

'But in the case I knew of, the man married to get an heir.'

'Charles has lived, secluded on his Northumberland estate, for eight years, very happily with his lover who, as far as the rest of the world is concerned, is his steward.'

'Ah.' Eva thought about it. 'That makes no difference to me, the thought of the title.'

'Good.' Bel beamed back. 'But it might to Sebastian, don't you think? Only he would never mention it, because he is so loyal to Charles.'

'So you think I should just find him and…propose?' It sounded the most frightening thing she had ever done. She could not imagine what it would feel like if he said *yes*.

'I think that I will inveigle him into escorting me to Lady

Letheringsett's masked ball the day after tomorrow, and if you cannot find an excuse to carry him off and do the deed, then I wash my hands of the pair of you.'

'But I am not invited…' Bel with a plan was proving every bit as hard to resist as her brother.

'Then come and let me present her to you. She'll have arrived by now, I have no doubt. She'll invite you, never fear.'

'But if Jack finds out, he won't come.'

'Trust me.' Bel grinned. 'I will tell him at length how disappointed I am that the fascinating Grand Duchess Eva has declined! He will feel quite safe. Now, let's see if we can fix your feathers.'

'Don't you have to dress up?' Freddie enquired, obviously disappointed. He was perched on the edge of Eva's bed, watching while Fettersham dressed her hair to accommodate the half-mask she was to wear.

'No, just masks. It isn't a masquerade with fancy dress, but there will be a grand unmasking at midnight.'

The mask was pretty, she decided, holding it up so the dresser could thread the ribbons back into her coiffure to hold it securely. It was covered in tiny golden brown feathers, making her eyes seem a richer, deeper brown in its shadows.

Her gown was amber gauze over bronze silk, the neckline swooping low to expose the swell of her breasts and a generous décolletage. Eva was dressing for Jack tonight. Since that first night he had never seen her in anything but practical clothes. This was going to be a revelation.

'Jewellery, ma'am?' Fettersham proffered the selection the jewellers had sent. Diamonds, of course, or citrines or amber to match the dress. Eva hesitated, then chose diamonds set in gold with a diamond aigrette for her hair.

She glowed, as she intended to, an offering to a man whose scruples must be overcome. She had seduced him once, on his own turf, now, on hers, the world of ballrooms and etiquette, she felt her confidence building. He would say *yes,* she had to believe it.

'Mr Ryder will like that gown,' Freddie said confidently. 'I think you look very pretty.'

'Why, thank you.' Eva stared at her son as his words penetrated. 'Why do you think Mr Ryder will be there to see it?'

Freddie sucked his cheeks in and managed to look like a cheeky angel. 'You are all fluttery, Mama.'

'Impudent child,' she scolded. 'Off to bed with you!'

Fluttery, indeed! The little wretch could read her like a book, even if he did not know the first thing about the relationships between men and women. *Just like his papa,* she thought. Louis had always been able to read her mind—except when he chose not to for his own ends, like that dreadful day in the vaults. She sincerely hoped her innocent son had not the slightest inkling of the sort of things that flitted through her mind when she thought of Jack.

'What a fabulous gown!' Lady Bel pounced on Eva as soon as she had entered the ballroom. 'And such a lovely mask— I wouldn't have known it was you if I hadn't been looking out very carefully. It is so nice to be out of mourning, although I shall be in such trouble if Mama finds out. I have four more weeks to go, really.' She swept Eva down one side of the crowded ballroom, ignoring the chattering throng, the men with their quizzing glasses scrutinising every masked lady, the towering floral displays and the glittering lights.

'Is this not a brilliant idea of mine?' Bel congratulated herself as they arrived in a slightly quieter semi-alcove.

'Because of the masks, no one is announced, so he will not have the slightest suspicion.'

'Where is he?' Eva craned to see. It appeared hopeless, then the crowd moved and there, leaning one shoulder against the pillar opposite, was a tall, dark-haired man in severe evening black, his mask a plain black slash across his face, his white linen the only relief from the starkness. She would have known him anywhere, and known, too, that, despite the relaxed half-smile on his lips, the casual attitude, he did not want to be here, that this evening was a penance undertaken to give his sister pleasure.

'I left him there and made him swear to wait for me,' Bel explained. 'There is a retiring room right behind that curtain, and the key is in the lock.'

'Do you know the location of every retiring room in London?' Eva asked, amused despite her tension. 'You make me suspect you have numerous outrageous flirtations.'

Bel coloured. 'I am boringly chaste—and unchased,' she said lightly. 'Go on, he is all yours. And good luck!'

Eva skirted round to approach Jack from behind. She paused, studying him. His hair had been cut since he got back; she could glimpse the whiter skin at his nape, and the memory of how that skin had felt under her fingers, against her mouth, took her breath.

There was so much noise with voices raised in conversation and the orchestra just trying its first few chords that she knew he could not have heard the soft tap of her slippers on the parquet floor, but as she reached the point where she could have stretched out and touched him, he pushed himself away from the wall and turned.

'You.' He kept his voice low, but it reached her none the less. His whole body was poised to move, the tension she had sensed on the quayside in Lyon was vibrating through him. He had hardly had to look at her and he knew her.

'Jack…' Eva held out her hand, but he did not take it. 'I need to talk with you.'

'This is Bel's doing, I take it?' His mouth was a hard line and Eva realised he was furiously angry.

'Your sister told me you would be here. Jack—' No, he wasn't Jack Ryder here. This, in the glamour of the ballroom, in his exquisite tailoring, his signet glowing dark on his hand, this was the other man, the one she had never met. 'Lord Sebastian. Please, there is a retiring room just here, I believe.'

'Very well.' Punctiliously he held the curtain back, opened the door for her and waited while she slipped inside.

'Will you turn the key? I do not wish to be interrupted.' She glanced around. A *chaise* against the wall, two chairs, a pretty little marble fireplace set across the corner, that was all.

'Jack…Sebastian. What do I call you?'

'Nothing,' he said harshly.

'You left without saying goodbye.' Eva meant it as a prelude; he took it as an accusation.

'It was better that way. I had hoped not to have this conversation.'

'What conversation? How do you know what I want to talk about?'

'I assumed you have changed your mind about wanting our *affaire* to end.' Jack's eyes were bleak, although his tone was neutral. 'I do not want it to end, either,' he added. 'But I know it is the wise thing. The only thing for two people circumstanced as we are.'

'No. That is not what I meant to say. I agree with you: an *affaire* is impossible here.' That, she was pleased to see, took him aback. 'But like you, I wish it were not.'

'Then why are we here?' Jack asked. The black mask made him seem different somehow, more aloof, more dangerous. 'In a locked room? Just one more time, perhaps?' Eva moved in a flutter of silk and gauze, needing to be closer, needing to see his eyes more clearly. She saw his control snap, suddenly without warning, like lightning from a clear sky. She was in his arms, crushed against his chest, his eyes were blazing into hers and his mouth came crushing down to silence her gasp of protest.

Damn it, did she think he was made of iron? She had taken him by surprise, with his guard down, and she came in silks and feathers and a cloud of subtle perfume that enhanced the scent of her and spoke of sin and sweetness and soft, soft skin. He was aching for her, had been aching with the bone-deep agony of something broken ever since that chaste night in Brussels.

He had expected it to get better; it got worse. He had thought it was purely lust and had tried to assuage it in the obvious manner. But he found his feet would not carry him over the threshold of the discreet house of pleasure that had enjoyed his custom so many times before.

If it were lust, then no other woman than this one, the one he could not have, could slake it. But it was not lust. He had admitted it to himself already—now he had to live with the reality of it. Love. He had found the strength to do the right thing and now she flung all that hard-won self-control back in his face, as though it did not matter, as though he would rather have slashed his own wrist open rather than walk away from that house without a farewell.

He had gone to the War Office and made them very happy with the rocket notes and then he made the effort to put Jack Ryder behind himself until this madness at least became a manageable agony. He had his hair ruthlessly barbered into the newest crop. He filled the white nights when he could not sleep with gaming, and won an embarrassing amount of money. He visited his tailor and ordered lavishly. Nothing helped, and, to add insult to injury, the highly fashionable, clinging knitted black silk of his evening knee breeches could not have been better designed to demonstrate the violently carnal effect Eva was having on him.

Then she had moved, bringing her warmth, her scent, to lash his senses, and he lost control.

Anger or lust or sheer desperation? Jack had no idea, and with Eva's body crushed against his, with her mouth warm and moist and soft under his, he stopped thinking. Her gown, already low over those milk-white breasts, slid away under the pressure of his hands and she spilled into his palms, the perfect weight so familiar, so arousing. He stooped and took one nipple in his mouth, nipping it, fretting it with his tongue mercilessly so that she cried out, gripping his hair, not in pain, but to urge him closer.

Closer? If she wanted closer, then she would have closer. There were buttons under his fingers, then they were free, the gown slipping down, over the curve of her hips, the perfect roundness of her buttocks. Under it she wore only the finest of petticoats, the simplest of corsets. They were no obstacle, it was moments and then she was naked except for her silk stockings and her mask, the effect wildly, indecently erotic. Behind the mask her eyes were wide and soft and fevered in its feathery shadows.

Almost roughly he pushed her down on to the *chaise* and began to tear off his own clothing. He was so hard for her, so aroused, the clinging silk almost refused to be removed. Impatient, he tugged and heard her gasp as she saw him. Had she forgotten his body so soon, or was this simply the result of the days of abstinence from her?

But Eva showed no fear, not of his anger, not of his size. She reached for him, drew him down to her, wrapped her long, slim, strong horsewoman's legs around him and pulled him hard to the core of her. She was wet for him, quivering, the scent of arousal fuelling his own state to the point where he thought he would lose all control before he even entered her.

There was no finesse, neither of them sought that, only possession, only oblivion. She cried out as he entered her without any preliminary caress, but the cry was feral, triumphant, demanding and he answered her by driving hard into the centre of her, again and again as she writhed and gasped and called his name, over and over until he felt her convulse around him and he somehow found the strength to wrench himself away before the tremors of her ecstasy sent him over into his.

Chapter Twenty-One

Eva came to herself to find Jack's weight still crushing down on her, the *chaise*'s hard bolster digging into the small of her back in the most uncomfortable fashion. They were hot, they were sweaty, she could hardly breathe and she had never felt physical pleasure like it. From outside the volume of noise from the music and the guests beat against the door; inside, the only sound was their panting breaths.

Slowly Jack raised his head so he could look down into her eyes. The black mask made him seem almost sinister, but the harsh lines of his mouth were softened, and the shadow of a smile lurked at the corner. With a sigh he dropped his forehead to rest against hers. She closed her eyes as his lashes brushed against her own lids and his breath stirred warm on her mouth.

'We are not very good at this abstinence thing, are we?' he enquired.

'No. It seems not. Jack…I cannot breathe very well.'

He levered himself up and sat at her feet, arms along the carved rail of the *chaise,* head thrown back. Naked except for the mask, he looked magnificent in the candlelight, his muscles long and smooth and powerful. She looked at the hand lying relaxed on the carved wood and felt the heat flood through her at the memory of what those elegant, clever, wicked fingers had been doing.

'Thank you.' She scrambled up until she was curled against the head of the *chaise,* just far enough away not to feel the heat of him, just far enough not to yield to the temptation to bend closer and run her tongue tip down his arm. 'Strange to say, I did not come here for this.'

'No? Eva, please, put something on. The effect of that mask and the silk stockings is quite outrageously arousing.'

Eva glanced down at herself, then at Jack, whose body was all too obviously stirring into life again at the sight of her. She dragged on her underthings. 'You'll have to tie my laces. I cannot get into this gown unless I am laced tight.'

He got up and came to do as she asked. Eva could hear the catch in his breathing as he gathered up the strings. She put her hands at her waist, drew in a breath and nodded. Jack pulled. 'More.' He pulled again. 'Enough. Tie them in a bow—although my dresser will know. Goodness knows what I am going to say to her.'

Jack stepped back as soon as the corset was done. 'And the buttons on my gown, as well. I am sorry, I cannot reach.' She stood as still as she could while he buttoned the amber silk. 'Thank you. Now, I will take care of my hair while you dress.' She found she could not look at him, she was nervous now.

The overmantel glass reflected back the entire room; Eva forced her eyes to focus only on her hair. This might be the last time she would ever see Jack naked, share the intimacy of getting dressed together. This might be the last time they ever kissed, caressed. The last time if she did not get this right.

'Well? What is it, Eva?' Jack stood at the foot of the *chaise,* his colour a little heightened, his neckcloth in a considerably simpler knot that he had arrived with, but apparently unruffled.

Eva sat down, certain her legs were not going to carry her, and gestured for him to sit likewise.

'I want to ask you something. And to tell you something,' she began. 'I need you so much it hurts to be without you.' It was out, far too abruptly, without any of the subtlety she had rehearsed. And the word she had sworn to herself she would use—love—would not pass her lips, not without some hint from him that he felt the same.

'Eva—'

'No, let me finish. I did not intend to feel like this. It is not just our lovemaking, although that is wonderful. When I asked you to be my lover, I was honest in my reasons, in what I told you. I said I was with a man I desired and trusted and liked. I thought I wanted physical pleasure, physical comfort, a strong man to hold me. That is all true. And then I found I cannot live without you.'

'Eva.' His head was down; he was regarding his clasped hands as though they held the answer. 'Eva, you honour me, and I—but that makes no difference to our problem. For you to take a lover, now you are back in the full glare of the public eye, is impossible if you wish to avoid scandal.'

'Jack, please look at me.' He looked up, met her eyes, his own still and watchful, and very dark. She sat quite still, her own hands, with a desperation to stop her from reaching for him, knotted in her lap. 'You do not understand. I am asking you to marry me.'

He was so silent that she thought he had not heard her. Then he stood up with the violent grace she had seen him use when he was fighting. From the other side of the little room, as far as he could get from her, he said, 'Are you insane?'

'No! I mean it.' His reaction shocked her. She had expected surprise, doubt, an argument. Not outright hostility.

'Have you forgotten who—what—you are?'

'I am the Dowager Grand Duchess. But I am not of the Blood Royal. My father was a French count, my mother the daughter of an English earl. You are the son of a duke. There is no disparity between our breeding.' She had thought that out very carefully. If Louis could marry her, then she could marry Jack.

'How very convenient that you discovered my bloodlines,' Jack said coldly. 'What would you have done if you had found I was plain Mr Ryder, simply an agent and an adventurer?'

'I have no idea,' Eva said flatly. 'I learned to need plain Mr Ryder, but I did not know just how much being separated from you was going to hurt until I got here. How do I know what I would have thought, what I would want to do, if you were not Lord Sebastian?'

'Not a convenient Maubourg title, then? That would have sorted out plain Mr Ryder. You might still want to come up with some sort of tinsel decoration, some sort of specially created title for me, or a senior rank in your army perhaps? Yes, that would do it. A handsome sash to wear on my new blue-and-silver uniform—or you could ask the Prince Regent to design something: he specialises in fantasy.'

'Stop it! You do not need a title, you have a perfectly good one of your own! If you want to take an interest in the army, then I am sure that would be very acceptable. What is the matter with you? Do you not want to marry me? Is there someone else after all?' He had never said those words, she realised, cold sweat beginning to trickle down her spine. She loved him, had hoped, when she asked him to marry her, that he would confess that he loved her, but had not felt able to say so. It seemed she had made a terrible misjudgement…

'No. There is no one else.' Jack took two strides, came up against the corner of the room and turned again, frustrated by the confining space. 'Don't you think, ma'am, that I might prefer to do the asking? Does it not occur to you that I have a life—two, actually—in this country? Marriages into Royal families happen for dynastic reasons, for heirs—there is one already; for international allegiance—I cannot bring that; for wealth—I am sure my resources are paltry in comparison to yours. What they are not intended for is so that the lady in question can enjoy the attentions of her lover without causing a scandal.'

'But that isn't why—I told you, I need you!' Eva got to her feet, her head spinning. This was not how it was supposed to go. She had told him how she felt, she made an offer that was the honourable one, fitting for both of them, and he threw it back in her face. Anger was beginning to stir under the misery.

'That is extremely flattering, ma'am. But as you know, I already have an occupation and being transplanted to virtually the Alps so I can service the sexual needs of a lady— however alluring and charming—does not fit in with my plans for my life.'

He did not even try to avoid it as she slapped him, hard across the cheek. Shaking her stinging fingers, Eva stared aghast at the scarlet mark of her hand branded across his livid face. She had hit so hard it would probably bruise.

'It is so much more than sex,' she whispered. 'So much more. I thought you felt the same. I was wrong. I am sorry, so sorry I spoke. I will go.'

'Eva.' Jack took her arms, holding fast as she tried to twist away. All she wanted now was to escape this humiliating heartbreak. 'Eva, What I feel for you went far beyond what happened just now in this room. You have been lonely, frightened, left to do your duty at whatever cost to yourself. I came along and gave you excitement and freedom and affection. It is not me you want now, and I cannot give you what you need. I am English, Eva, I live here, this is my home. I have purpose, identity, independence. I cannot give that up to find myself in a country not my own, where I have no role, where my life is bounded by the constraints of who I have married.'

'If you loved me, you would not say that,' she flung at him.

The silence between them seemed to fill the room. The music faded, the loud voices that had roared like the sound of the sea beyond the door became a whisper. 'If I loved you, my answer would be the same,' Jack said steadily. 'I cannot be caged into the life you offer me and, if you tried, I would finish by hurting you. I think you need to go back to Maubourg, Eva. Take Freddie, it is safe to travel now with the escort the Foreign Office will arrange for you. Go now, and forget me.'

Her hands were shaking so much that Eva could hardly unlock the door. She managed it at last, turning as she opened it for one last look at him. 'How can I forget?' she whispered. 'I love you.' It was safe to say it, he could not have heard her, the orchestra was just drawing a particularly noisy country dance to a triumphant conclusion amidst enthusiastic clapping. The dancers coming off the floor engulfed her, swept her away from the door as the Rhône had carried her, dizzy, weak, unable to fight her way to the edge of the room.

'Eva!' It was Bel, tugging her arm. That hurt; she remembered vaguely Jack gripping her just there, a hundred years ago. 'Come and sit down.' She steered Eva to a chair in an alcove. 'What happened?'

Eva could only shake her head, dumbly. Words seemed to have deserted her. 'You need a drink.' Bel looked around her.

'Why is there never a waiter when you need one? Theo! Yes, I know it is you, no one else in London is that tall with auburn hair, you numbskull. I need two glasses of champagne, at once. And a glass of brandy. Shoo!' She pushed the indignant young man off into the throng. 'My scapegrace cousin Theo,' she explained. 'Did he say no?'

Eva nodded.

'Why? Why on earth would he say no?'

'Because he does not love me, I suppose. Because I made a mull of it, because he does not want to end up as an adjunct to his wife in a foreign court.'

'You told him you love him? No?' Eva shook her head. A whisper he could not hear did not count. 'Why ever not?'

'Because I thought he realised that was why I was asking him, and then he told me he did not love me, so what was the point?'

'He told you?' Bel stared at her. 'In so many words? He actually said *I do not love you*?'

'He had told me he would not marry me and then he said his answer would be the same whether or not he loved me. I think.' She shook her head, too stunned by the whole experience to trust her memory any more. The young man—Theo, was it?—came back with a waiter at his heels. Bel took a brandy glass, pressed it into Eva's hands and then scooped the two champagne flutes off the tray. 'Thank you, Theo.'

She waited until her cousin had retreated, then said, 'Drink it!' Eva tossed back the brandy, reckless now for something to take the edge off the pain, while Bel took a reviving drink of champagne, then removed the empty brandy glass and substituted the other flute for it. 'I will be drunk,' Eva protested.

'Good. I'd get tipsy and then go home if I were you, there isn't any purpose in waiting here for the unmasking, you'll only be miserable.' Bel sipped her drink, brooding. 'He may well think better of it in the morning,' she offered at length.

'I doubt it. I hit him.'

'Good.'

They brooded some more, the brandy and wine burning dully through Eva's veins. She recalled the last time she had been tipsy—a most infrequent happening in her well-regulated life. That had been with Jack in the inn and she had been utterly indiscreet. She felt more than indiscreet now, she felt desperate for action, to get away, not stay trapped here in this foreign country, miles from home.

'There's Lord Gowering,' Bel observed. 'See, in the red-sequined mask with one shoulder higher than the other. He directs all the agents in the Foreign Office, though you wouldn't think he was a spymaster to look at him. I have half a mind to go and tell him he should sack my brother for not taking care of you.'

The tall, stooping man was heading in their direction. 'Introduce me,' Eva said suddenly.

Bel shot her a startled glance, but got up and accosted the man. He bowed over Eva's hand. 'I had not expected to see you here, your Serene Highness. I understand we have to thank you for some very interesting armament designs. You are none the worse for your journey, I trust?'

'Perfectly recovered, I thank you, my lord. So much so that I wish to leave immediately for the Continent, with my son. I believe the butler and footmen at my present lodging are your men—I would like to borrow them for the journey.'

'But, of course, ma'am.' She gestured to the seat beside her and his lordship took it. 'There will be no difficulty with papers, naturally, but we had not expected you to wish to return so soon.'

'I am anxious about my brother-in-law, the Regent,' Eva explained, hearing her own voice fluently explaining how her son wanted to go home very badly, how she felt quite rested now—all as though there was some ventriloquist behind her speaking these words while she writhed in dumb misery. It must be the brandy. And years of training.

'Very well, ma'am, I will have papers for the staff sent to you first thing tomorrow. I wish you a safe and speedy return home, and we will hope to see you again in London when travelling conditions are a little less…exciting.'

He bowed himself off, leaving Bel staring at Eva. 'What am I going to tell Sebastian?'

'Nothing,' said Eva flatly. 'Nothing at all if you can help it. Bel, thank you for your support, your friendship. I would have loved to have you as my sister.'

'And I you. Oh, Eva, don't give up on him.' Bel took Eva's hand and squeezed it.

'I think for my own sanity, I must do so.' Eva stood up and shook out her skirts. 'Could you tell our hostess that I have a migraine and had to slip away?' She hesitated, Bel's hands in hers. 'Goodbye, Bel. Look after him for me.'

As she hurried away through the crowd, she caught Bel's wrathful parting words. 'Box his ears, more like.'

Jack stayed where he was after Eva had gone, waiting for his reddened cheek to subside enough to show himself again. The marks of her fingers would probably be there in bruises tomorrow; she had hit with intent to hurt him, and succeeded.

How he had had the strength to do the right thing and turn her down he had no idea. At least she had said nothing about loving him—he did not think he could have coped with that. She was lonely in that great castle, who could blame her?

What they had shared had been a revelation for her, but they could not recreate those feelings, not in the humdrum world of court life.

It would be a disaster if they married and he loved her too much to risk it. Jack began to pace, the part of him that was trying to be fair, trying to understand, giving ground again to his pride and his temper. What had possessed her? He should have been the one doing the asking, not her. He should be the one with title and wealth and position to offer, not her. He could not be bought like a toy, and a husband was not something that was easy to throw away when you tired of him, either.

Leave England? Leave the estate that he had inherited from his maternal grandfather? Leave the rolling countryside, the broad river valleys, the green hills for a foreign country where he had no role except to please the first lady? He wanted sons who would be Englishmen, he realised, not exiles in another country where their half-brother had a status wildly different from their own.

Damn it! She should have guessed all that, she should never have asked him. He was an English gentleman, not some foreign gigolo—

'So you are skulking in here.' Hell and damnation, it was his interfering sister. Jack glared at Bel and she whipped off her mask and glared back. 'My goodness, that is going to mark,' she observed, apparently with some satisfaction, walking up to touch her fingertips to his cheek.

'Thank you, I do not need a second opinion on that,' he said tightly. 'I collect I have you to blame for this idiotic situation.'

'I suggested the ball and this room,' Bel said, sitting with some grace on the rumpled *chaise*. 'You are entirely to blame for the situation being idiotic.'

'You consider that I should have accepted her Serene

Highness's flattering offer, do you?' He had never felt so out of charity with his sister.

'As you love her, I would have thought that was a logical thing to do.'

'Who told you I love her?' He saw the trap the moment he put his foot into it. Bel looked smug. 'I just did, didn't I?'

'I had guessed, that was why I wanted to help you both. Has it not occurred to you, numbskull, that she loves you, too? Or are both of you so determined this is all just about sex—' Bel went scarlet, but pushed on '—that you cannot see what is in front of your faces? Do you really think a woman like that is going to do something as difficult as asking a man to marry her if she did not love him?'

'She does?' Jack discovered his legs were feeling decidedly odd. The only place to sit was beside his sister, so he sat on the end of the *chaise* next to her and rubbed his hands over his face. 'Damn this thing.' He yanked off the mask and threw it on the floor. Bel just looked at him.

Eva loved him? He loved her, so it was not impossible, just something he had never dared to contemplate. She had wanted his lovemaking, his company, his friendship—was that not all she had wanted? Now his mind brought back the image of her face as she turned to him, her hand on the key of that door. What had she said, her lips moving, but no sound reaching him above the swell of the music?

He had learned to lip read as a useful espionage skill, but it needed a lot of concentration. This was Eva: she deserved that concentration. He closed his eyes, searched for the picture of her moving lips, his own moving as he tried out the words. *How can I forget? I love you.*

'Why did she not say so?' His sister, a woman, might be able to explain this mystery.

'Because she is shy, because she was afraid you would reject her, because she rather thought her idiot lover might have some inkling without having to be hit over the head with it,' his loving sister snapped.

'Oh.'

'So, what are you going to do about it?' Bel demanded after they had sat in silence for minutes.

Jack sat staring at the crumpled scrap of black fabric at his feet. 'Nothing.'

Chapter Twenty-Two

'What! Jack, you love her—now you know she loves you and you still say you will do *nothing?*"

'Bel, she is a Grand Duchess, for goodness' sake. I am a younger son.'

'Of a duke,' she retorted. 'Your breeding as a scion of one of England's oldest houses is as good as anyone's in this country. You know what you are, Sebastian John Ryder Ravenhurst? You are a snob.'

'A *what?*' Jack twisted round on the *chaise* to stare at her.

'A snob,' Bel repeated. 'An inverted snob. You refuse to justify your own position, to stand up for who and what you are because she has that title. One she married, not one she inherited, mind you. One of these days you could be a duke—your son certainly will be.'

'Bel!' She had truly shocked him now.

'You think I do not understand about our brother and his situation? If he is happy, I am certainly not going to judge him. And you are an English gentleman; the Mauborgians should be grateful to have you as their Grand Duke's stepfather.'

'Mauborgeois,' Jack corrected absently.

'So, what are you going to do now?' Bel demanded again, ignoring his interjection.

'Nothing,' he repeated.

'Nothing.' His sister sprang up and regarded him, hands on hips. 'Nothing. Because your pride will not accept you having to stand one step behind your wife on state occasions. Because you will not compromise on how you live your life. Because people might talk. I could box your ears, Sebastian Ravenhurst, but a better woman got in first.'

The door slammed behind Bel. Jack stayed where he was, staring at the painted panels, trying to make some sense of his feelings. His head ached, his face ached, his heart…*ached* was an altogether inadequate word for how that felt. With a groan he flung himself back full length on the *chaise* cushions and found his nostrils full of the scent of Eva.

Pride, compromise, status, love. It was a word game, a riddle he had no idea how to read.

'How long may I stay in Maubourg?' Freddie demanded as the carriage rolled over London Bridge.

'Until the new term. This is not the end of school, young man, you know your papa wished you to be educated as an English gentleman.' Eva carried on settling all her things for the journey. Books into door pockets, her travelling chess set on the seat, some *petit point* in her sewing bag. Freddie's seat was cluttered with packs of cards, books, something he was whittling out of wood and a box of exercises Herr Hoffmeister insisted he took with him. They were doomed to stay there, Eva suspected—the tutor was taking a holiday, much to Freddie's well-suppressed glee.

'Why did Papa not let me come home for holidays?' Freddie persisted.

'I think because he wanted you to be thoroughly English,' Eva explained. 'Then when you were older you would have all the contacts you needed for diplomacy, and your English would be perfect.' Which it was. Now, they had slipped back into a mixture of French and the Maubourg dialect; she did not want her son arriving home sounding like a foreigner.

'I missed you.'

'I missed you, too.' She suppressed the nagging suspicion that Louis had wanted their son to grow up with less feminine influence, or even that, as Napoleon's influence grew, he had doubts about having married a half-French bride. Whatever it was, he had never chosen to explain himself to his wife, merely citing her tears as evidence that Fréderic was better off at school. 'Still, now you are so much older, I am sure Papa would have wanted you to spend your holidays in Maubourg.'

Freddie nodded thoughtfully. 'And I can study with Uncle Philippe so I will learn how to be a proper Grand Duke.'

'Yes, my love.' She smiled at him, tears of pride shimmering across her vision so that he became a blur. Last night, amidst the chaos of the preparations for their sudden departure, she had found no opportunity to shed the tears that filled her heart for Jack until she had reached her bed, and then, alone at last, she had wept for what might have been, but now never could be.

'Uncle Philippe is a very good Regent, isn't he?'

'Yes, dear.'

'But he doesn't know about things like sport and adventures and things like that, does he?'

'No, I don't think those interest him.' Her brother-in-law was the scholarly one of the family.

'I do wish you were going to marry Mr Ryder after all,' Freddie said.

'Freddie! Whatever makes you think—?'

'I thought you loved him. You were very sad when he went away and didn't say goodbye. And the way he looked at you. I may not know much about these things,' her nine-year-old son said with dignity as she gaped at him, 'but I can tell when two people like each other a lot. I don't understand why he didn't ask you to marry him.'

'Possibly because I am a Grand Duchess,' Eva said more sharply than she intended.

Freddie nodded. 'I did wonder about that. But then, he's a duke's son, isn't he? One of the chaps at Eton recognised him and told me. I know it's a long time since you've really been in England,' he explained earnestly, 'but it's a very important family; perfectly eligible. Do you think I ought to write and give him permission?'

'Freddie!'

'It is a difficult question of etiquette,' her son pondered, apparently oblivious to his mother's horrified expression. 'I shall have to ask Uncle Bruin. I mean, Mr Ryder is a lot older than me, after all.'

'Twenty years,' Eva said weakly.

'Old enough to be a proper father, and young enough to be fun,' the Grand Duke opined solemnly. 'Just right, really.'

'Freddie, promise me, really, truly, promise me you will not write to Mr Ryder,' Eva begged.

'Sure? Well, tell me if you change your mind, Mama.' Freddie found his pocket telescope and proceeded to risk motion sickness by trying to use it while the vehicle was moving.

Eva slumped back in the corner of the carriage. Bel thought he loved her. Her own son thought he loved her. She had hoped he loved her. But Jack had not said it. Were they all wrong—or was he deliberately not telling her?

* * *

Two days later Eva was still pondering. They were travelling at a reasonable speed, one of the footmen up on the box beside the driver with a shotgun, the other man, with Grimstone, riding on either side of the carriage. There had been no problems, no apparent danger—it seemed Antoine's plotting had died with him.

She looked out at the countryside, contrasting it with England and with Maubourg. She seemed never to have found a real home—their French château was a distant memory, she had been in England only a short while before Louis had married her, and Maubourg was hers by marriage, not by birth.

Jack struck her as a very English Englishman. She was not sure what that meant, but she had seen a change steal over him after they had landed, a sense that he was home, that he had taken a deep breath and relaxed. She had asked him to leave that without a single thought to how it would feel for him, without even asking what lands he held, how attached he was to them.

She had fallen in love with the man, without ever seeing him in his true context. How could she hope to understand him? How could she know what she was asking him to give up for her?

Layer upon layer, Eva realised as the carriage rumbled over the cobbles in Lyon three days further on, she had failed to understand Jack. She should not have made that proposal; instead, she should have told him she loved him and waited for his response. She should not have demanded, she should have found some way of letting him know it was all right to propose—if he did love her. And she should never have started this without thinking through how she could compromise her way of life to fit with his.

She still could not imagine how that could be achieved. There was the Rhône, swirling past the road. The river that had almost taken her life, if it had not been for Jack. 'Not long now,' she said cheerfully to Freddie, and fell back into thought about compromise. But how? There was her son, her duty—and a country hundreds of miles from England.

The first sight of the castle struck Freddie dumb. Eyes wide, he stared, then, as the carriage rumbled over the bridge and began to climb the steep streets to the great gate, he darted from side to side, searching for familiar landmarks, places he could recognise.

There was a clatter of hooves and Grimstone spurred ahead, going to warn the castle of their arrival. And then they were there; guards were spilling out through the gate to line up on either side, townspeople coming running to see what was afoot.

The carriage drew up, the footman let down the step and reached to hand Eva down. 'No.' It was Freddie. With a dignity she did not realise her small son possessed, he said, 'Excuse me, Mama,' and climbed out first. Then he stood by the side of the door and held up his hand for her to take, making a little ceremony out of her appearance.

His expression as he looked at her was pure pride. Pride for himself, pride in her and a glowing pride at being home where he belonged.

Pride. Eva hung back as Philippe appeared in the gateway and walked steadily towards his nephew. Freddie started forward, almost at the run, then collected himself and walked up to his uncle.

'Your Serene Highness, welcome home.' The man bowed to the child and suddenly all the dignity was gone. Freddie threw his arms around his uncle's neck.

'Uncle Bruin! We're back!' He twisted round. 'Mama, see, Uncle Bruin is well again.'

'Yes, so he is.' Eva came forward, both hands held out to Philippe. 'Thank Heavens for it.' But in the back of her mind the word lingered. Pride. Pride and honour. So important to men, so easily forgotten by women who loved them.

'I am so sorry I left you,' she murmured to her brother-in-law as he took her arm to take her into dinner, hours later.

'It was the right thing. Your place was with Freddie, and by going you threw all Antoine's calculations into disarray.' The Regent patted her hand as he helped her to her seat next to him at the round table the family used when they dined informally alone. With Antoine gone, there was just the three of them now. Philippe's wife had died many years before, leaving him childless.

'You look well,' Philippe observed as the soup was served and the footmen retired to give them privacy. 'It may have been an odd holiday, but it has done you good to get away.'

'For the first time in over nine years,' Eva said. 'Yes, it was a…change. And the long days in the open air were invigorating.'

'I never understood why you did not go away before.' Philippe passed her the bread.

'Louis preferred that I did not travel,' she began.

'Louis has been dead almost two years,' his brother reminded her gently. 'You have been very obedient to all his wishes.'

Yes, she had, Eva realised. The rule that Freddie must stay in England, the rule that she did not travel. Yet Philippe was a more-than-competent Regent, it was hardly that she needed to be there all the time—only when Freddie was here in the holidays. And the rest of the time he was in England…

Compromise. Suddenly, in her mind's eye, she could see a

compromise, a plan she could lay before Jack. He might still reject it—and her. But she had to go to him, put things right somehow, even if all that meant was that he felt he could write now and again to Freddie.

'Freddie. Philippe.' They broke off in the middle of an intense discussion about Napoleon's tactics at Waterloo that involved the salt cellars, a mustard pot and a bread roll, and turned to her politely. 'Would you both mind very much if I go back to England?'

'When?' Philippe looked startled, but her son's face was one big grin.

'Tomorrow. There is something I need to do.' She smiled back at Freddie. 'Someone I need to see.'

Eva was apologetic to her escort. She could take Maubourg men with her on the journey back, she offered. Grimstone and his two companions must be travel weary and saddle sore.

'No, ma'am.' The butler-turned-bodyguard was adamant. 'The guv'nor would expect us to stick with you, however long it takes. Where are we off to now, if I might ask, ma'am?'

'England,' Eva said firmly. 'Straight back to London.'

'Yes, ma'am.' The butler managed an estimable straight face. It sat oddly with his battered pugilistic features. 'Whatever you say, ma'am. Back to London it is, then.'

She did not leave until well on in the afternoon the next day. Partly it was because she wanted to enjoy the sight of Freddie rediscovering the castle, partly because she wanted to be completely sure that Philippe was well, but also because she was determined to retrace the route she and Jack had taken and to stay in the same inns. So, unless she was going to arrive ludicrously early at the first one, she needed to delay her departure. She was not certain what she would do when they reached the area where they had slept out under the stars, but she would deal with that when she came to it.

It was about six in the evening when the carriage, driven by a very bemused driver, deposited the Grand Duchess of Maubourg on the threshold of one of her more humble inns.

It was the same innkeeper who greeted them and he blinked a little at the sight of her again so soon, and with only servants at her back and no husband. But he did not recognise her true self this time, either, cheerfully ushering in *Madame,* lamenting that her esteemed husband was not travelling with her, and assuring her that the same bedchamber as last time was free. They had no other guests, he explained, directing her escort to a spacious attic room, although a hunting party was due in two days. What a fortunate occurrence that *Madame* could have the whole place to herself; he would light a fire in the parlour, for he was sure rain threatened and the temperature was dropping, did she not agree?

The promised rain came not as a shower but as a torrential downpour that made her think of the night before the battle. Then she had had only an open-sided hovel and straw to keep her dry and warm. And Jack's long body curled around her. But now she was in a snug parlour, surrounded by the carved woodwork and brightly painted earthenware the Maubourg peasants excelled at producing.

On the wide wooden mantel there was even the commemorative tankard that had been produced to celebrate her wedding to Louis. A good thing the image of her was so unlike. It was good of Louis though, she had always thought so. The handsome aloof profile stared blankly at the insipid representation of the new bride. So young, so innocent and so easily moulded to the dutiful wife her husband had demanded. Eva got up and turned the vessel around so the portraits faced the wall and the Maubourg crest was towards the room. That was better. She was another woman now.

There was a fire in the hearth to send red light chasing across the whitewashed walls and the curtains were drawn cosily across the casements. Distantly from the taproom she could hear the men talking. Here she was alone, but not lonely, thankful for the peace and the privacy to think about Jack. She had to get it right this time. Then upstairs was the bed they had shared, the memories of their first night together to relive when she finally felt sleepy. That first night—with a bolster down the middle of the bed!

Eva smiled. What would Jack think if he could see her now, nostalgically retracing their steps across France? Would he think her foolish, or would he understand?

The rain lashed down harder; it almost felt as though the sturdy little inn was a ship in rough seas, the waves battering at its sides. If it was like this tomorrow, she would not move on. It was madness to risk men and horses on roads that could become mountain torrents. Strangely it did not disturb her, the prospect of delay. She had made up her mind—she was travelling back to Jack almost fatalistically. He would be there when she arrived, she knew it.

There was a bustle outside, doors banged and the innkeeper shouted for the ostler. Some chance traveller caught in the storm, perhaps. Eva put down the book she had not been attempting to read and went to twitch aside the curtain. In the erratic light of the wind-tossed lanterns she saw that the ostler, huddled under the inadequate shelter of a sack, was leading a big horse towards the stable. Its coat was black, streaming with water, the saddle already soaked. She caught a glimpse of the skirts of a many-caped greatcoat as the rider vanished into the shelter of the porch.

A lone man, then. It seemed, unless he was content with the common taproom, that she must lose her privacy. Eva shrugged. She did not mind. One of the footmen could come in, too, to cover the proprieties.

'Such a surprise, *monsieur.*' The innkeeper was jovially greeting the newcomer. 'Come in, sir, come in! What a night to be sure, but you at least are certain of a warm welcome and your usual room. This way, sir, this way.'

A regular and favoured customer by the sound of it. But Eva was surprised that the innkeeper appeared about to usher him into the parlour, without a word to her.

'Here we are, sir.' The door swung open, making the candles gutter wildly. A tall figure, its bulk increased by the soaked greatcoat, filled the door. Water poured off the coat, pooled around the booted feet. The man's hat was in his gloved hands, but it could not have done much good, for his hair was plastered to his head.

The candles steadied as he took a step inside and Eva came to her feet. He looked weary, this traveller, there were shadows under the grey eyes and lines at the corners of his mouth that were new, she would swear, but as he saw her he went white, and under the blanched skin the bruised shape of four fingers stood out starkly.

'Jack. Oh, my God. Jack.' And then she was across the room, into his arms, her own around his neck, his soaking clothing leaching freezing wet into hers. And the heat of her love swept through her as he bent his head and his ice-cold lips met hers.

Chapter Twenty-Three

'*Madame! Madame?* Here, you, you can't go in there and…
Guv'nor!' Grimstone came pounding down the passageway
from the taproom, big fists clenched, then skidded to a halt,
his expression one of almost comical astonishment as Jack
turned, Eva in the crook of his arm.

'Thank you, Grimstone. *Madame* is quite safe with me.'

The bodyguard backed off, grinning. 'We're in the
taproom, guv'nor, if there's anything you need.'

'Divine intervention, probably,' Eva thought she heard
Jack mutter. 'You can get my boots off,' he added more
loudly, standing on one foot while the man tugged from the
back. The boot slid off with an unpleasant squelch and they
switched to the other.

'Landlord! A hot bath as soon as possible, if you please,' Eva
ordered, her hands already dragging off the heavy greatcoat.
'You are soaked, right through. You'll catch your death, Jack.'

He shrugged off the greatcoat and coat together, bundled
them into Grimstone's arms and turned back to her. 'Don't
fuss, sweet, I am tough enough to stand some rain.'

'You look like a half-drowned rat. Come to the fire.' She

tugged, but he stood his ground, then stooping, swept her up in his arms and made for the stairs. 'Jack!' Eva registered the staring faces around them break into broad smiles and buried her face in Jack's shoulder. 'Jack,' she whispered, half in sheer embarrassment, half with the joy of being able to say his name.

'Forget the hot water,' he threw back over his shoulder as he climbed. 'I'll ring later.'

'Jack!' she was still protesting as he shouldered open the door and set her on her feet inside the bedchamber.

'Eva.' The door closed with a thud and the key clicked. 'Eva, what in Heaven's name are you doing here? Has there been an accident? Where's Freddie? You should have been in Maubourg by now.'

'He is, we were. I mean, we arrived yesterday. Freddie is with his uncle.'

'So why are you here?' Jack stood dripping, the water still trickling down from his hair and regarded her steadily. Oh, Lord, she had made such a mess of his face.

'I was coming back. To England.'

'But why are you here? If you left this morning, you should be well on your way by now.' He did not ask why she was returning, she noticed with sinking heart.

Jack would think her a foolish and romantic woman, but there was nothing for it but to explain. 'I wanted to stay in the inns we had used. And I could hardly turn up at ten in the morning at this one, could I? I have been here just two hours.'

He smiled then, his mouth curving into a tender line that made the tears start in her eyes. 'Why were you coming back? Had you forgotten your bonnet?'

'No.' She could not joke about it. And she had to say it now. 'I was coming to see you and say I was sorry. I handled it so badly.' She could not stand to be the focus of those intelligent grey eyes—they seemed to see right through her, into the muddle and fear inside. 'I thought about status and what I ought to do as Grand Duchess, not what I wanted to do as a woman. I hurt your pride, I made demands without thinking what you would need or want. I did not tell you the important thing.' The words stuck in her throat. Dare she say them? Once said, they could never be unsaid.

But he did not ask. Of course, he did not want her to say it. Eva felt her heart sink, all the warmth his presence had surrounded her with shrank away. Why, with her handprint on his face, would Jack want her explanations?

'Aren't you going to ask me why I am here?' The deep, amused voice did not sound like the angry man she had left at the masquerade.

'I assume you were driven here by the storm.'

'As it happens, I was heading for this place. Eva, has it not struck you as rather strange that I am here at all?'

'Oh.' She stared at him. 'Of course. I was thinking so much about you it never occurred to me. You should be in London!'

'I should be where you are,' he said gently, taking her hand and pulling her to him. 'I wanted to spend one night here before going on to the castle. One night to remember the first one, one night to get my speech in order.'

'Speech?' She was feeling stupid, numb, Somewhere a voice was whispering that this was going to be all right, but she dare not heed it.

'The one where I fall to one knee and kiss your hand.' He knelt in front of her and lifted her hand to his lips with his cold, damp one. 'The one where I tell you I love you and ask you to marry me.' He waited patiently, his lips curving into a smile against her knuckles.

'But you said…' She stumbled to a halt, gazing down on

the bent head, the otter-sleek wet hair, the vulnerable, exposed nape. 'You love me?'

'I love you. I should have told you then, in London. Instead I said a number of stupid, angry things. Eva, I let my pride get in the way of how I feel about you. I reacted without thinking about how we could make this work, and I know we can.'

'And I did not even think about how it *needed* to be made to work. I did not think about compromise, I just wanted you in my life. My old life, as though I could uproot you, demand that you fit into the court at Maubourg.'

'We need to invent a new life.'

'Oh, yes.' A new life, with Jack. Who loved her.

'There was an important thing you had to say to me,' he prompted.

'I have never said it to any man before.' Eva tugged at his hands until he rose and stood very close, looking down at her. Her heart was banging against her ribs. She had to explain that this was not an easy thing, a thing she had given before. She searched for the words. 'Louis did not expect me to love him, and although I respected him very much, I never felt anything more for him than that. But I want to say those words to you, and for you to know how important they are for me.'

'Which is why it is hard to say.' Jack nodded. 'I understand. If it were not important, it would be easy, that is how I felt. I have never said those words, either.'

'I love you.' Eva put one hand on his shoulder and lifted the other against the bruises on his cheek. His skin was stubbled and cold, but she felt as though she was warm right through from that one touch. 'I love you with all my heart, and I wish very much to marry you.' And then it was suddenly easy to say. 'I love you, I love you, I lo— Jack!' He swept her up in his arms again and carried her to the bed. She stared up at him from the soft white quilt. 'Jack, you must get warm, you are soaked through.'

'I intend to get warm, very soon.' He had discarded his neckcloth, his numb fingers were fumbling the buttons on his shirt; she knelt up on the bed to help. He tossed it aside and she found that her hand was pressed flat against the front of his breeches, against the only hot part of him. 'Just as soon as I get these off.' He moved her hands away and unfastened the fall, pushing them off so he stood naked and magnificent and completely unashamed in front of her, showing her just how much he wanted her. 'There. Now you can warm me up.'

'Dry your hair first,' Eva said shakily, half-convinced she had fallen asleep in front of the parlour fire and was dreaming this.

'Undress.' Impatient, Jack reached for a towel and began to rub his hair, his eyes never leaving her.

There was no disobeying him, there never was. Eva slid off the bed and began to unbutton her gown, heeling off her slippers. She should undress slowly, she thought, tease him, but she was too impatient. Her fingers moved faster and faster, pulling at her petticoats, yanking at her corset strings, fumbling with her garters until she was naked.

Jack tossed the wet towel on to the tumbled heap of her clothes and turned to sit on the bed, pulling her towards him until she was standing between his legs.

'Now then, your Serene Highness, how do you propose going about this?'

'Like this.' Eva put her hands on his shoulders for balance and climbed up so she was kneeling on the edge of the bed, straddling the narrow hips, her thighs pressed tight against his flanks, the heat of her tantalising, just above the thrusting erection. She wriggled, seeking just the right angle, making him gasp and clutch her waist, then she slid down in one hard movement to take him, all of him, possessing and possessed.

Eye to eye they were still, her breasts pressed against him, his barely controlled, panting breath fretting their nipples together into an almost unbearable friction. Then she leaned her weight in, feeling the inner muscles gripping and holding the whole hot wonderful length of him as they fell in a tangle of limbs, back on to the bed.

Jack rolled her, his voice a growl, his mouth everywhere, tasting and licking and kissing as though to reclaim every inch of her. 'I love you,' he gasped in her ear, 'I love you.'

'I love you,' she answered, only to find his kiss swallowing the words as his mouth sealed over hers, drawing the breath and the soul out of her body. He drove into her, harder, deeper than she had thought possible, and began to move, driving her wild, her body arching under his, her legs curled round his hips, her heels locked, urging his taut buttocks down.

'I love you.' Which of them spoke? She did not know, only that the world was turning into black velvet night, that she was spinning in space, that the pleasure flooding her body was his gift to her, just as she gave him all the love in her heart as he reared up, taut with ecstasy above her, gasped her name and collapsed into her embrace, their bodies still locked in delight.

Jack was conscious of determined hands dragging the covers up over his body, opened one eye and found he was burrowed comfortably into Eva's bosom. Bliss. He extended his tongue and touched one pink nipple and was rewarded by a squeak of outrage and a giggle. He shifted his position and began to give the stiffening peak serious attention.

'Jack—not again! My love, we ought to eat.' *My love.* He closed his eyes again and just luxuriated in the words.

'Must we?' he managed at length.

'Yes.' Eva wriggled upright, a deliciously arousing activity in itself. 'We have made love a positively indecent number of times and I am starving.'

'Mmm,' he agreed. Her change of position had brought his head into her lap; his tongue was quite prepared to explore down here, as well.

'Jack!' It was the imperious Grand Duchess voice. He rather thought he had not been dragged out of trouble by his ears since he was six, but he yielded, flopping over on to his back to smile up at her sleepily.

'Dinner,' he agreed. 'I'll ring.' His legs supported him as far as the bell pull, just. He yanked at it, then struggled into his shirt and breeches. 'Where? Here?'

'Yes.' Eva had slid out of bed and was groping amidst her clothes, complaining because the wet towel had made her stays damp. 'Oh, bother it.' She tossed her underthings aside, dragged on her gown, pushed her bare feet in to her slippers and went to braid her hair into a thick tail down her back.

There was a tap at the door. Jack put out his head and found Grimstone there, his expression so blank it was positively insolent. 'Food. Wine. Here. Quickly.'

'Guv'nor. It's one o'clock.' There was a pause. 'In the morning.' Another pause. 'I'll find something.'

Jack closed the door and leaned on it. 'Do you know what time it is?'

Eva's eyes were wide. 'I heard. Poor Grimstone.'

'I am sorry. Are you very tired?'

'No. Not at all.' His love twinkled at him wickedly. 'I had a very nice sleep after the last time.'

'Eva, we have to talk before we get to Maubourg. We have to have decided how this is going to work before we talk to Freddie and your brother-in-law.'

She got up and went to clear the small table that would take their food. With her hair in its simple plait and her rumpled skirts, she looked deliciously domestic. 'I had thought—and you must tell me if this is not all right—that we could be in England when Freddie is at school and then here when it is the holidays. But I do not know whether you have an estate in England.' She shook her head ruefully. 'I am so ashamed, I never even took the time to find out about your home.'

'That is a good compromise.' Jack found himself thinking about Knightsacre, how he had neglected it, how it needed a mistress to love it back into life. 'My estate is called Knightsacre. You would like it, Eva, it is in the West Country. Soft, green land, rolling hills, wide, clear rivers. You could learn to be the mistress of the house—it is three hundred years old, but with no towers and no dungeons. I have neglected it for years: it is waiting for you.'

'Oh, yes. I can imagine it, imagine you riding home from wide acres to the steps of an English mansion that we will make home again for us. But here—what will you do in Maubourg? Will you not be bored? That was what I was going to think about on the journey.'

The knock on the door halted her worries while Grimstone carried in his spoils from the kitchen and set them out. 'This all right, guv'nor?'

'Good, thank you. You go to bed now.'

'We're taking it in turns to sit up. Don't like to leave the place unguarded, not with *Madame* on the premises.' He inclined his head sharply to Eva and took himself out.

Jack pulled up a chair and waited for Eva to sort out the

platters of bread, cheese and cold meats. 'You are worrying about me being bored—does that mean I have to work?' His mouth quirked. 'I was expecting to have a very smart cocked hat and to stand one pace behind you during ceremonials, looking handsome.' Her dismay at his teasing must have shown on her face. 'I am sorry, sweet. I thought I would be an additional tutor for Freddie—teach him to shoot and fence and improve his riding. And I wonder if there is something I can do to promote agriculture—growing flowers for perfume is all very well, but the arable crops look woeful.'

She reached across the table and touched his hand. 'You will be his father, not his tutor; he will love the attention. Thank you.' She took a sip of tea and frowned. 'Jack, will this stop your work for the government?'

'It will stop my private work. As for the government, I will have to see. I would not be able to do anything that could compromise the duchy.'

'Or dangerous.' He raised one eyebrow. 'Oh, all right, anyone would think it is fun! Well, nothing involving rescuing ladies, that I insist upon.'

'Very well.' He could promise that, at least.

'Jack,' she said again, still frowning in thought.

'Yes?' He watched her and tried to come to terms with being happy. It felt very odd.

'Before, when we have made love, you were very careful. Tonight you have not been.' She blushed rosily. 'I liked it even more. But does that mean you do not mind if we start a family?'

'I would like to, very much.'

'Oh, good.' Her smile made him feel he had given her the earth and the sea and the sky. It made him feel so powerful that he could do anything. 'A boy and a girl?'

'A boy and two girls,' he corrected. 'We need to keep the

numbers even, and the girls will look like you, which will be delightful.'

'Very well. How wonderful if we had started our family tonight.'

'How soon can we get married?' He had not thought of that. A baby. There must be no scandal. And this was not something that could be achieved with a quick licence from the Bishop.

Eva frowned, a slice of bread halfway to her lips. She really did not look like a Grand Duchess. He tried to remember the imperiously angry creature he had found in her chamber the first night.

'Two weeks,' she pronounced. 'I will tell the Archbishop he must sort it out.'

Oh, yes! Imperious was back. 'Make it three,' he suggested. 'Then we can get the English guests here. I'll start a list.'

They carried the notebook and pencil back to bed, leaning shoulder to shoulder as they planned the wedding. 'Who gives you away?' Jack asked, and was answered by a soft murmur. Her head was on his shoulder, her eyes closed. He prised the paper from her hands and snuggled her back into the bed, then slipped out to douse the candles. As he got back she turned, curled her arm around his chest and snuggled close. Jack closed his eyes on the darkness and smiled. He had told her he would always come back for her, and he had. The miracle was, she had been there for him.

It had not occurred to Eva that anyone would recognise her. Their first visit, and then last night, had lulled her into a sense of security. But when they came downstairs the next morning they found in the entranceway Grimstone and both footmen, ostensibly discussing the state of Jack's boots with the landlord. There were also a plump woman, several maids and the ostler.

'*Madame,*' the landlord said seriously, breaking off the discussion and hurrying to the foot of the stairs. 'I must tell you, my wife has recognised you. I just wanted to say that all here are loyal supporters of the Grand Ducal house and we would sooner cut out our own tongues than gossip. You may be assured of our utmost discretion.'

She felt ready to sink, but Jack merely shook the startled innkeeper by the hand 'You are all invited to the wedding,' he said largely. 'Grimstone, see to it. Oh, yes, and a coat of arms for over the door. *By Appointment.*' He murmured in Eva's ear in English. 'I can do that, can't I?'

'Freddie can. You had better ask him.' She was going to collapse into giggles at any moment, which was probably better than strong hysterics, which seemed the alternative option. Jack was getting the hang of this very rapidly; she had forgotten that in his trade acting was a vital skill.

'I had better ask his permission to marry you, don't you think?' he added, handing her up into the coach.

'You would both be crippled with embarrassment,' Eva protested.

'Nonsense. I will be very solemn, call him by his title every other word. He'll love it. Then we can drink a toast in best Napoleon brandy.'

'Jack, he's nine!'

'I did say best brandy.' He grinned unrepentantly as she shook her head at him. 'Now brief me about everyone I am going to meet.'

'Well, as you've sent Grimstone on ahead, I should imagine the entire court will have turned out.' Eva made herself concentrate—staring like a moonling at her gorgeous lover and husband-to-be would have to wait. 'First of all there is Philippe…'

* * *

The entire court and the full Guard of Honour and all the staff appeared to have turned out. Jack helped her down amidst a trumpet fanfare and wild clapping from the onlookers.

'How do they know?' he hissed, nodding towards the townsfolk.

'They don't, but this is obviously an Occasion.'

'I am going to design myself a uniform,' Jack remarked as they solemnly paced across the flagstones to where Philippe was waiting, Freddie grinning hugely at his side. 'Something very severe and black with just a hint of silver braid.'

'There is no need, my love.' Eva waved graciously to the cheering crowd, her other hand very obviously resting on Jack's arm. She felt so proud she thought she was going to float. 'I have thought of a suitable office and title for you, and it doesn't come with a uniform.'

'None?'

'Not a stitch,' she said as they arrived at the foot of the steps. 'Master of the Bedchamber.'

Jack stopped and looked down at her, his eyes dark, and she wondered for a moment if the joke offended him. Then he tossed his hat at the crowd, took her firmly in his arms, and kissed their Grand Duchess full on the mouth. As the crowd roared its approval, he lifted his lips just enough to murmur, 'An office for life, I collect, my darling. I accept, with all my heart.'

Harlequin® Historical
Historical Romantic Adventure!

From *USA TODAY*
bestselling author

Margaret Moore

A LOVER'S KISS

A Frenchwoman in London,
Juliette Bergerine is unexpectedly
thrown together in hiding with
Sir Douglas Drury. As lust and
desire give way to deeper emotions,
how will Juliette react on discovering
that her brother was murdered—
by Drury!

*Available September
wherever you buy books.*

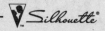

REQUEST YOUR FREE BOOKS!

Harlequin® Historical
Historical Romantic Adventure!

2 FREE NOVELS PLUS 2 FREE GIFTS!

YES! Please send me 2 FREE Harlequin® Historical novels and my 2 FREE gifts (gifts are worth about $10). After receiving them, if I don't wish to receive any more books, I can return the shipping statement marked "cancel". If I don't cancel, I will receive 6 brand-new novels every month and be billed just $4.94 per book in the U.S. or $5.49 per book in Canada, plus 25¢ shipping and handling per book and applicable taxes, if any*. That's a savings of 20% off the cover price! I understand that accepting the 2 free books and gifts places me under no obligation to buy anything. I can always return a shipment and cancel at any time. Even if I never buy another book, the two free books and gifts are mine to keep forever.

246 HDN ERUM   349 HDN ERUA

Name	(PLEASE PRINT)
Address	Apt. #
City	State/Prov.	Zip/Postal Code

Signature (if under 18, a parent or guardian must sign)

Mail to the **Harlequin Reader Service**:
IN U.S.A.: P.O. Box 1867, Buffalo, NY 14240-1867
IN CANADA: P.O. Box 609, Fort Erie, Ontario L2A 5X3

Not valid to current subscribers of Harlequin Historical books.

Want to try two free books from another line?
Call 1-800-873-8635 or visit www.morefreebooks.com.

* Terms and prices subject to change without notice. N.Y. residents add applicable sales tax. Canadian residents will be charged applicable provincial taxes and GST. Offer not valid in Quebec. This offer is limited to one order per household. All orders subject to approval. Credit or debit balances in a customer's account(s) may be offset by any other outstanding balance owed by or to the customer. Please allow 4 to 6 weeks for delivery. Offer available while quantities last.

Your Privacy: Harlequin Books is committed to protecting your privacy. Our Privacy Policy is available online at www.eHarlequin.com or upon request from the Reader Service. From time to time we make our lists of customers available to reputable third parties who may have a product or service of interest to you. If you would prefer we not share your name and address, please check here. ☐

HH08R

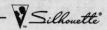

SPECIAL EDITION™

NEW YORK TIMES
BESTSELLING AUTHOR

DIANA
PALMER

A brand-new Long, Tall Texans novel

HEART OF STONE

Feeling unwanted and unloved, Keely returns
to Jacobsville and to Boone Sinclair, a rancher
troubled by his own past. Boone has always
seemed reserved, but now Keely discovers a
sensuality with him that quickly turns to love. Can
they each see past their own scars to let love in?

Available September 2008
wherever you buy books.

COMING NEXT MONTH FROM

HARLEQUIN®
HISTORICAL

- **THE OUTRAGEOUS LADY FELSHAM**
  by **Louise Allen**
  (Regency)
  Her unhappy marriage over, Lady Belinda Felsham plans to enjoy
  herself. An outrageous affair with breathtakingly handsome major Ashe
  Reynard is exactly what she needs!
  *Follow **Those Scandalous Ravenhursts** in the second book of
  Louise Allen's sensual miniseries.*

- **A LOVER'S KISS**
  by **Margaret Moore**
  (Regency)
  A Frenchwoman in London, Juliette Bergerine is unexpectedly thrown
  into hiding with Sir Douglas Drury after they are mysteriously attacked.
  *As desire gives way to a deeper emotion, what will become of Juliette's
  reputation?*

- **THE BOUNTY HUNTER AND THE HEIRESS**
  by **Carol Finch**
  (Western)
  Evangeline Hallowell is determined to catch the dirty, rotten scoundrel
  who stole her sister's money. But pretending to be a hard-bitten bounty
  hunter's wife means things are bound to go awry....
  *Danger lurks and wild passions flare in the rugged canyons of
  Colorado.*

- **POSSESSED BY THE HIGHLANDER**
  by **Terri Brisbin**
  (Medieval)
  Peacemaker for the MacLerie clan, Duncan is manipulated into
  marrying the exiled "Robertson Harlot." Despite shadows lurking
  over their union, Duncan discovers a love for Marian, and will stop
  at nothing to protect her....
  *The third book in Terri Brisbin's Highlander miniseries. Honor,
  promises and dark secrets fuel this medieval tale of clan romance.*